BARLOCH

The Wind as Witness

Best wishes,

Diarmid MacArthur

A Barloch investigation

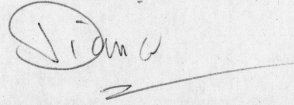

Copyright

Prologue

Figures, as one, in the dark.
Fumbling. Fighting?
Mumbled words of hate, carried away on the wet wind.
'...take yer hands aff me...'
'...be sorry...'
The sound of a blow, skin against skin.
'Aaaah, ya bastart, Ah'm...'
A scream of pain, a moan, cursing,
More fumbling, more fighting.
A raised arm.
Figures in the dark, one on the ground, im-
mobile, another running.
Only the rain falling as tears of grief...
  ...and the sigh of the wind as witness.

Chapter 1

Four months.

Just four months until Hogmanay heralded in a
new year, a new decade...and, hopefully, the start of a
new chapter in the life of Constable Alan McInnes.

He pulled up the collar of his police-issue gaberdine coat
as he continued his routine late evening tramp along the
unseasonably cold and damp main street of the little Renfrewshire village of Barloch. At the moment, Hogmanay
seemed an eternity away as he rather half-heartedly pulled
at the rusty security grill protecting the rain-streaked
window of the village's Scottish Co-operative Society
electrical goods shop. Amongst the rather random display
of the latest hairdryers, electric irons and the new-fan-
gled transistor radios were a couple of black-and-white
television sets, a prime target for a petty thief. Even with
the attractive terms on offer, Alan knew full well that
the price was out of the reach of the modest earnings of
both himself and his social circle. Like everyone else he
knew, he rented and, as his father frequently pointed out,
at least the televisions got fixed quickly when anything
went wrong—as they did, with unfailing regularity.

It had been a routine, straightforward shift, apart from
the inclemency of the weather. Constable McInnes had
been called to the reported theft of a bicycle (which,
by all accounts, was barely roadworthy) then, when he
had turned back into the windswept Main Street, he

had come across three youths sitting astride their motorcycles and noisily revving their engines. Recognising one of them as a local lad, about six years younger than himself and a former pupil of the local school, he approached the members of the leather jacket and winkle picker attired group, who had looked challengingly at him. He had reckoned there were two ways to deal with the situation and he had addressed the local youth.

'Evenin' Hamish. I see you've got a new bike there—a BSA Bantam, eh? Looks a good wee machine.'

Hamish Calder had blushed slightly at the familiar approach but responded nonetheless.

'Em, aye, Mr McInnes. Jist got it at the weekend. Second-hand, like.'

Alan made a show of inspecting the bike, noting that the other two had stopped gunning their engines. He looked at one of the other machines.

'Triumph Tiger Cub—that's a smasher, always fancied one of those myself...'

A few minutes later, with a reasonably friendly admonishment about noise in a built-up area, the three young bikers drove off, leaving the Main Street in peace once more. Alan had walked on, his face reddening at Hamish's parting comment.

"Tell Miss Wright that Hamish wis askin' efter her..."

*

He trudged on, narrowly avoiding a dog's mess that was slowly dissipating on the wet flagstones; he shuddered as a gust of rain-laden wind sent rivulets of cold water down the back of his neck. So much for it being the end of summer: it felt more like a March day. He smiled to himself. Maybe

8

he and Nancy Wright would have a summer wedding (in a year or two, of course), he resplendent in a new suit, his bride eye-wateringly beautiful in the white dress upon which she would undoubtedly (and quite correctly) insist.

He shook his head; of course, he'd have to ask her first... and she'd have to say "yes", hopefully ushering in this new chapter in PC Alan McInnes's life. Hogmanay seemed as good a time as any, he thought, suddenly aware of a nervous clenching of his stomach—what if she *did* say no?

His world was already changing, though. At the recommendation, and invitation, of his sergeant, Donald Tait, he had joined the local Masonic Club, whose rather sombre red sandstone building he was about to walk past. Alan's father hadn't been happy, mumbling that promotion should be on ability alone and not what club you belonged to, what handshake you used. But Alan was nobody's fool; he had already sat, and passed, his sergeant's exams, promotion would hopefully be only a matter of time. His ultimate goal, however, was to join the Criminal Investigation Department; Detective Sergeant McInnes, C.I.D.—now that *really* had a ring to it.

There was an empty semi-detached police house next door to Sergeant Tait's, but that was the last place Alan wanted to move into with his new bride. Under the scrutiny of his superior officer he would be expected to attend the weekly church services, tend the garden, grow roses... no, he and Nancy should surely be able to afford a nice wee house on the edge of the village, where a new development was already under way. Nancy Wright was a schoolteacher at the Barloch primary school, where she earned a reasonable salary. Although Alan hadn't met her parents, he was aware that they were what he'd call "well-off" (by his standards, at least) although this hadn't influenced his choice of ladyfriend in the slightest. Alan had first met Nancy whilst attending a road safety event in the school playground; he had plucked up the courage to engage her in conversation, then, just before he had left...

The smile of that happy memory faded as he became aware of a noise. He was approaching one of the many little secluded, covered pends and vennels that led off Barloch's main street and he could hear whispering, a giggle...he pulled out his heavy torch, shining it briefly on the adjacent wall. The batteries were low, he'd need to replace them soon. There was an unlit gas streetlamp just outside the pend but he could make out the name, which he knew well enough: "Braid's Close", a narrow walkway leading between the adjacent houses to Harris Square at the rear. He took a few steps and swung the faltering beam of the torch into the darkness. The pool of yellow light fell onto something pale and, in an instant, Alan realised that it was a girl's thigh, adorned by a slender suspender strap attached to a black stocking-top; her flimsy-looking skirt hoisted above her waist and her pants appearing to be somewhere around her knees. The whispering ceased as he swung the beam upwards, catching the girl's face. She was pretty enough, in a hard sort of way, with dark hair piled up on top of her head. Her full lips, currently drawn back in an expression of surprise (or anger, perhaps?) were painted scarlet.

'Mary Campbell! What the hell d'you think...?'

The mention of her name galvanised the young woman into action. In what seemed like a single movement, she hoisted up her pants and pulled down her skirt. Then, without a backward glance and with a clatter of heels, she scurried off through the pend, leaving her partner behind. As Alan moved the beam away from her face towards the young man, currently struggling to pull up his navy-blue jeans, he heard Mary call out.

'C'mon, afore he sees ye an' tells ma mammy!'

It was too late for that, mused Alan. He would be going to visit Mrs Campbell as soon as he started tomorrow's shift, although he doubted if the woman would care that much, her own moral values having been questioned more than once. He took a step down the pend, shining the torch on the man's face. Young but already heavy-jowled, a rough, unshaven chin beneath a slightly vacant expression; Billy Benson, a local ne'er do weel.

'An' as for you, Benson...'

Like a hound in pursuit, the well-built young man was off his mark, chasing his ladyfriend until the darkness of the unlit pend enveloped him. Alan shook his head and let out a long sigh. Although they were all born and bred in Barloch and had attended the same small village school, he already felt a world apart from these people. Their only excuse was, he supposed, quite simply that there was nowhere else for courting couples to go, the village offering little in the way of nightlife for young folk other than a few church-related activities such as badminton.

It wasn't worth pursuing them—they would already have disappeared into the dark backyards of Harris Square. Wearily, he turned and started his tramp back along the main street; the rain seemed to be heavier, the evening cooler. He passed the dark windows of the masonic club, its arms and date of founding emblazoned above the door. Onwards to the "Hole in the Wa'" bar, sitting on the corner of Main Street and Factory Street, already disgorging the group of Monday night drinkers, cigarettes and pipes lit, collars turned up, flat caps pulled down. A few nodded to him; Alan was a weel-kent face.

He turned the corner and headed down Factory Street towards the loch, a sharp whistle causing him to glance upwards. At the bottom of the street, a steam locomotive rumbled noisily across the furthest of three railway bridges that crossed the lower end of the street, the ensuing noise indicating that it probably had a rake of mineral wagons in tow. It was undoubtedly heading for Glensherrie Steelworks, just across the border in Ayrshire. The smoke and steam of the engine's exhaust glowed red above the cab as it clanked and clattered on through the station as it headed southwards. In a few minutes, the noise had diminished; just like the steam trains themselves, thought Alan, who rather liked trains. After all, his father had been a railway guard until a shunting accident had caused him to give up his work. Railways, however, were just another aspect of his world that were changing as the ubiquitous diesels began to challenge the once mighty steam engines. He walked on down the street, under the first bridge, then the second, welcoming the temporary respite from the rain as he shone his waning torchlight inside the station entrance towards the long, feebly lit ramp that ran up to the island platform. He felt there had been a sound, a slight movement, but the space was empty. Probably just a rat, seeking shelter; he didn't blame it.

'Hello! Anybody there?'

His call was answered by silence while his nostrils twitched as he sniffed the air, detecting a sharp, acrid smell. He shrugged, assuming it was just the exhaust from the locomotive, then switched off the torch and walked on, around the corner, the dark waters of the Bar Castle loch stretching off to his left. He speeded up on this unlit and lonely section, striding past the steep bank that led up to the little goods yard where his father now worked as a night watchman. In a few minutes, he'd look in and have a cup of tea, brewed on the brazier and thick as tar. His father was a man of few words but Alan knew that the night shift was long and lonely and fifteen minutes in the company of his son, albeit mostly spent in silence, would help relieve the monotony. He had heard a rumour that British Railways was considering closing the yard and, with a twinge of concern, he wondered what his father would do then. Just another bridge to cross as and when he reached it, he supposed.

Constable Alan McInnes bent his head down at the onset of a fresh shower of driving rain; his world was, indeed, changing and, briefly, he wondered what surprises, pleasant or otherwise, the nineteen-sixties, just four months away, would hold.

Chapter 2

Glasgow: the Second City, the beating industrial heart of Scotland, the upper reaches of the mighty River Clyde a conjoined mass of shipyards, works and docks. The latter provided the artery by which goods flowed out from and into the city, despatched by an army of stevedores and a fleet of carts and lorries for onwards transit to the City's numerous merchants and traders. Grain, agricultural produce, tobacco, whisky, timber—the list was endless, most of it safely despatched to its intended destination.

Most, but not all...

As a grey dawn light appeared in the smoky sky that lay over the City's East End, shadowy figures moved amongst the cranes, the crates, the ropes and the rats of King George V dock. There were muttered, guttural words, the striking of a match, the tang of strong tobacco. A package exchanged, a consignment diverted. "The insurance'll pay"; "They can bloody afford it"; "It'll no' be missed"...a plethora of reasons, a raft of excuses.

All for a grubby envelope containing a few pounds, to be spent later that day in the pub, in the bookies, in a brothel...

"Aye, we're the boys awright...!"

*

'Mary! Mary! For God's sake, lassie, will ye get a move on or ye'll be late. Ah've got a couple o' tattie scones on for ye.'

Meg Campbell glared down at the two triangular scones that were sizzling in their slathering of lard, having already burnt the first two beyond recognition. The weekday morning routine seldom varied in the Campbell household but it was unlike Meg to spoil these meagre rations. She let out an angry sigh; she struggled to keep her daughter fed and could have done without the waste, albeit small. She yelled again, louder this time.

'MARY! C'mon girl!'

Since leaving school, her daughter had struggled to keep a job and if she turned up late, only six weeks in to a position in the office of the local cooperage, she could find herself very quickly unemployed again.

'Mary! MARY!'

She glanced at the clock that was cheerfully ticking on the scullery shelf; twenty-five past eight. Mary started work at nine and, although the cooperage was only a ten-minute walk away, by the time she plastered make-up on her face it was unlikely that she'd be on time. Turning the gas off, Meg stormed out of the scullery, through the cramped living room and into the narrow hallway. She banged noisily on the door of her daughter's bedroom as she yelled.

'For God's sake, move yer erse, ye dinn'ae want tae lose yer bloody job...'

As Meg had expected, this final summons elicited a loud thumping from the floor above and a muffled shout.

'Keep the damned noise down, for God's sake.'

Meg muttered a few expletives about "mindin' yer own business" and gave one final shout.

'Mary, for God's sake, whit's keepin' you?'

She gave a loud peremptory knock on the door

and barged in, stopping suddenly in her tracks;
a second later, she let out a loud scream.

'Oh Jesus...!'

*

'Oh dear goodness, what a racket!'

Isa McInnes wiped her hands on her pristine floral apron and trotted out to the hallway, where the offending noisy item sat on a polished oak table. She glared at the black bakelite telephone, wishing it had never been installed, as all it ever seemed to do was bring tidings of evil into the peace of their little household. Still, she was proud of her son, Alan—he'd make a good policeman, she was sure and, if that necessitated a telephone being installed, then so be it. The implement let out another long ring and she lifted it rather fearfully. Her husband had only just gone to bed after the night shift and he wasn't a sound sleeper. Alan was on back-shift and could do with another hour or so. She raised the phone to her mouth before adopting her best telephone voice.

'Barloch two-three-one, Mrs McInnes speaking.'

'Isa, is that you? Its Don...em, Sergeant Tait here.'

There was still a gentle lilt to his voice and Isa McInness smiled; she had always had a soft spot for Donald Tait, ever since they started junior secondary school together all those years ago, remaining in the same class until they left to make their respective ways in the world. From the Mull of Kintyre originally, his family had moved to the village when he was ten, his father having gained employment at the steelworks. Sadly, Donny had returned from the War a changed man and the death of his beloved wife, Jeannie, several years ago had added another layer of sadness to the once-handsome sergeant.

'Hello Donny, how are you?'

'Och, doin' awa', Isa, just doin' awa'...listen, is yer laddie aboot, Ah'd like a wee word, if that's okay?'

'I'll just get him, Donny, can you hold on a wee minute? I'll put the phone down.'

Very gently, she placed the handset down on the oak table, more out of concern for the latter's surface than for any damage to the infernal instrument. She was a slightly built woman and could move like a panther when the need arose; she tip-toed up the stairs and knocked softly on the door to Alan's room.

'Alan, son, are you awake?'

She could hear a faint snore in reply; she opened the door and crossed to the bed, gazing down for a moment on the handsome young man that her little boy had become. The regulation-cut, but still sleep-tousled dark hair, the full lips, slightly parted, the morning-stubble—her son was a good catch and, if the way he spoke of Nancy Wright was anything to go by, he was already on the hook. Her smile faded slightly; she hadn't yet met Nancy and would reserve judgement but, as she leaned forward to gently shake her pride and joy into wakefulness, she beamed. If she was being truthful with herself, *no* woman would ever be good enough for her Alan...

*

Twenty minutes later, Constable McInnes came down the stairs, shaved and dressed in his uniform but with his highly polished size eleven boots carried in his hand. He sat at the table and pushed his feet into them.

'What did Donny want, son?' asked Isa, looking over her shoulder.

He looked up, shaking his head; his mother's habitual familiarity with his superior officer always made him slightly uneasy.

'No' sure, Mother, he just asked me to come down to the station right away. I'd best be gettin' a move on.'

He tied the lace on the second boot and stood up.

'Right, I'll be off.'

She turned and gave him a rather severe look.

'You'll do no such thing—you're going nowhere until you've had your breakfast. After all, you're supposed to be off duty today, what with you being on the night shift. Sit yourself back down.'

On the oil-clothed table she placed a plate, laden with two fried eggs, two lorne sausages and two slices of fried bread.

'But Mother, Sergeant Tait said—'

'I don't care what Sergeant Tait said. Come on now, before it gets cold.'

Alan sat back down with a sigh of resignation, although the smell of the fried food was making his mouth water. He lifted his fork and started to eat as Isa poured him a cup of strong tea.

'And you can just slow down—you don't want to be getting an ulcer like your father.

'Aye, Mother,' replied Alan, with a smile. An argument with Isa McInnes, especially where food was concerned, was seldom, if ever, won.

*

Isa closed the door gently behind her son, not wanting to waken her husband. Gilbert McInnes was a good man, a man who, throughout his life, had done his best for his family.

Isa knew that he struggled with the constant pain from the injury; she knew, too, that his mind still held untold horrors from the Great War, of which he never spoke. But he had never wronged her, he had never lifted a finger, never looked at another woman...

She walked briskly back through to the small kitchen and started to clear away the breakfast dishes, placing them as gently as she could in the Belfast sink. They had a good enough life, never short of food, never without coal; she had been a primary-school teacher before she'd met Gilbert, back in the days when she was expected to give up her job when she married. But she had been a frugal young woman and had saved a little bit of money; and, as a competent violinist in her youth, she still gave a few weekly lessons to the children of better-off Barloch families. After the First War, Gilbert had obtained a reasonable job as a goods guard on the railways and had received some compensation money after the accident; things could have been a lot worse, she supposed.

She and Gilbert had tried for years but she had never managed to conceive; the doctor had put it down to the shrapnel that he still carried in his body. Then finally, miraculously, she had become pregnant and had given birth to a healthy baby boy. She felt the familiar tears well up in her eyes and, drying her hands on her pinny, she sat down and took out a delicate lace handkerchief. They had both been so proud, the shock of dark hair on the baby's head testament to her own father's heritage. From the outset, Gilbert had been a good father, caring and providing both for Isa and Alan. However, as the baby grew to be a tall, good-looking boy and as that boy had become a handsome young man, Gilbert McInnes seemed to become increasingly distant, withdrawing into himself and struggling to communicate with his adult son. Isa put it down to pain from his injury and the onset of old age, but, in her own darker moments, her inherent Christian faith told her that there would come a day where, somehow, she would be held accountable...

She stood up quickly, drying her eyes. This would never do, this wallowing in self-pity, raking over the past. She went to the pantry cupboard, removing a bag of flour and a pat of butter. As her mother used to say, 'When it's a' goin' agin' ye, ye can aye dae worse than bake!'

*

It was after ten o'clock before Alan finally entered the little village police station. One of his fellow constables, Kerr Brodie, was standing behind the public desk, or "bar," as they called it. He looked up and grinned.

'Sarge is efter ye, Alan.'

Alan smiled back.

'Aye, he phoned up the road but ma mother made me have ma breakfast first.'

'Quite right too—bluidy nuisance, that phone, if you ask me, far too easy tae get in touch wi' us these days!'

'Right enough, Kerr. Anyway, I'd best awa' through before he gets too hot under the collar.'

'Aye. Oh, an' by the way, he's got someone in wi' him.'

Alan gave his colleague a questioning look but Kerr grinned again.

'Ye'll find oot soon enough...'

*

Alan knocked on the door of Sergeant Tait's office. A gruff

voice responded.

'Aye, come awa."

He opened the door to the small room, more akin to a large cupboard with a barred window, then blinked as the thick, blue fug of tobacco smoke nipped his eyes. Donald Tait was puffing on a rather foul pipe, while the woman sitting across the desk from him was sucking greedily on the last dregs of a cigarette as she clutched a chipped mug of tea in her other hand. Alan recognised the woman immediately.

Clad in a shabby dress beneath an old raincoat and with her grey hair tied back in a tight bun, Meg Campbell had lived in Barloch for as long as Alan could remember, although she was still viewed as an outsider, having moved down from Glasgow many years before he was born. He also knew that she was generally disliked and had few friends; she was a mean-mouthed woman with a quick temper and, over the years there had been a good few complaints about her public behaviour. Tait puffed at his pipe and exhaled slowly; he looked weary, Alan thought.

'Constable, ye'll know Mrs Campbell?'

'Yes, Sergeant. Good mornin', Mrs Campbell.'

The woman's lips twitched slightly but she remained silent. Donald Tait spoke again.

'Mrs Campbell's concerned aboot her daughter, Mary. Apparently she never came home last night, isn't that richt, Mrs Campbell?'

The woman's face changed from its seemingly permanent scowl to one of concern, Alan noticed. The words tumbled out of her mouth as she spoke.

'Naw, she never. It's no' like her, she's a good lassie, she's no' done anythin' like this afore. Ah'm fair

worried, so Ah am. See, ma man hasn'ae came
hame yet, he's oan the night shift doon at the works,
must've missed his train, so Ah came doon here.'

Tait and Alan exchanged a brief glance; if Meg Campbell was disliked, Hugh Campbell was almost universally
hated. The man was a loud-mouthed bigot who, when
drunk, was inclined to lash out at anyone who disagreed
with him. He frequently spent a night in one of the two
small cells at the rear of the police station. He was known
to spend a considerable amount of his meagre salary
on drink, leaving Meg to struggle by on what was left.
He was also rumoured to have a gambling habit, often
taking the train to nearby Paisley on a Saturday where
he would spend the afternoon in the bookmaker's shop.
Tait took a final puff then laid his pipe on the table, indicating that the interview was almost concluded.

'Aye, weel you awa' hame an' wait
for him, Mrs Campbell...'

He turned to face Alan.

'Mrs Campbell here's given me a wee list o'
Mary's friends. Ah've told her that its mair
than likely she's spent the nicht wi' one o' them.
Ah've said that you'll go roon' an' check...'

He turned back to the woman.

'...an' Ah'm sure she'll turn up in nae time at a'. In
fact, it's likely enough that she's already at her work.
Constable, it micht be worth checkin' there first?'

'Yes, Sergeant, sounds like a good idea.'

Rather stiffly, Donald Tait stood up and, with some
reluctance, Meg Campbell followed suit. She seemed
to derive a modicum of pleasure from being the centre of attraction, even if it was while in a police sta-

tion reporting that her daughter hadn't come home!

'You awa' an' see Mrs Campbell oot—an' we'll be in touch, din'na you worry.'

Alan escorted Meg Campbell to the front door then walked back through to the Sergeant's office, knocking again. Once invited inside, Tait indicated for him to sit down.

'Likely as no' the lassie's been worse fur the wear an' stayed ower at a friend's hoose, don't ye think? Like mother, like daughter.'

Alan took a breath.

'Aye, well, I'm no' so sure, Sergeant.'

'Oh?'

Tait lifted and re-lit his pipe, his expression of curiosity inviting Alan to continue.

'Y'see, when I was oot on my round last night, I caught her up Braid's Close with thon Billy Benson.'

Tait frowned.

'Did ye now? An' whit were they up tae?'

Alan could feel the colour rise in his cheeks; Tait smiled.

'Aye, aye, enough said, lad. An' whit happened?'

'They made off, Sergeant, down into Harris Square. The streetlight was out, I didn't see much point in followin' them, they'd soon have disappeared along Harris Street.'

Tait puffed thoughtfully on his pipe for a minute; he took it out of his mouth, pointing the stem at Alan.

'Hmm. Weel, ye were richt no' tae say anythin' tae Meg Campbell. God knows whit she micht have gone an' done. Or worse, if she telt that husband o' hers, weel, the man's a bloody menace, if ye'll pardon ma language.'

'Aye, he is so.'

'Any idea where we can get a hold o' this Billy Benson?'

'Aye, I have, Sergeant. My father said he'd seen him workin' on McGeoch's coal lorry down next to the goods yard. Been there a few weeks now, I think.'

Tait nodded.

'Good, maybe he's settlin' doon at last, he's aye been a bit o' a bad lot. Richt, if ye fancy a bit overtime, get yersel' ower tae the cooperage an' see if Mary Campbell's turned up for work. If she has, jist leave her be, dinn'ae want tae go makin' unnecessary trouble fur the lassie, Ah can hae a word wi' her later aboot wastin' police time. But if she's no' there, can ye head ower tae the coal yard an' see if Benson's aboot?'

'Right, Sergeant, I'll get off now an' I'll let you know.'

He stood up and took the three paces to the door. As he opened it, Tait called after him in a tone of innocence.

'Did ye manage tae get yer breakfast afore ye came?'

Alan wondered if he'd got away with being half an hour later than scheduled; obviously not.

'Em, aye, Sergeant. My mother had it made, didn't want tae hurt her feelings...'

Tait smiled, his eyes twinkling as he nodded.

'Aye, Ah thocht as much.'

Chapter 3

Constable Alan McInnes had never met Neil Lawson, the manager of Glen Cooperage, although he knew the man by sight. He took an instant dislike to him, with his flashy suit, his slicked back black hair, his thin Errol Flynn-style moustache and his pan-loafy accent. However, his dislike was quickly replaced by concern at the troubling news that Mary Campbell hadn't turned up for work that morning; Sergeant Tait had been wrong after all. Alan thanked Lawson and had opened the office door when the manager gave his parting shot.

'And if you *do* happen to see Miss Campbell, Constable, you may advise her not to bother turning up for work tomorrow. Her employment is terminated forthwith.'

Alan stopped half-way through the door, pausing for a moment, choosing his words carefully. He turned back to face Lawson, his shoulders squared and his features set in their most official manner.

'I regret that is outside the scope of my duties, Mister Lawson. Good day t'you.'

He closed the door behind him and, as he walked through the outer office, he was aware of the secretary stifling a slightly girlish giggle. He daren't look—he might have been tempted to give the rather attractive Alice Quinn, a former classmate, a conspiratorial wink; and that would never do.

*

It was only a ten-minute walk to the yard, situated behind the station that accommodated both the local goods depot and McGeoch's coal yard. The sky was a leaden grey but at least the rain had stopped and it was reasonably warm. The village was quiet, most of the inhabitants being at their places of work. He walked down Kirk Street, home to three of the village's churches, passing under the railway bridges that mirrored those in Factory Street. He then turned left onto the rise that led up to his destination. As he entered the gates, he was rather dismayed at the level of dilapidation on view; it was invisible during his nocturnal visits to his father's watchman's hut. The ground was strewn with random pieces of discarded equipment and general debris, mostly overgrown with willow herb and weeds. One solitary goods van sat in the siding that led to the goods shed and the various buildings carried an air of semi-dereliction. The entire area was certainly showing considerable signs of neglect and he suspected that the rumours of closure might well be true. He walked across to the little brick office that bore a blue-painted sign "McGeoch & Son, coal and coke merchants". To the rear of this, two overall-and-flat-cap-clad men were shovelling coal from the nearer of two battered grey coal wagons and into sacks, which sat in a neat row. There was no sign of either of McGeoch's two Albion coal-lorries. He knocked on the office door and a female voice replied.

'Aye, come in, it's open.'

He entered, taking off his uniform cap; the woman looked up at him through a cloud of smoke from the cigarette that dangled from her thin lips, then took off her rather elaborate, upswept spectacles.

'Oh, it's yersel', Alan, How are ye—

tak' a seat, Ah'll put the kettle on.'

Alan had been in Peter McGeoch's class at school, although he wasn't the "Son" referred to on the name-board—that was his older brother, Paul. Peter, the younger of the two, had gone on to technical college and was now working as a technical teacher at a school in Paisley. Alan pulled out the visitor's chair that was tucked under the desk and sat down.

'How's Peter doin', Mrs M?'

He had called her that for as long as he could remember.

'Aye, he's doin jist fine, so he is. Happy as Larry, by aw' accounts. How's yer mother, Alan?'

'Och, she's fine too, Mrs M.'

The welcome mug of tea was placed before him, accompanied by a thick slice of sultana cake.

'Made it masel' jist on Sunday.'

Alan smiled; Mrs McGeoch's baking was legendary. He took a bite of the succulent, dark cake.

'Mmm. Haven'ae lost yer touch, Mrs M.'

She smiled as she masticated her own slice.

'So whit brings ye down here, Alan?
No' anyone in trouble, Ah hope?'

'I hope not either—I'm just wantin' a wee word with Billy Benson.'

Her expression darkened slightly.

'Aw, whit's the big lump gone an'done noo?'

'Well, nothin' as far as I'm aware, Mrs M. It's just...well, I saw him last night, with a young lady, and she seems to have disappeared.'

As soon as the words were out, he regretted them. Even though he hadn't mentioned her by name, it was likely that, before the day was out, Mary Campbell's

disappearance would be common knowledge. Mrs Mc-
Geoch must have noticed his expression; she smiled.

'Dinn'ae you worry, Alan, lad, Ah'll no' say a
word; but Billy's no' here the noo, he's awa' oot on
the lorry. He'll be back aboot half-twelve for his
piece. Now, wid ye like another slice o' cake?'

*

Alan returned to the police station and reported his findings,
such as they were, to Sergeant Tait, who pondered on the
news for a moment. He took a puff of his pipe.

'Weel, it sounds like Mary Campbell *has* gone astray,
then. Ah thocht she'd have just turned up at her
work wi' a bit o' a sarry heid. Worryin'...worryin...'

He put down his pipe and reached for his notebook, flicking the pages then squinting at his notes.

'Hm, micht be worth ha'ein' a word wi'
her freends richt enough. Thing is...'

He looked up at Alan, who hadn't been invited to sit.

'This first yin, Patricia Doyle, Ah know that she works
doon in the steelworks offices so she'll no' be at home.'

'What about her mother, Sergeant?'

Tait considered the question.

'Aye, she micht be in, but her faither's a quarryman up at the Glenshiel quarry an' they bide in a
cottage aboot twa miles up the quarry road. Frae
here, ye're aboot three miles there, three back an'
ye'll miss Benson if ye head up there the noo.'

Alan turned his head and looked down at
Tait's notebook. The print was neat but un-
usually large and he suspected that Sergeant
Tait was likely in need of reading glasses.

'What aboot Betsy White?'

Tait shook his head.

'Works in wan o' the mills up in Johnstone, as does her mither, an' ye're no' traipsin' awa' up there. Naw, ye'd best hang fire an' wait 'til Benson turns up, see whit he has tae say for himsel'.'

He pulled an ancient silver watch from his jacket pocket.

'It's near twelve the noo, ye'd be as well bidin' yer time then awa' back doon tae the yard. Ah'll be keen tae hear whit Billy Benson has tae say for himsel.'

*

Alan was sitting in the small front office with a mug of tea while Kerr Brodie was standing with his back to the coal fire that, despite the season, was crackling merrily in the grate. He consulted his rather fine wristwatch, a birthday gift from Nancy. He smiled—surely she wouldn't have given him such a gift if she didn't—

'Penny for them, Alan?'

'What—oh, em, nothin', Kerr, I've got to go back doon tae the coal yard at half-twelve, I need a wee word wi' Billy Benson.'

Kerr snorted, took a final draw on his cigarette and threw the butt into the fire.

'Him! Big lump o' nothin'—was in my class at school. He's no' the brightest, that's for sure. Whit's he supposed tae have done onywey?'

Alan shrugged.

'No' sure if he's done anythin', Kerr, but you know Mary Campbell's gone missin'? Never came home last night.'

Kerr Brodie nodded.

'So that's why the Sarge wis bein' so nice

29

tae the mither—never usually gives her the time o' day. Where does Benson fit in?'

'I caught them up Braid's Close aboot ten o'clock last night, when I wis doin' the rounds. Skirt up, pants doon, you know...'

Kerr winked.

'Doesn'ae surprise me, mind ye, Mary's got a bit o' a name for hersel' over the past wee while.'

'Really?

'Aye, fast an' free, if ye ken whit Ah mean.'

'Interestin'' Alan responded, with a frown. 'I was under the impression that she and Benson had been seein' a bit of each other recently.'

'More than a bit if ye ask me,' retorted Brodie. Alan gave a weak smile—he didn't particularly like such vulgar remarks. He stood up.

'Right Kerr, best make ma way down, don't want to miss the bugger.'

*

Alan didn't make haste for the coal yard, however, figuring that if Benson detected his presence he might well jump off the lorry and make a run for it, like he had done the previous evening. The clouds had cleared and the sky was now a beautiful shade of blue as he walked slowly down School Street until he heard the ringing of the school lunch bell at twelve-thirty. Within minutes, a host of children of all ages came running down the hill, eager to get home for their lunch. Or maybe they had a few pennies to spend in the local baker's shop, where pies, bridies and sausage rolls, fresh out of the oven, had tempted him as a young schoolboy. But some of them, he knew, would be heading for the loch, their sandwiches wrapped in greaseproof paper. There, they would seek out unwary newts and water-beetles, dive-bombing them with stones while attempting to emulate the chatter of British airmen on a bombing sortie—just as he had done not so very long ago. It would be a while before World War Two became a distant memory; indeed, for some, such as Donald Tait, it would probably never become so.

He arrived at the yard entrance and was dismayed to find that McGeoch's lorries were still not in evidence. Mrs McGeoch was standing outside the office door, shaking her head.

'They're no' back yet, Alan. Dinn'a ken where they are, maybe they've had a puncture or a breakdoon.'

'Never mind, Mrs M, I'll just wait—I didn't want tae scare him off.'

She smiled up at the handsome young constable.

'Aye, wan look at you in yer uniform is enough tae—'

She was interrupted by a long, piercing scream, emanating from the area of the loch. She frowned.

'Bloomin' weans, it's the same every day. Whit a racket...'

The scream sounded again, joined by a second. Alan could feel the hairs on the back of his neck stand up; this wasn't the sound of schoolchildren at play. He looked at Mrs McGeoch, whose expression had turned to one of concern.

'What the—'

The screams were now interspersed with feeble cries for help. Alan turned and started to run, as did the two men who had been loading the coal sacks. He called over his shoulder.

'You've got a telephone, Mrs M—can you call the Sergeant, tell him there's trou-

31

ble o' some sort doon at the loch.'

*

Alan was a fit, strong young man and, despite his heavy
boots, he quickly left behind the two coal workers, habitual
smokers by their laboured breathing and the expressions on
their pasty, grey faces. Within minutes, he was on Lochside
Road where a group of six young boys, ten or eleven years
old, were huddled together. As he approached, he could see
that two of them appeared to be the centre of attention and
were in a state of near hysteria. He recognised one from
his road safety event at the school, a tall, gangly child with
a shock of red hair. Despite his height, he was universally
known as "Wee Tam", a consequence of sharing his first name
with his father, "Big Tam". Gently pushing the other, curious
children aside, Alan knelt down and took off his helmet.

'Now then, Wee Tam, what is it, what's
the matter? Have you hurt yoursel'?'

Tears were streaming down the child's face
and he was shaking uncontrollably. His friend
was in a similar condition. Alan reached out
and took the youngster by the shoulders.

'It's all right, Wee Tam, you know who I am, don't you?'

Wee Tam nodded but continued to sob, rivulets of
tears running down his sallow, rather grubby cheeks.
At the sound of footsteps, Alan turned round; the two
workers were approaching, closely followed by Mrs
McGeoch. Alan breathed an inward sigh of relief as
the woman bustled through and knelt beside him.

'There now, there now, Wee Tam, come
oan, sit oan ma knee. Here, wid ye like a
wee bit cake, it'll mak' ye feel better...'

As Mrs McGeoch soothed Wee Tam, trying in vain to pat down his mop of unruly
red hair, Alan spoke gently to the boy.

'So whit's the matter, Wee Tam? Whit's aw' this screamin'
aboot?' he asked, in as soothing a voice as he could muster.

Wee Tam pointed vaguely towards the loch.

'Doon there, Mister, doon in the watter.'

'Whit's doon in the water, Wee Tam?'

'A body, Mister, a deid body, aw' blood an' everythin'...'

*

The wait seemed interminable, although it only took
Sergeant Tait about ten minutes to arrive on his Velocette
LE motorcycle, the Barloch station not yet able toafford the
luxury of a motorised vehicle. By this time, Mrs McGeoch
was kneeling with both the traumatised boys enfolded in
her arms as they continued to sob. As Alan stood up, he
looked down at the woman in wonder. They were made of
different stuff, the likes of Mrs McGeoch, and he knew full
well that his own mother would have behaved in exactly the
same manner. He nodded to Sergeant Tait but, as he walked
towards his superior, he was aware of two of the other boys
furtively sidling towards the loch, presumably for their own
share of the horrors on offer.

'Here, you two, get yerselves back here
right now!' he barked. 'Stay where you are an'
don't be goin' anywhere near that loch.'

By this time a small crowd had gathered and Sergeant
Tait was looking decidedly worried. He beckoned to
Alan, who leaned down to hear the whispered words.

'Ah'll awa' doon' an see whit's whit—you keep

this lot at bay, dinn'a let onybody doon tae the water. Brodie will be here in a minute, he's oan foot.'

Alan looked along the road where, sure enough, Kerr Brodie was trotting towards them. Rather stiffly, the sergeant dismounted, laid his bike carefully on the ground and headed through the undergrowth towards the waters of Bar Loch. Alan and Kerr stood with their backs to him, keeping a watchful eye on all and sundry while ignoring the numerous questions.

'Who's deid, Mister?'

'Wis it the Commies whit done it, d'ye think, Mister?'

Alan was disappointed; having been first on the scene, he had hoped to accompany the sergeant in his search for the body. Then a jolt ran through him as he realised that he had never actually seen a corpse before, far less one with "blood an' everythin'", according to Wee Tam's description. Maybe it was for the best, especially as he had a strong suspicion as to whom it might be.

It took Sergeant Tait less than five minutes to return; there was a clamour of voices, all asking the same question—who was the victim? Tait was tight-lipped but his expression was grave. He approached the two constables, turning his back on the agitated crowd.

'Ah'm awa' back up tae call in the CID. Beyond oor scope, this sort o' thing. Make sure naebody goes near that loch, mind.'

Kerr Brodie's face had drained of colour but, still, he asked, 'D'ye think it's murder, Sarge?'

'No' for me tae say, laddie.'

'Em, an' who is...um, was it...?'

But Tait was already lifting his bike, much to the disappointment of the two constables and the crowd.

Chapter 4

'I'd rather you didn't, if you don't mind, Sergeant.'

Detective Sergeant Gordon McGinn stifled a sigh, sliding the offending cigarette back into the packet, which he then placed in the pocket of his navy-blue suit. He clambered into the driver's seat of the powerful police Wolseley, closed the door with a resounding clunk and pressed the starter. It was going to be a long journey. He cast a rather resentful sideways glance at his superior officer, the term "austere" springing into his mind. Clad in a plain, clerical-grey suit, the man had short dark hair, greying at the temples, small but alert eyes and a clean-shaven face, seemingly devoid of either expression or emotion. His thin lips were still pursed in an expression of distaste.

Detective Inspector Gabriel Nisbet had transferred from the City of Glasgow Police and had arrived at Paisley's Criminal Investigation Department some eight months previously. Within a relatively short space of time, the man had made himself highly unpopular. Looking more like a Free Presbyterian minister than an inspector of police, he was taciturn to say the least; he didn't smoke, no-one had known him to take a drink and all that McGinn knew of his superior's private life came from the plain gold wedding band that he wore on his left hand. However, that he was a competent detective wasn't in question; he had already uncovered and arrested a few of the hierarchy in a lucrative black market cigarettes-and-alcohol syndicate. He had tracked down the perpetrator of an attempted murder and had foiled an attempt to rob a Post Office van. Gordon McGinn had learned a lot; unfortunately, not when to keep his mouth firmly closed.

'So, sir, I'm assumin' it's a murder we're investigatin', eh?'

Nisbet didn't reply immediately; as always he seemed to be weighing and measuring his words before he spoke. McGinn, who had taken the call from Sergeant Tait, was about to wish he'd done the same. When the inspector finally spoke, his tone held a rather derisive sneer.

'You would be wise not to assume anything, McGinn. To "assume" makes an ass out of "you" and "me".'

McGinn gritted his teeth as Nisbet continued.

'You see, if we assume anything, we arrive with a pre-conceived idea of what may have happened. All we know at this stage is that a body has been found, in a loch, and with a serious head injury to the rear of the cranium...'

Who did the man think he was, the bloody Police Doctor...? Nisbet went on.

'...which could, of course, mean that the victim fell backwards and struck a solid object, that they fell in to the loch and were hit by a vessel of some sort, or that they were, indeed, a victim of an attack.'

McGinn interjected.

'Not sure if there's that many vessels *on* Barloch, sir.'

Nisbet turned and scrutinised his sergeant.

'You're not *sure*, McGinn? Unless you can categorically state that there are no vessels on the loch, then we cannot rule out that possibility. As with the other two, it is simply a process of elimination. And, of course, we will have to wait until the pathologist arrives and gives us his opinion, which will have a strong bearing on the case. I take it you telephoned him?'

Of course I bloody did, thought McGinn.

'Yes, sir. It's Dr Miller that's on call, he'll be on his way by now.'

'Good; a sound chap, Miller. Watch, slow down here, McGinn, there's a school just around the corner and it'll be coming out soon, we don't want an accident.'

Detective Sergeant McGinn bit the inside of his mouth; God, he could fair do with that bloody cigarette now!

*

The rest of the journey was made mostly in silence; McGinn was a competent driver, despite Nisbet's observations, and soon they had taken a right turn off the main road to Irvine, heading down the road leading to the village of Barloch. The sergeant was also, by nature, a gregarious type and sitting in silence didn't come naturally to him.

'Don't really know this part o' the world too well, sir. Nice countryside though—that'll be Bar Loch on the right, I'd imagine.'

'Mm? Oh, yes, I suppose so. Right, I think the road should be here...'

McGinn indicated and turned right, crossing over a narrow, hump-backed bridge. To their left, a grassed space led across to the railway embankment, a green diesel multiple-unit trundling sedately across its summit, heading away from the station towards Glensherrie.

'Right, McGinn, that's Kirk Street up to the left there...ah, here we are. Usual crowd of damned onlookers. Pull in here, don't want any of these brats clambering all over the vehicle.'

McGinn pulled in at the side of the road and quickly

exited the car, pulling his cigarettes from his pocket and lighting up before Nisbet got the opportunity to object. He buttoned up his suit jacket, rather tighter than it had been when he had purchased it, and the two officers approached the now slightly depleted crowd. Constables McInnes and Brodie were still standing guard, while Sergeant Tait chatted in quiet, sombre tones with a tall, sparse figure clad in clerical grey and wearing a dog-collar. McGinn smiled to himself; put that collar around the inspector's neck and he'd certainly look the part! The two older men puffed on their pipes as they conversed, Tait turning towards the approaching figures.

'Sergeant Tait?' asked Nisbet.

'Aye, that's me...'

He indicated the two other uniformed officers.

'...and constables Brodie and McInnes.'

'Detective Inspector Nisbet, Sergeant McGinn, Paisley CID. So, tell me what's happened—and can I ask you not to put your own slant on this please, just adhere to the facts.'

McGinn could see his fellow sergeant bristling already but, with a strong effort of will, Donald Tait recounted the bare facts of the discovery. McGinn took notes on a small pad as Tait spoke, then there was a pause once the older man had finished. Nisbet nodded as if in approval.

'I see. Good. Now, the pathologist is on his way, a Doctor Miller, so can you get your men to send him down as soon as he gets here? Right, shall we have a look?'

McGinn resisted the temptation to shake his head; Nisbet managed to make it sound as if they were off to view Sergeant Tait's bloody garden. As he caught his counterpart's eye, a brief spark of understanding flickered between the two men; they both knew the type of superior officer they were dealing with.

Nisbet briefly stopped to speak to the two constables, who confirmed what Tait had already told them. As Tait led the two detectives towards the loch, the inspector turned back towards Alan.

'McIntyre, I take it you've allowed nobody to attend the scene? I hope nothing's been disturbed.'

'No, sir,' replied Alan, his face set as in stone.' Not a thing, nobody's been down as long as we've been here. Em, and it's McInnes, sir.'

Nisbet favoured him with a frown.

'Hm. Right then, Sergeant?'

As they walked away through the boggy grass, Nisbet continued.

'You see, it is vital that such a scene is secured and that nobody has the opportunity either to tamper with or to contaminate the crime scene—if, in fact, a crime has been committed.'

Sergeant Tait rose to the bait

'Looks pretty like it tae me, Inspector.'

'Yes, well, as I was just saying to Sergeant McGinn earlier—'

'Richt, just yonder, sir' interrupted Tait, pointing to where, a few yards away, the body lay face down in about a foot of water, hands spread-eagled and with one leg twisted to the side. A lone magpie was sitting on the corpse's shoulder, as if about to peck at the already decaying flesh. It hopped then flew away with its characteristic "cak-cak-cak."

'Aye, wan for sorrow richt enough,' mumbled Tait.

'I beg your pardon?'

'Och, nothin', Inspector. Richt, here
we are, an' it's no' a pretty sicht.'

*

The crowd was gradually dissipating and Alan McInnes was
getting rather bored standing guard. The police doctor had
arrived in a brand new Land Rover, resplendent in shiny dark
green. Alan had never seen one before and he was impressed
at its appearance, although it seemed an odd car for a doctor
to be driving. Dr Miller had climbed out, a vision in tweed
plus-fours, a deerstalker hat and a pair of green rubber boots,
emblazoned with the name "Hunter"; the man obviously
knew what to expect! He seemed a decent sort, Alan had
thought, spending a few moments chatting before heading
down the group at the lochside. An ambulance had followed
not long after, its blue light continuing to circle slowly on
its roof while the two uniformed ambulance men leaned on
the bonnet as they smoked in silence; he didn't envy their
forthcoming task. After a few minutes, he heard Sergeant
Tait calling out.

'McInnes—can ye come doon here a wee minute?'

Alan exchanged a glance with Kerr, then set off through
the boggy scrubland, swallowing hard. He had a strong
enough stomach but he had heard tales of people vom-
iting on their first encounter with a body in such circumstances and he certainly didn't want to let himself
down, especially as he had a pretty good idea of the
identity of the victim. He arrived at the small group,
where Dr Miller was kneeling and the other three stood
and watched. With a deep breath, he took the last few
steps and joined them, looking down at the sad remains. He looked up in astonishment, catching Ser-

geant Tait's eye. The older man shook his head sadly.

'Aye, lad, no' exactly whit I expected either.'

*

The police photographer had arrived and photographed the body in situ. Once satisfied, he stepped back, allowing the officers to move towards the corpse. Surprise had overtaken Alan's misgivings and, with some considerable effort, accompanied by rather pointed instruction from both the doctor and Inspector Nisbet, they managed to turn the body over onto its back. Alan stood up, wiping his hands on his trousers; despite the smearing of mud and the bloating that was already starting following immersion in the water, there was no doubt. He was looking down on the mortal remains of Hugh Campbell.

Chapter 5

Dr Miller, satisfied that he had gleaned all available evidence from the scene, summoned the ambulance-men. Hugh Campbell's body was lifted rather unceremoniously onto the canvas stretcher, covered with a sheet and removed to the safety of the ambulance. A few onlookers tried to get closer for a glimpse of the corpse but they were quickly admonished by Alan and Kerr. As the ambulance disappeared along the road and over the bridge, its blue light still flashing in a desultory fashion, the few remaining bystanders walked away, leaving two trench-coat clad individuals, one holding a press camera. As they approached, obviously looking for a statement from the police, Nisbet glared at them. His expression was sufficient; the two men turned and walked back to their Austin and drove off, empty-handed.

'Damned press,' muttered Nisbet. 'Poking their noses in.'

He turned to Sergeant Tait, who was looking exhausted.

'See that nothing gets out—I don't want this affair public knowledge just yet.'

Tait sighed.

'Ye'll be lucky there, sir. It's only a wee village, word travels fast. Speaking o' which...'

He looked at Alan.

'We'd best go an' inform Mrs Campbell that we've found her husband. Aye, an' that her daughter's still no' turned up either. Poor wummin.'

'Her daughter?' asked McGinn.

43

'Aye,' replied Tait. 'Seems her lassie, Mary, never came home last nicht, but we're thinkin' that she probably had a bit too much tae drink an' maybe spent the nicht at a friend's hoose.'

'I see,' replied McGinn, rubbing his chin. 'Is there any other family?'

Tait shook his head.

'No...weel, Meg's got an older son frae a previous marriage.'

McGinn and Nisbet exchanged a glance.

'Ye see, her first husband wis killed at Dunkirk an' she re-married Hughie Campbell. The older boy... whit's his name...oh, aye, Colin, he's in the Merchant Navy an' Ah couldn'ae tell ye when he wis last hame. Didn'ae get on wi' the stepfather an' he left years ago. Naw, Meg Campbell's aw' on her ain—an' she hasn'ae a freend tae speak o'—well, no' in the village, anywey.'

Nisbet frowned.

'She's not well-liked, then?'

Tait shook his head.

'The wummin has a sharp tongue and keeps hersel' close, if ye ken whit Ah mean.'

Sergeant McGinn nodded and looked back at Nisbet.

'Could we get a WPC down from Paisley, sir? Might be best, under the circumstances.'

Nisbet let out a snort of annoyance.

'Hmph, that might take some time. As the sergeant has pointed out, it's a small village.'

'My mother would maybe go wi' you, Sergeant.'

As soon as he said it, Alan could see the look of both gratitude and relief on Tait's weary features.

'Aye, she micht at that, she's got a big heart, has

44

Isa. Once we're back up at the office, Ah'll give her a wee call, see if she can spare the time.'

'Good, that's that sorted out,' stated Nisbet. 'Now, where are the two boys who found the body?'

'Mrs McGeoch took them back up to the coal office, sir.'

'And where's that, Constable?'

'Just up the bank there,' he replied, pointing to the steep slope across from them. 'The yard road leads off Kirk Street, just round the corner.'

Nisbet turned to McGinn.

'You go up with the constable and take a statement from them. We need to know if they noticed anything apart from the body, if they touched or took anything—'

'They're just bairns, sir,' interjected Sergeant Tait.

'They may well be, Sergeant, but they are also witnesses. They discovered the body, you just don't know what children might get up to. They may have seen something before they saw the body, lifted it and forgotten—accidentally or otherwise.'

'Right, sir' said McGinn, turning and walking away. 'This way, McInnes?'

'Aye, sir, along here then turn right, up Kirk Street,' replied Alan, grateful to be leaving; he didn't warm to Inspector Nisbet and, judging by the expression in his face, neither did Sergeant Tait.

*

A few minutes later, the two officers turned up the ramp leading to the goods yard. Suddenly, Alan stopped, swearing softly under his breath. McGinn turned and gave him a quizzical look.

'Somethin' on your mind, McInnes?'

'Aye, sir. I was actually down here to interview a chap called Billy Benson. Works on the coal lorries.'

'Oh aye— an' what was that about?'

'Em,, well...Mary Campbell, the girl that's missin'—she was the daughter o' the victim, of course.'

McGinn nodded.

'Aye, when your sergeant mentioned that you'd been keeping an eye out for a missing girl, I'm pretty sure that was who he'd expected the corpse to be.'

'Aye—and I suppose I did as well. You see, I saw the girl last night wi' this Benson fellow and I'd been waitin' for a word with him when the boys started screamin' down at the loch. I'd completely forgotten, what with all the excitement.'

McGinn smiled grimly.

'Excitement? Aye, I suppose you could call it that! Will Benson be here now, d'you think?'

'Probably not—he'll likely be away back out on the lorry, deliverin' the coal. I'll need to come back down about five o'clock, see if I can speak to him then.'

'Well, we'd best let the Inspector know all this as soon as possible, he doesn't appreciate things bein' kept from him, if you know what I mean. See, when you get involved in CID work, whenever you think a crime may have been committed, it pays to see if there have been any other unusual occurrences around the same time, criminal or otherwise. They might no' be related—but, then again they might.'

McGinn paused.

'So what d'you think o' Inspector Nisbet, then?'

The question was innocent enough, but Alan wasn't going to let himself fall into any trap.

'No' really my place to say, sir.'

McGinn laughed, a cheerful chuckle.

'Very diplomatic, son. He's a bloody good detective, mind, but he's a hard man to like.'

'I know what you mean—is he local?'

'No, he came down from Glasgow earlier this year. All I know about him is that he's married an' that's only on account of the wedding band he wears. Could even be a widower, for all I know. Doesn't seem to drink, doesn't approve of smokin'

...speakin' of which...'

McGinn delved into his pocket and took out his cigarette packet, offering it first to Alan; Capstan full strength, un-tipped, he noticed.

'Em, no thanks, sir, I don't smoke either.'

McGinn chuckled again as he removed a cigarette then delved into another pocket, taking out his matches.

'Aye, bad habit, right enough; at least, so my wife tells me. You'd get on well with Inspector Nisbet, mind.'

He stared at the pack for a moment, a distant look on his face; it was a look Alan had seen before.

'Picked up the habit in the Merchant Navy. Full strength, too, straight away. Difficult times, though, needed somethin' to get us through those damned Atlantic Convoys...'

Alan recognised the ghosts passing across McGinn's features—he had seen them before on Sergeant Tait's face, on the rare occasions that he mentioned the war. McGinn looked up.

'You'd be too young, of course?'

'Aye, I was only six when it started.'

'What about your father?'

'He was a railway guard.'

McGinn nodded, still holding the matches and the unlit cigarette.

'Aye, a reserved occupation. They didn't get off lightly either, mind you.'

'No, they didn't. He was in the First War, though.'

'Really; God, they had it a hell o' a lot worse than any o' us. He ever talk about it?'

Alan shook his head.

'Never. He picked up some shrapnel but he just puts up wi' it.'

McGinn nodded; a few moments passed, memories awakened.

'You enjoy policin', McInnes?'

'Aye, I do, sir. Generally it's a quiet wee village. This is the first time I've had experience o' anythin' o this sort. Em, the thing is...'

McGinn tilted his head to one side in question.

'Ah'd really like to join the CID, do whit you're doin'...sir.'

McGinn smiled.

'Would you, now? Hmm...by the way, it's Gordon McGinn.'

The sergeant extended his hand and Alan, unsurprised at the gesture, extended his own. They shook in the customary Masonic manner, a few words were exchanged and, within seconds the two men had an understanding and a bond; a bond of which Alan's father would, no doubt, have strongly disapproved.

'Good man. Right, we can talk about all that later, best get up an' see these two poor wee buggers.'

He struck the match, lit his cigarette and inhaled deeply before breathing out the strong blue tobacco smoke and blowing out the match. Although an abstainer, Alan was surrounded by smokers and the habit didn't particularly bother him. However, there was something about the smell of that curiously strong tobacco, overlaid with the acrid, sulphurous smell of the freshly struck match, that struck a chord in his memory. It was probably nothing, he thought. And yet...

They walked on until they reached McGeoch's coal office.

'This it, then?'

'Aye, sir, but they're no' inside.'

Alan pointed further up the yard, where Mrs McGeoch was standing, a boy on each side of her holding her hands. A small, black and rather rusty steam engine was busy shunting wagons in the goods yard and the boys, as with all boys of their age, were transfixed. With an indulgent smile, McGinn started to walk over and the trio turned as the officers feet crunched on the mixture of clinker and dirt.

'Hello, Alan,' Mrs McGeoch said with a smile. 'The lads are jist watchin' the wee engine shuntin' the trucks.'

Wee Tam looked up with a rather toothless grin.

'Aye, mister, it's rare!'

Alan knelt beside the boy, who had what looked like chocolate smudges on his face; Mrs McGeoch was doing a grand job. He pointed at the engine.

'That wee engine there is called a "Jinty",
Wee Tam. See, it's got three wheels each side,
which makes a total o' how many?'

Wee Tam's brow's furrowed, his
lips moving as he counted.

'Six, mister!'

'Good lad, you're right, the Jinty has six
wheels and they're joined with that big rod

on the side. It's called an "oh-six-oh".

Wee Tam repeated it, committing it to memory, as Alan continued.

'Now, see those big tanks on the side, they hold the water that makes the steam.'

'Where dis the watter come fae, mister?' asked Wee Tam's friend.

Alan pointed further along the yard.

'See that big tower over there, with the grey tank on the top—that's called a water-tower. When the tanks are empty, they drive the Jinty over there an' fill the tanks from that big bag that's hangin' doon, see?'

The boys looked over with a sense of wonder. McGinn cleared his throat and Alan stood up.

'Em, sorry, sir...'

'Don't worry, McInnes, I've got a wee lad myself, he'd love it down here. Best be havin' a word though. Mrs McGeoch—I'm Sergeant McGinn, Paisley CID, would you mind if we used your office?'

She gave him a slightly disparaging look.

'Aye, only if Ah can sit in wi' them—they're just bairns, Sergeant, an' they've had enough shocks for the wan day, if no' a lifetime.'

He nodded his assent and they set off towards the small office. Wee Tam, still holding her hand, looked up at Mrs McGeoch and pointed at the two coal trucks in the adjacent siding, where the labourers were continuing to empty the contents of the furthest one into sacks.

'Is the wee eng...the Jinty...takin they twa' wagons awa' today, Mrs M?'

She shook her head.

'Naw, Wee Tam, the men are still emptyin' it, see?

50

It'll be Thursday afore the engine comes back an' takes them. It'll leave us twa full yins, loaded wi' coal fur the village. Yer mammy gets her coal frae us so you micht even be gettin' some o' that stuff there!'

Wee Tam looked again in wonder, the earlier events completely forgotten; for the moment...

*

The interview didn't take long; with the resilience of youth, the boys recounted their grisly find in a matter-of-fact way and Alan was sure that they had neither touched anything nor gone too close to the body. Sergeant McGinn also seemed satisfied as he closed his notebook.

'Right, boys, you did very well.'

He delved into his trouser pocket and pulled out some coins, passing each boy a shiny sixpenny piece.

'Here, you can get yourselves some sweeties on the way home.'

The boys looked at the coins in astonishment, probably several times what they normally received as pocket-money. Mrs McGeoch, too, regarded the sergeant in a considerably more kindly manner.

'Ah'll keep the laddies here until their folks get home,' she announced. 'The school's finished an' there's nae sense sendin' them oot on the streets now.'

'Thanks, Mrs McGeoch, that's a good idea,' replied McGinn; he and Alan both knew that it would also keep the boys' first-hand experiences quiet—for the time being.

'What time's the lorries back, Mrs M?'

'Ony time soon, Alan, jist when their roonds is done. You'd likely no' get a chance tae speak tae Billy earlier, wi' wan thing an' another?'

'No, an' I still need to—maybe even more so now.'

Mrs McGeoch's face looked grave as she stared up at him.

'Wis it...wis it her, the lassie he wis with?'

Alan shook his head.

'No, Mrs M, thankfully it wasn't.'

'Thank the Lord. But who...?'

'I'm very sorry, Mrs McGeoch,' replied Mc-Ginn, 'but we can't say at the moment, although I daresay you'll find out soon enough.'

She pursed her lips frustratedly, but Alan knew that the sergeant was all too correct.

*

They reported back to the police station, Alan first having asked Mrs McGeoch to try to keep Benson at the yard should he come back early. Kerr Brodie gave them a nod as they entered.

'The Inspector's in Sergeant Tait's office—ye've tae go through.'

Alan knocked; instead of Tait's gentle beckoning, he was answered with a curt "come."

Tait was absent, presumably enroute to break the tragic news to Mrs Campbell and Alan wondered if his mother was with him. He hoped she wouldn't be annoyed with him but he knew that she had a big heart; she wouldn't see even a woman such as Meg Campbell left alone and uncomforted when receiving such devastating news. Nisbet appeared to have commandeered Tait's desk, the sheaf of the sergeant's paperwork having been summarily pushed to one side. Instead, Nisbet had his notebook, as well as several sheets of lined foolscap pages, in front of him.

'Well—what did the boys have to say?'

McGinn gave a brief synopsis of the interview, with which Nisbet seemed content. The sergeant sat down across from his superior while Alan remained standing, there being no additional seats in the cramped office.

The Inspector said, 'Right, we have two separate incidents here; Hugh Campbell, a murder victim—Dr Miller has confirmed that Campbell was, indeed, murdered—and Mary Campbell, a missing girl, the daughter of said victim. Did you notice anything about Hugh Campbell?'

McGinn turned and looked at Alan, with the ghost of a wink.

'McInnes?'

'Em, yes sir, he had some nasty lookin' scratches on his face.'

A pause.

'Indeed. Well spotted, McInnes. Does that suggest anything?'

McGinn answered this time.

'Probably in a fight. Most likely with a woman—it would need a pretty good set o' fingernails to inflict that kind of damage.'

Nisbet was writing with his pencil, a neat, precise script, Alan noticed.

'Yes. So we have Hugh Campbell, presumably in an altercation of some sort, with a woman, who has scratched his face. He is then hit on the back of the head, probably with a rock, according to Dr Miller. We also have his daughter gone astray...and still missing?'

He gave Alan a questioning glance.

'Yes, sir. We haven't been able to locate her as yet. She didn't turn up for work this morning.'

The pencil scratched again.

'Hm.'

'Sir?'

'Yes, McInnes?'

'When I was on my rounds last night, I came
across Mary Campbell, the missin' girl, em...well,
bein' intimate with a certain Billy Benson.'

Nisbet snapped his pencil down on the desk.

'Why wasn't I told?'

McGinn interjected.

'The discovery of the body took precedence, sir. McInnes
was waiting to interview Benson, who works on the coal
lorries, when the boys discovered Campbell's body.'

Another pause. Alan wondered if it was intentional;
it was certainly unsettling. Finally Nisbet spoke again.

'I see. Have you since spoken to Benson?'

'No sir, he's away out on deliveries again
but I'm goin' back down to the yard in about
half-an- hour. I'll speak to him then.'

'Very well. So, we may have a suspect.'

'I really don't think Benson's capable o' murder, sir...'

Nisbet glared at Alan.

'You don't *think*, Constable? Unless you can categorically state that Benson is incapable of murder,
then "not thinking" is irrelevant. The blow must have
required some force—is this Benson well built?'

Alan nodded, his face reddening at the reprimand. McGinn cast him a sympathetic glance.

'Yes sir, he is. It's a hard physical job on the coal lorry.'

'So he'd be perfectly capable of inflicting such a blow?'

Alan decided it was best not to argue.

'Yes sir, he would.'

The Inspector paused again, this

time consulting his notes.

'So, we have Benson in a relationship with Mary Campbell. We have Campbell senior, apparently in an altercation with a girl. We have the girl still missing and the father murdered.'

He looked up.

'At the moment, then, I'd say we have two potential suspects; Benson...and Mary Campbell. We need to find both of them, as soon as possible. Right, McInnes, get back down there right away and wait for this Benson, we don't want him slipping through our fingers. Bring him back up here for questioning, might loosen his tongue a bit. I'll get—what's your colleague's name, McInnes?'

'Constable Brodie, sir.'

'I'll get Brodie to commence a *proper* search for the girl; that doesn't appear to have been instigated as yet...'

Alan bit the inside of his mouth in anger; there had barely been time.

'...and when Sergeant Tait returns, we'll see if we can draft any additional officers to the case.'

Nisbet stood up.

'McGinn, you'd best go with McInnes, in case this Benson fellow decides to resist.'

Chapter 6

Their sombre task completed, Sergeant Donald Tait and Mrs Isa McInnes walked back along Glenhead Street in a silence that was far beyond companionable. They had known each other nigh on sixty years, playing as toddlers even before they had gone to Barloch Primary School. They had shared hardship, sorrow and happiness; they needed no words, silently drawing strength from one another.

As they turned to walk down School Street, Donald finally spoke.

'Yer laddie's doin' well.'

She smiled.

'I'm glad to hear that, Donny, and he does seem to be enjoying the job—he told me he'd passed his sergeant's exams too.'

'Aye, first go an' all—he's a bricht one, so he is.'

They walked on in silence, then Isa spoke again.

'Of course, Gilbert wanted him to follow him into the railways but, well, look what happened tae him...'

Donny Tait gave her arm a sympathetic squeeze.

'Aye, right enough, Isa, ye wouldn'ae wish that on anyone. Naw, Alan's got the makin's o' a fine policeman, like ye said he's passed his sergeant's exams an' promotion'll come soon enough.'

'He's got a young lady now, too.'

Tait smiled.

'Has he noo? Richt enough, Ah thocht there wis a wee

spring in his step recently...who's the lucky lassie?'

'Nancy Wright—she's a teacher at the school.'

He nodded his approval; they walked on
for a few more minutes, then the sergeant
spoke again, his tone more sombre.

'Ye ken, thon Meg Campbell's a richt strange
wan, there's no gettin' awa' frae it.'

Isa shook her head.

'It's odd, Donny, I can't understand it; I
mean, I know she's beside herself over Mary
goin' missin' but I'd have expected...'

Her voice tailed off; she took out her lace
handkerchief and wiped away a tear.

'There now, lass—Ah ken whit ye mean, though.
But thon Hughie Campbell wisn'ae an easy man.'

There was another short silence.

'I don't know if you noticed, Donny, I held
her hand at one point; then I put my hand
on her arm and she flinched. It felt swollen—I think she's got a nasty bruise there.'

Tait nodded his agreement.

'Wouldn'ae be the first time Ah've seen her wi'
a black eye—or a split lip, for that matter. He
wis aye quick wi' his hauns, wis Campbell.'

They walked on down School Street then
stopped at the corner of Ladeside Road.

'Well, this is me, Donny.'

He gazed into her soft brown eyes. She looked up
at the grizzled, careworn man that the handsome,
dark-haired youth from her past had become.

'Ah dinn' ken whit Ah'd have done without ye today, Isa. Ye're wan in a million, so ye are.'

With great gentleness and fondness, and with a surreptitious glance to ensure no-one was watching, he took her dainty hand and gave it a squeeze. She returned it, then pulled away.

'Oh Donny, when did we become old?' she sighed, 'and although I couldn't exactly say it was a pleasure...'

'Enough said, lassie, enough said.'

She turned way before any more careless words spilled out, then looked over her shoulder to where he stood, watching her walk away.

'You look after yourself, Donald Tait.'

'You too, lass, you too...'

*

Alan was back at the coal yard, accompanied by Detective Sergeant McGinn. The two Albion lorries stood in the yard as they entered the office, to find Mrs McGeoch in conversation with Alec, her husband. The burly, dirt-begrimed man turned and extended his hand, shaking Alan's hand with a grip similar to that of McGinn, whom Alan introduced.

'So the wife says ye're efter a word wi' Benson?'

'Yes, Mr McGeoch, is he about?'

Alec McGeoch looked troubled.

'Weel, that's the funny thing. We cam' back up for wir lunch tae find a' this carry on, Benson went aff tae see whit wis happenin' an' never came back.'

Alan and McGinn exchanged glances.

'Any idea where he might have gone, sir?' asked McGinn.

Alec McGeoch shook his head.

'Sorry, Sergeant, nane. He jist buggered off an' never came back. He'd been doin' okay, too, Ah wis beginnin' tae think the boy had final-

58

ly settled doon. Seems like Ah wis wrang.'

'Any o' the other men know where he went?'

'Naw, they jist said he told them he was goin' tae see whit aw the fuss wis aboot, Never came back. Left us a man doon', that's why we're so bloody late back.'

Mrs McGeoch gave him a frosty look.

'Sorry, pet, Ah'm jist angry wi' Benson.'

The two officers took their leave, having a quick word with the remaining coalmen as they passed. None of them seemed to have any idea of where Benson had gone, nor did they think he had been acting strangely that morning. Finally, the two officers walked back down the ramp towards Kirk Street. McGinn took out his cigarettes and lit up, the smell sparking that same, perplexing memory with Alan.

'So what now, McInnes? Where does this Benson fellow live?

'His father's a quarryman up at the Glenshiel Quarry; he stays in a cottage a few miles up the hill at the back o' the village. Actually, one o' Mary Campbell's friends lives next door. If we go up we could have a word wi' her at the same time, see if she's heard anythin".

'Good idea, McInnes. Just as well I've got the Wolseley. Come on then, let's go for a wee hurl.'

*

Quarry Row consisted of two sets of semi-detached, single-storey stone cottages, sitting behind a low stone wall; all of which had been hewn from Glenshiel quarry, another mile or so up the rough track that ran along the River Sheil glen. The garden of the first was overgrown with weeds, the paved path cracked. All four chimneys, however, showed a curl of smoke, indicating that the occupants were now at home. McGinn pulled the Wolseley over to one side of the track and the two officers got out. Alan scanned the four dwellings.

'I think the Bensons live in the first one.'

They walked through the gate, which was hanging on its post by one hinge, and up the uneven path. McGinn banged on the door, to which they heard a reply

'Aye, in ye come, it's open.'

They pushed open the paint-peeled wooden door and found themselves in a narrow room. At one side, a fire was burning in a range and there was a pervading smell of bacon and eggs. An older man, his shirt unbuttoned and braces hanging by his side, was sitting at a rickety table, finishing his meal. He looked up at the two men.

'Aye-aye...oh, it's yersel', Alan. How're ye doin'?'

'Aye, fine, Mr Benson. Yoursel'?'

'Och, just gettin' by. Whit can Ah dae for ye?'

'We're looking for your son, Mr Benson' replied McGinn.

'Billy?' Benson senior shrugged. 'Hav'nae seen him this afternoon—in fact, Ah dinn'ae see much o' him at a' these days. He's got a lassie—weel, so he says.'

'Oh? Any idea who she is?' asked Alan.

Benson grinned, revealing stumps of teeth.

'Weel, he tells me it's Mary Campbell, though Ah'd have thocht she'd have set her sichts a bit higher. Though maybe Ah says it whit shouldn'ae. But he's got a job now, on McGeoch's lorry, so he's dain' his best.'

The grin faded.

'Here, whit's up—he's no' in trouble, is he?'

'Mr Benson, when did you last see you son?' asked McGinn.

'This mornin'— came doon an' he wis

60

lyin' sleepin' oan the settee there.'

'D'you know what time he came home last night?'

Benson shrugged.

'Nae idea. Ah turn in about nine—there's nae electric up oor way yet an' onywey, it's a hard shift Ah've got up the quarry, Ah need ma kip. Billy's got a wee room up in the loft but the creakin' o' the stairs wakens me up, so if he's late, he sleeps oan the settee. Like Ah said, he wis here this mornin'.'

'He didn't turn up for work this afternoon; any idea where he might have gone?'

Benson shrugged again and took a slurp of tea.

'Naw, nane, sorry. Likely he's awa' doon the pub, spendin' aw' his new-found wealth.'

'Mind if we have a look around, Mr Benson?' asked McGinn. Benson gave a humourless laugh.

'Please yersel, Sergeant, it'll no' tak' ye long. There's this room, there's ma bedroom, another wee room fu' o' junk, then there's Billy's space up above. Oh, an' dinn'ae forget the ootside toilet and the wee coal shed up the back...let me know if ye find him, won't ye?'

'What about Mrs Benson...'

Alan cringed at the question as Benson's face clouded over.

'Deid these past fower years, thank's fur remindin me...'

*

They didn't find Billy Benson; as indicated by Benson senior, there was no trace of him either inside or outside. They exited, Benson asking Alan to "mind me tae yer auld man."

'Well, that was a waste o' bloody time, McInnes. D'you think Benson senior's tellin' us the truth?'

Alan considered the question.

'Aye, I'd say so—he's pretty straight, is old man Benson, I don't think he's hidin' anythin".

'Fair enough. Right, where does this Doyle girl stay?'

The next block of cottages were slightly larger, obviously designed more as family homes. They walked up to the first and Alan knocked; a woman, her hair in a net and a spotless floral apron tied around her ample form, answered the door.

'Aye?'

'Mrs Doyle?'

The woman squinted at Alan.

'You're Isa's boy.' It was a statement rather than a question. Alan nodded.

'Mrs Doyle, we're tryin' to trace Mary Campbell and I believe that Patricia's friendly with her. Can we have a word with her, please?'

The woman turned her head.

'Patricia—the Polis is here tae speak tae ye.'

*

Patricia Doyle was unable to provide any useful information regarding Mary Campbell. They had travelled to Paisley the previous Saturday to attend the cinema, where they had been suitably scared by the film *North by North-West*. Afterwards, they had bought a fish supper then got the train home, parting company at the station. Patricia hadn't seen her friend since and hadn't expected to until the following weekend. She had been surprised at Mary's disappearance and, when asked about Billy Benson, she had given a knowing smile.

'Aye, she seemed fond o' him, richt enough, though

62

God knows why. Ach, he's a weel-enough built boy but he's no' whit ye'd ca' bricht, if ye get ma meanin'...'

Mary hadn't indicated to Patricia when she'd next be seeing Benson, nor did she think it likely that Betsy White had seen her friend either. She had briefly met Betsy and her mother in the village that afternoon and their friend's disappearance hadn't been mentioned. The two officers returned to the Wolseley with little further information although, by her expression, they had brought a load of worry on to the slim shoulders of Patricia Doyle. As they closed the gate, she had called, a little tearfully.

'Ah hope ye find her, Mr McInnes. Ah know she's got a bit o' a reputation but she's a'richt, really. She an' Billy...weel, they were close, Ah don't think he'd harm a hair oan her heid, honest Ah don't.'

As McGinn started the engine, he gave Alan an odd look.

'D'you know *everyone* around here, McInnes?'

Alan grinned.

'Aye, pretty much, sir. Born an' bred, that's me.'

*

Inspector Nisbet seemed unimpressed by their efforts.

'Hm, you've not managed to find out a great deal, have you, McGinn?'

'There wasn't a great deal to be found out, sir. Benson might well turn up tonight—as might Mary Campbell.'

The customary pause ensued.

'Maybe, but somehow I think it unlikely.'

He looked up at Alan.

'McInnes, what about trains? Benson might have taken a train somewhere—have you checked?'

'No sir, an' the stationmaster will be away now, it'll

63

be the assistant. I'll go down first thing and ask him.'

'Do that.'

Sergeant Tait interjected.

'Mind ye're on back shift, lad. ye've already done a shift an' a half today.'

'That's okay, Sergeant, I'm quite happy to assist.'

The ghost of a smile flickered across Nisbet's stony face.

'Good, McInnes, that's the spirit. Right, McGinn, we'll call it a night now and come back in the morning. Sergeant Tait, if anything transpires, call the Paisley Office and either myself or Sergeant McGinn can be contacted.'

The two officers departed, McGinn giving Alan and Tait a nod as he left. Tait let out a weary sigh.

'Thank Christ that yin's awa'. Dear God Almighty, he's wan o' the worst Ah've ever encountered.'

'Aye, Sergeant, he's a difficult man to warm to, right enough.'

'Richt, you get yersel' awa' home an' get some rest...'

'But I'm supposed to be on the back shift today.'

'Aye, Ah ken, but dinn'ae you worry, Brodie an' I will cover the shift, you've done mair than enough for wan day, especially as ye've volunteered tae be back doon in the mornin."

'Okay, if you're sure, Sergeant, I'll be off.'

Suddenly, Tait's mouth dropped open.

'Here—Ah've jist had a thought.'

Alan stopped half way to the door.

'What's that, Sergeant?'

'Maybe the twa o' them's eloped!'

Alan saw the smile begin on Tait's lips and he grinned back.

'Aye, wouldn't that be one in the eye for Inspector Nisbet! 'Night, Sarge.'

As he was leaving the office, Tait called out.

'An' tell yer mither again that Ah'm richt
grateful for a' her help the day.'

Alan smiled in reply, vaguely aware of a brief and
unfamiliar softening of Tait's careworn features.

*

Inspector Nisbet and Sergeant McGinn had almost reached
the outskirts of Johnstone, the mill-town situated just a
few miles outside Paisley, before Nisbet spoke. McGinn
had been aware of his boss's eyebrows furrowing in silent
thought from time to time and decided it was best to remain
silent, an effort which would have been greatly relieved by
a cigarette. Finally, Nisbet gave a sigh; he sounded weary,
McGinn thought.

'We need to find this Benson fellow; I'm certain that he's the key.'

'D'you think so, sir? Em, you don't think there's any
possibility that the two of them are in cahoots? Both
the Doyle girl and Benson's old man seem to think that
Mary Campbell and Benson were an "item", so to speak.'

The customary pause ensued.

'She disappeared last night, McGinn. Benson
was at work until lunchtime today. No, I think he
knew what we'd find at the loch and made off.'

'But surely, if he was the killer, he'd
have made off before now, sir?'

'Not necessarily. Benson might have thought no-one
would find the body until later; presumably he didn't
consider the presence of the schoolchildren at lunchtime. However, it is eminently possible that he's also

killed Mary and secreted her remains elsewhere.'

McGinn chewed his lip; already it was proving to be a somewhat complex case. Nisbet continued.

'No, my working theory, if you like, is that Benson has murdered Mary; the father, somehow, suspected this and Benson subsequently killed Campbell senior. We need to find him—I wish bloody McInnes had had the foresight to speak to the stationmaster earlier.'

'To be fair, sir, we didn't know Benson had run off until after five. We were busy following other leads until then.'

'Hm, I suppose that's true. Well, if the girl hasn't turned up overnight, we'll need to get more officers down and start searching the loch, the woodlands etcetera. Could be a costly operation, too, I'll need approval from the Chief Superintendent, of course. Oh, and tomorrow, I want to have a word with the Campbell woman myself...'

Another pause.

'...what d'you make of Constable McInnes, McGinn?'

Gordon McGinn suppressed a smile; was Alan McInnes making a favourable impression with the inspector?

'Seems a sound man, sir. Certainly has a good local knowledge and the people seem to trust him, if you know what I mean.'

'You think that they might be more prepared to open up to him, is that what you're implying?'

'I suppose it is, sir. He has a kind of "way" about him.'

'Hm. I'll maybe take him when I go and see the widow.'

McGinn briefly wondered if McInnes would use the opportunity to voice his interest in the CID; hopefully not, if he had any sense. He merely replied with a simple "good idea, sir."

Silence ensued for a few more minutes until Nisbet spoke again, staring straight ahead, his voice flat and devoid of emotion.

'Em, I don't know if I mentioned it, I will be on leave on Thursday. Funeral to attend.'

McGinn was surprised; he didn't imagine that anything as mundane as a funeral would keep Nisbet from his work.

'I see, sir.'

The pause was considerably longer than usual.

'It's my grandmother; passed away two weeks ago. Very sudden—heart attack, apparently.'

An even longer pause.

'I'm sorry to hear that, sir. Were you close?'

Nisbet continued to stare straight ahead, his words entirely devoid of emotion and coming out as if being read from a script, thought McGinn.

'She brought me up. My mother died when I was an infant and it fell to my grandmother to look after me. Either that or adoption, I suppose. She was a good Christian woman, though. Her faith saw her through.'

McGinn dared to ask.

'What about your grandfather, sir—is he...?'

'No, he died during the Clydebank blitz, he was an Air Raid warden. The "all-clear" had sounded but Jerry had decided to drop a few parachute mines for good measure. Unfortunately, my grandfather fell victim. I was away at he time—in the Highland Light Infantry— my grand-mother didn't write to tell me, didn't want to upset me, I suppose. Wasn't there to support her...anyway, the funeral is in Maryhill at ten, there'll be the customary luncheon and I felt it best to stay and represent my family, although there are precious few...' His thoughts seemed to drift away for a moment. 'Anyway, I'll be back on duty on Friday.'

McGinn was stunned; it was the most information that Nisbet had revealed about his private life and it was rather tragic, he supposed. He wasn't sure what to say.

'I'm very sorry, sir, if there's anything—'

'There is, just get this bloody case solved, Mc-Ginn...watch, the traffic's slowing at these lights...'

*

Alan McInnes had cleared the rather mountainous serving of mince, creamed potatoes and carrots that his mother had placed before him. It had been a very long day. He pushed his chair back and clasped his hands over his stomach as Isa affectionately ruffled his dark hair.

'You were needin' that, son. Been a long day for you.'

'Aye, it was that, thanks Mother.'

'It was good of Sergeant Tait to cov-er for you tonight, he's a decent man.'

There was the faintest snort from Gilbert McInnes, currently bathing the angry red stump of his low-er left leg in salt water. Beside the basin sat a carved wood-and-steel prosthetic foot, together with a large wad of padding. Alan looked across at his father.

'Mother's right, Sergeant Tait could just as easi-ly have insisted that I did the back shift. Inspector Nisbet has asked us all to be in tomorrow mornin' to start the search proper for Mary Campbell.'

This time it was Isa McInnes who respond-ed, with a long sigh. Alan looked back up at her, noticing the lines, the look of concern.

'How was she, Mother?'

Isa shook her head sadly..

'Just...well, it was like she hadn't taken it in, she seemed more concerned about her daughter than her husband.'

'Don't bloody blame the woman,' interjected Gilbert. 'That Hughie Campbell was a right nasty bugger.'

'Gilbert!' exclaimed Isa. 'Language, please.'

'Och, Ah'm sorry Isa, but it's true. Ah've seen him in many a foul mood, spoilin' for trouble. No, the woman's probably best off withoot him.'

Isa McInnes banged Alan's plate down noisily on the wooden counter.

'That's a terribile thing to say, Gilbert McInnes. No matter what, he was her husband—'

'Oh, for goodness sake,' interrupted Alan. 'Look I've had a long, hard day, can you please no' argue an' let's have a bit o' peace. C'mon, let's see what's on the television...'

*

Emergency Ward 10, one of Isa's favourite programmes, had just finished on the relatively new Scottish Television channel and Gilbert, who had been dozing, stood up.

'Richt, Ah'll get ready an' away doon the road. Ah'll no see ye the nicht then, Alan?'

'No, Father, I'm headin' off tae bed myself now.'

Gilbert kissed his wife on the cheek, their harsh words seemingly forgotten. Alan accompanied his father to the door, helping him on with his heavy donkey-jacket.

'Father, last night, when you were on watch, you didn't hear anythin', by any chance?'

Gilbert McInnes scowled.

'An' whit wid Ah be hearin', exactly?'

Alan shrugged.

'I don't know—it's just, well you know what happened down at the loch, I just wondered if you'd heard raised voices or anythin'...och never mind, you were probably a bit far away.'

'Aye, it's a good wee bit tae the side o' the loch, likely Ah wouldn'ae have heard a thing. Richt, Ah'll be seein' ye...'

Alan closed the door, standing with his back to it for a moment. When he had arrived at his father's little hut, its brazier glowing cheerfully, Gilbert McInnes had been fast asleep; was that how he spent most of his watchman's duties, Alan wondered.

Chapter 7

Wednesday morning saw a gloomy grey sky blanketing the village of Barloch, from which a fine precipitation fell and seeped into Alan's clothing. He looked up at the hills behind the village, currently shrouded in mist, and smiled, recalling his father's advice

"If ye can see Bar Law, it's goin' tae rain—if ye cann'ae see Bar Law, it's rainin' already..."

His smile turned grim as he turned towards the village police station, remembering the task in hand. Two dark-coloured police vans sat outside and a few uniformed officers were standing about, talking in lowered tones as they smoked; Alan noticed that they were all wearing rubber boots. One constable nodded as he passed and entered the station, where Kerr Brodie was standing beside a further two unfamiliar officers, fishermens' waders pulled up over their uniform trousers. Kerr jerked his thumb over his shoulder.

'Mornin' Alan, the Inspector's wantin' a word wi' you.'

'Thanks, Kerr. I take it there's been no news?'

Kerr shook his head.

'No' a cheep.'

'Are you goin' out with the search?'

'Don't know yet, Sergeant Tait hasn'ae said but likely he'll want tae man the fort an' send me oot in the rain.'

Alan knocked on the office door and heard Nisbet's curt response. He entered, finding Nisbet seated once more in

Sergeant Tait's chair with Tait, looking decidedly put out, seated across from him. McGinn stood with his back to the blazing fire, presumably in an attempt to soak up some heat in anticipation of the damp and dreary task ahead.

'Ah, McInnes, I've spoken to Sergeant Tait and we've organised the men into groups to search the area for Mary Campbell.'

Alan nodded silently.

'Now, I want to have a word with her mother and, as you are acquainted with the woman, I want you to accompany me.'

'Em, I wouldn't say I was *acquainted* with Mrs Campbell as such...'

'You're a local and the woman knows who you are, McInnes. She's more likely to talk with you in attendance rather than to two complete strangers. I'll just finalise the search details and we'll be on our way. She lives nearby, I believe—we'll walk, then. That's all just now, we'll finish up here and I'll be out in a few minutes.'

'Em...sir?'

'What, McInnes?'

'Did you not want me to go and ask the stationmaster about Benson?'

Nisbet stared at Alan for a moment; the younger man waited for the near-inevitable reprimand which, to his surprise, wasn't forthcoming.

'Yes, you're correct, I did. Very well, you go down just now and see what he has to say. Don't take all morning about it, mind, I want to get on and speak to the Campbell woman.'

Sergeant Tait gave Alan a rather sympathetic look as he left; as he entered the front office, Kerr handed him a mug of tea.

'Gonna be a long day.'

Alan took a sip.

'You're tellin' me, Kerr.'

*

Alan turned off Kirk Street and walked up the long, covered ramp that led to the station, a near mirror-image to the entrance at the opposite end. At the top, a wooden and glass structure sheltered the space below, allowing daylight to filter through its grimy windows. He walked along the deserted platform and entered the wooden ticket office, where he found stationmaster Bert Oliphant, a large, bushy-bearded man, in conversation with Alex Combe, one of the porters.

'Hello Alan—how's yersel?'

'Aye, grand, Mr Oliphant.'

'An' whit brings ye down here today—are you no' out lookin' for the Campbell lassie?'

Alan shook his head as the porter sidled out of the door. Word certainly got around fast in Barloch.

'I'm helping the CID inspector who's in charge—we're looking for Billy Benson and I wondered if you'd seen him at any point yesterday.'

Oliphant frowned.

'Aye, Ah'd heard he'd done a runner. He's a big lump o' a laddie but Ah widn'ae think he'd hurt on-ybody. Here, ye surely don't think he...?'

'I'm sorry, I can't really comment, Mr Oliphant. It's just that...'

He stopped himself; it was all to easy to let snip-pets of information slip that would soon be-come distorted and spread as truthless rumours, potentially hindering the enquiry.

'Well, the CID man from Paisley, Inspector Nisbet, wants a word with him.'

Oliphant smiled knowingly.

'Aye, Ah've heard a' aboot *him*—had a pint wi' yer sergeant last night, he's no muckle impressed wi' the man.'

'No, he's no' the easiest person to get along with.'

'Anyways, in answer tae yer question, Ah'm sorry, laddie, but Ah've no' seen hide nor hair o' Benson since last week an' that wis only when Ah saw him headin' oot on McGeoch's lorry.'

They chatted for a few more minutes and Alan took his leave. As he approached the exit ramp, Alex Combe was sweeping the platform. He looked at Alan in a conspiratorial manner.

'Em, Mr McInnes?'

'Yes, Mr Combe?'

Combe looked about, presumably to make sure the stationmaster was well out of earshot.

'Ye were askin' aboot Billy Benson?'

Had the man been listening outside the door, Alan wondered.

'I might have been; why, d'you know something about him, Mr Combe?'

'Aye, weel, Ah micht...thing is, when the Glasgow train pulled out yesterday, jist after wan o'clock, Ah saw this fellow come oot from behind the canopy that covers the ramp—the wan along at the other end, ye ken.'

Alan was intrigued.

'Yes—go on.'

'Weel, the train wis near awa'— it's still the old suburban carriages, ye see, nae corridor, jist a' thae

wee doors. The mannie runs and manages tae get
the last door open and gets himsel' inside.'

'And was it Benson?'

Combe didn't answer; he just shrugged, a slightly uneasy expression on his wizened features.

'It's important, Mr Combe—we really need to speak to him.'

'Weel, Ah didn'ae really see his face but his build wis
much the same. Broad shouldered, like, he wis dressed for
the coal lorry an' his back wis a' coal dust. He wis a wee bit
bow-legged, jist like auld Benson. Ah thought he wis just
dodgin' his fare, it happens sometimes, an' Ah called oot,
but Ah wis too late, the train wis past the platform end.'

'And you didn't tell Mr Oliphant?'

Combe shook his head gloomily.

'Ach, he'd jist gie me a tellin' aff for no' stoppin' him.
Ah mean, whit wis the point, the man wis awa'.'

'I suppose so; and I suppose he could have got off at pretty much any of the stations up the line – if he was careful
enough and managed to sneak out the way he sneaked in.'

'Aye, weel, as ye'll ken there's Kilmirrin, jist about
four miles awa', then there's Johnstone Lower, then
the line joins the main line at Elderslie. Efter that,
weel, it's a' stops tae St Enoch's up in Glasgow.'

Alan nodded; at least it was something.

'Right, Mr Combe, that's a big help.'

'Ye'll no' say anythin' tae Mr Oliphant?'

Alan suppressed a smile.

'Hopefully I won't have to, Mr Combe. Thanks.'

*

It was nearly ten o'clock before Alan arrived back at the police station to find inspector Nisbet standing in the outer office, wearing an impatient expression.

'About time, McInnes. Any news?'

Alan related the story that Combe had told him.

'Hm, that's interesting. I suppose he could be anywhere, though. I suggest that you and Sergeant McGinn have another word with the father this afternoon, see if he knows of anywhere along the line that the son may have gone. Right, let's be off, I'd hoped to have been away sooner.'

*

Inspector Nisbet, accompanied by Alan, set off up School Street and turned right into Glenhead Street. The soft, Scottish rain was still falling and Alan shuddered, partly from the damp, partly in anticipation of the forthcoming interview.

They arrived eventually at the council estate, built between the wars and already starting to show its age. Most of the properties were well kept, their net curtains white and the gardens neat and tidy, although Alan knew that there had been issues with damp and infestation. Some houses, however, showed signs of neglect, the gardens overgrown and the dark, uncurtained windows seeming to stare unseeingly out at the magnificent view they commanded, over the loch to the hills on the opposite side. They continued uphill until they arrived at Cruicksfield Oval; Alan pointed to a particularly decrepit-looking ground-floor property in a block of four so-called "cottage flats". The building sat on a steep slope, with a flight of concrete steps leading up to it. A sheet of cardboard appeared to be covering a broken window.

'Here we are, sir, just along a bit. The

one with the broken window.'

Nisbet looked around, his nose wrinkling slightly at the vague smell of cat urine. He pointed at the broken window.

'Hm. What happened there, d'you know?'

Alan shrugged.

'Not exactly, sir. It happened last Thursday, Mrs Campbell didn't actually report it herself, it was her upstairs neighbour...'

Alan pointed at the upper property and they both raised their gaze; the net curtains at the window above Meg Campbell's house suddenly fell shut.

'I see; it appears we're being watched.'

Alan smiled

'Aye, Mr Plunkett, local busybody. Complains about everythin' and anythin'.'

Nisbet ignored the comment.

'Right, best get it over with...here, who's that, d'you suppose? A bit out of place here, I'd say.'

A smart, British Racing Green Jaguar coupe sat at the kerb, adjacent to the path leading to the Campbell household. As they approached, the house door opened and two men exited, a tirade of abuse following in their wake. The door slammed shut and one of the men, a heavily built individual wearing a trilby hat and a black Crombie overcoat, turned and kicked the door. His associate, clad in a double-breasted navy pin-striped suit, noticed the two officers approaching and said something to his violently inclined associate. The two men walked down the steps then along the path towards the pavement, the gate to which was missing; Alan briefly wondered if it had been used for firewood. The be-suited man held a bowler hat in his hand, revealing slicked back brown

hair above a sallow, mean face. He smiled ingratiat-
ingly at Nisbet, who looked as if he'd seen a ghost.

'Penman—what the hell are you doing here?'

'Inspector, good tae see you again!'

By the expression on Nisbet's face, Alan surmised
that the chance meeting was anything but good. Nisbet glared at the man, while his associate hovered
behind him, ham-like fists clenched at his sides.

'What business do you have with Mrs Campbell?'

The other man, who had the broken nose and cau-
liflower ear of a boxer, replied in a harsh voice.

'Whit's it tae you?'

Penman turned and gave his friend
an admonishing look.

'Now, Tommy, we don't want to go upsettin' the officers...'

He turned back to Nisbet.

'...see, we had a wee bit o' business
with the late Mister Campbell...'

'And what kind of business would that be?' retorted Nisbet. Tommy replied with a sneer.

'Campbell owed us a bit o' money—ran up a
tab, we're jist lookin' fur what we're owed.'

'I believe that gambling debts pass with the deceased,' answered Nisbet. 'You have no right...'

Penman's "heavy" leaned forward and glared menacingly at Nisbet; Alan reached down, placing his
hand on the handle of his truncheon. The man
looked as if he could turn violent at any moment.

'We've every right, Mister Polisman, Campbell owed us.'

Penman put a hand on Tommy's
chest, gently pushing him away.

'Tommy's naturally upset—to be perfectly honest, the

sum *was* actually rather large, you see. Never tae mind, we just wondered if, maybe, Mr Campbell had life insurance.'

'I very much doubt that,' interrupted Alan, his tone as officious as he could muster. 'As you can see, the woman is living in poverty as it is.'

He stopped and looked up at the house. He caught a vague glimpse of Meg Campbell at the window, but she stepped back immediately. The upstairs curtains twitched once again. Alan glared at Tommy, his hand still resting on the truncheon.

'Here, was it you who broke her window, by any chance?'

'Now, now, Constable, that's a bit o' an accusation,' retorted Penman. 'Of course we didn't break Mrs Campbell's window. Probably just kids. Look, we'll be off now, I can see that we were mistaken. C'mon Tommy, we'll leave Mrs Campbell be.'

'If I catch you here again I'll be charging you with harassment, Penman. Won't look too good when your licence comes up for renewal.'

Penman turned and gave Nisbet a filthy look.

'Is that a threat, Inspector?'

'No, Penman, it's a bloody promise. Now, get out of my sight—and don't come back.'

Without a further word, Penman got into the driver's seat, Tommy lumbering around to the passenger side. With a powerful roar, the Jaguar sped along Cruicksfield Oval and disappeared round the bend. Nisbet sighed, a dark look on his pinched face.

'A right bad lot, that man. Right, let's see what she has to say.'

*

Nisbet rapped loudly on the door and, a few moments later, they heard shuffling footsteps.

'Aye, whit d'ye want?'

Nisbet looked at Alan and raised an eyebrow.

'Mrs Campbell, it's Constable McInnes—my mother visited you yesterday. Could we have a wee word, please?'

They heard the turning of a key and the door opened. Alan was shocked at Meg Campbell's appearance; her grey hair was matted and her apron was filthy.

'Ye'd best come awa' in.'

She turned and walked through the narrow hallway, leaving the two men to enter and close the door behind them. The house reeked of stale tobacco and the previous day's bacon fat. They followed her into the front room, where a dismal fire flickered in the grate, barely negating the draught from the broken window. She sat down and lit a cigarette; uninvited, the two officers sat down across from her on the worn settee. Nisbet placed his hand on the arm of the couch then removed it quickly, wiping it on his trousers as if to remove some unidentified sticky substance. Meg Campbell inhaled deeply on her cigarette as Alan regarded her; her eyes seemed to have lost focus and she gave the impression that her mind was elsewhere. She had aged considerably since the last time he had encountered her.

'Mrs Campbell—Meg—are you all right? Did that man, Penman, threaten you?' asked Alan.

She shook her head.

'Ach, Ah've been threatened by worse than that scrawny wee runt. Naw, Ah'm fine, thanks for askin.' Onywey, he cann'ae ha'e whit Ah haven'ae got tae gie' him.'

She sucked greedily on her cigarette, her

cheeks hollowing, Alan continued.

'What was it that he was looking for, Mrs Campbell.'

She shook her head again but remained silent;
there seemed no point in pursuing the matter.

'Well, as long as you're all right. This is Inspector Nisbet,
Mrs Campbell. He's leading the investigation in to...well...'

Meg Campbell swivelled her eyes to look at Nisbet and
Alan could see them widen slightly. Her mouth dropped
open, tobacco smoke trickling out carelessly, then she
closed her eyes and took another deep draw, turning
her head away and staring out of the window. Alan
supposed that the presence of a plain-clothes inspector probably had that effect on the public but he had a
vague suspicion that the woman had something to hide.
As Hughie Campbell's widow, it was highly probable.

'Ah've already telt Sergeant Tait everythin'—'

'Mrs Campbell' interrupted Nisbet, in a harsh tone
'I'm very sorry for your loss—naturally, we're investigating your husband's murder. However, we are also
concerned with your daughter's disappearance...'

Alan watched Meg Campbell carefully; mention
of her husband elicited no response but she flinched
slightly when Nisbet spoke of her daughter.

'...so I'd appreciate it if we could go over things again.'

Meg Campbell gave a weary sigh.

'Aye, awright.'

As Nisbet continued, Alan realised that
the man possessed almost no empathy. His
tone was neither sympathetic nor accusatory, merely devoid of feeling or expression.

'Good; now, is there anyone that you can think of
who might have wished your husband harm?'

'Whit—apart frae half the village?'

Nisbet stared at her and her belligerence subsided.

'Naw, no-one in particular. '

'What about your visitors, Mr Penman and his lackey?'

She shook her head.

'He didn'ae know Hughie was deid until Ah telt him—or so he said.'

'I see. Very well, what about Mary—can you
think of anywhere your daughter might have gone?
Any relatives that she may be staying with?'

Meg Campbell shook her head again, continuing to
gaze at the dreary outside world. Suddenly, she stood
up, throwing the butt of her cigarette in to the fire before
reaching for a box that sat on the tiled mantelpiece. As
she removed a fresh cigarette, Alan peered at the box-lid,
noticing the brand emblazoned upon it; State Express
555. A rather surprising brand for Meg Campbell to be
smoking, he thought, as the woman lit up, drawing deeply on the fresh cigarette before continuing to speak.

'Naebody. We've nae family.'

That wasn't strictly true, thought Alan.

'What about Colin, your other son, Mrs...'

She turned to Alan and snapped at
him, her eyes briefly flashing.

'Leave the boy oot o' this—he's got nothin' tae
dae wi' onythin'. Onywey, he's awa' at sea the noo
an' Ah don't want him gettin' bothered by the
likes o' you—he's made his ain way in life, an' nae
thanks tae that big bastart husband o' mine...'

Nisbet made a tutting noise before he spoke; Meg
Campbell ignored it, sucking again on her cigarette.

'Hm. I believe your husband didn't

get on with your older son.'

Meg Campbell turned and stared at Nisbet again for a few moments.

'Huh! Ye can say that again. That wis why he went tae sea, tae get awa'. Couldn'a blame the boy.'

'Did Colin get on well with Mary?' asked Alan.

Again a slight pause before she replied.

'He looked oot fur her, if that's whit ye mean. Made sure Hughie never laid a finger on the lassie. But he's been awa' these past ten year or so.'

'When did you last see your son, Mrs Campbell?'

Meg Campbell sneered at Nisbet's question.

'Christmas. He wis here fur an hour before Hughie started on him. Picked up his stuff an' walked oot, haven'ae heard a word frae him since. Onywey, Mary can look oot for hersel', Hughie widn'ae dare tae lay a finger on her nooadays.'

Cigarette between her lips, she folded her arms defiantly across her chest as she glared down at them and Alan saw Nisbet's brows furrowing for a moment. Her defiance seemed to evaporate suddenly and she dropped back down on the couch in a moody, depressed silence, answering the remainder of Nisbet's questions in a monosyllabic manner; the two officers finally took their leave with little useful information, Alan having urged her to report any further visits from Bernard Penman and Tommy, his pet "heavy."

*

They were walking back along Glenhead road before Nisbet spoke, his brows having been drawn in a permanent frown.

'I don't like it, McInnes.'

'What, sir?'

83

'Those two; as I said, Penman's a right bad lot— he has a reputation and I'd like fine to see him safely behind bars. As to the one called Tommy, seems like he's Penman's new enforcer.'

The Inspector gave a very rare, if rather grim, smile.

'I put his last one away for twelve years on an attempted murder charge a few months back. I don't think I'm a particular favourite of Bernard Penman.'

He stopped suddenly, turning towards Alan. The smile had vanished.

'Look, McInnes, you know this family... what d'you make of Mrs Campbell?'

Alan had been asking himself the same question.

'I don't really know the family *that* well, sir, but both Meg and Hugh had a reputation as troublemakers and the deceased spent a night in the cells more than once after causin' a disturbance. But Meg... well, she seemed really distant, as if she wasn't takin' it all in, somehow. I'd have thought she'd have been pretty intimidated by Penman and his lackey.'

'Yes, that's what I thought too.'

'Also, sir, my mother said that Meg seemed more concerned about her daughter than her husband's murder and, after today, I'd agree...'

He paused.

'Em, you don't think that Penman and the tough-nut would have had anythin' to do with *Mary's* disappearance, sir?'

Nisbet gave Alan a searching look.

'In what way, McInnes?'

Alan wasn't exactly sure.

'Well, I don't know exactly but...if Camp-

84

bell *did* owe them money, is there any chance they might have taken the girl?'

Nisbet gave a derisive snort.

'Kidnap? Huh, I think you're letting your imagination get the better of you, McInnes. No, Penman's an evil so-and-so but his style is more threats and violence, I don't think he's got either the intelligence or the courage to carry out a kidnapping.'

Alan wasn't so sure but Nisbet turned and started to walk again; his suggestion had been summarily dismissed.

'However, with Penman and his hoodlum involved, that does bring another possibility into the frame. If Campbell owed them money and refused to pay up...'

He shook his head and quickened his pace.

'I want you and Sergeant McGinn to get on with looking for this Benson fellow, even if it's just to eliminate him. But I'm pretty sure that he's involved in some way, whether or not he carried out the attack. And if Mary Campbell *is*, by any chance, in cahoots with Benson, he most likely knows where she is. In fact, he might even be with her, after all! This entire search might just be one damned big waste of time.'

They took a few more steps then Nisbet half-muttered, 'In which case there's going to be hell to pay with the Chief Super.'

*

Bernard Penman turned the powerful Jaguar left down Paisley's Well Street and pulled in at the side of the kerb, outside his bookmaker's shop. Thomas Lumsden had sat in a sullen silence all the way up the road, biting at the almost non-existent fingernails on his ham-like fists. He knew that he was in trouble and, once he had killed the engine, Penman turned and started to speak.

'You're a bloody fool, Lumsden, talkin' tae those coppers like that.'

Lumsden shrugged.

'Sorry, boss, Ye ken how Ah feel aboot the Law.'

'Aye, an' you know fine weel that I feel the same way; but there was nae bloody need to provoke them like that. I take it you know who that bastard Nisbet is?'

Lumsden shook his head.

'Naw, they aw' look the same tae me.'

'He's the one that put Larry Munn away. You want tae watch your step with Nisbet, Tommy, once he's on yer case, well...'

Lumsden merely grunted.

'And we've got a hell of a lot at stake here, I don't want the busies sniffin' around, d'you hear?'

Tommy Lumsden nodded as they exited the car, Penman locking the door. As they headed for the office, he continued.

'Actually, it might be best all round if you were tae lie low for a while; mind, I've got one more wee job for you afore you do...'

Chapter 8

Constable Brodie was wrong in his supposition; Sergeant Tait had, in fact, decided to assist with the search, leaving Brodie on duty in the police station. Tait was beginning to regret his decision.

Taking charge of the operation, he had split the additional officers into two teams, working towards each other along the shore of Bar Loch. The water had, on several occasions, come over the top of his boots and his feet were soaking. The fine, West of Scotland drizzle had seeped into the fabric of his coat, increasing both its weight and his personal discomfort; not for the first time, he realised that he was getting too old for this sort of thing.

The search had yielded nothing and, when he met up with the other team, headed (rather reluctantly) by Detective Sergeant McGinn, they stepped back on to the solidity of Lochside Road. McGinn lit a cigarette.

'Well, Tait, nothin' here, by the looks o' it. What d'you suggest now?'

Donald Tait pondered on the question; he really wasn't sure. There were the Parkside woods further along the loch, a dense, scrubland area with few paths—that would take days to search thoroughly. Then there were the various back-yards, outhouses, the abandoned works in Factory Street...he sighed heavily.

'Tae be honest, Ah'm no' sure she's here at a'.'

He consulted his watch.

'Hauf-twelve. The troops could probably do wi' a brew, let's head back tae the station, get the kettle on, an' Ah'll hae a wee think aboot where's best tae search next.'

McGinn readily agreed, as did the other damp and bedraggled officers. Twenty minutes later, they were drinking tea and munching a batch of freshly-baked scones that Isa McInnes had delivered that morning. Tait was in conversation with Kerr Brodie, working on a new search strategy, while Nisbet, McInnes and McGinn were ensconced in Sergeant Tait's office. McGinn was, once more, standing with his back to the fire in an attempt to dry himself out; Nisbet, who was studying his notes, looked up.

'Right, McGinn, I want you and McInnes to concentrate your efforts on finding this Billy Benson. Have another word with the father, see if he knows of somewhere the son might have been headed if he *did* get on that train.'

'Could be anywhere, sir' replied McGinn. 'The train stops at every station on the way to St Enoch's. For that matter, he might have headed even further away— there's trains run to London from the terminus.'

Nisbet shook his head.

'That costs money, McGinn and, by all accounts, that's a commodity that Benson didn't have. Easy enough to hop on a local compartment train without a ticket, not so easy on a corridor express, where there'll be ticket inspectors and the like. No, my feeling is that he's somewhere relatively local. I would like him found by today, if possible...'

*

Somewhat refreshed, Alan and McGinn were heading back towards Glenshiel quarry; Alan was relieved to be travelling in the comfort of the police Wolseley rather than trudging about at the edge of Bar Loch and he had the distinct impression that the Sergeant felt the same. They turned into the roughly finished road that led to the quarry, drawing level with the quarrymens' cottages. McGinn stopped the car.

'Might be worth checkin' the house, just in case.'

McGinn knocked on the door but there was no reply. Alan went round the back and had a look in the outside toilet and, as he walked back toward the cottage, McGinn came out of the back door.

'Wasn't locked—mind you, there's no' much worth pinchin'. But there's no sign of either Benson; right, let's get up to the quarry, see if we can speak to the old man.'

The Wolseley bounced and creaked its way up the narrow, rocky road, finally arriving at the large Glenshiel quarry. A grizzled, overall-clad workman, whom Alan recognised as the quarry foreman, stepped out of the brick-built office. McGinn would down his window and the man leaned down, regarding them shrewdly.

'Afternoon...oh, hullo, Alan, how're ye doin'?'

McGinn gave a wry smile; yet another local who recognised the young constable.

'Aye, fine, Mr Cafferty. This is Inspector McGinn, of the CID.'

McGinn nodded to the foreman, who responded.

'CID is it? Ye here on official business, like?'

'We'd like a word wi' Jimmy Benson.'

Cafferty narrowed his eyes slightly.

'Is he in bother?'

Alan didn't want to make trouble for the elder Benson; the man had enough woes in his life already.

'No, he's no', we're tryin' to track down that boy o' his.'

The foreman straightened up.

'Ach, him? Big daft lump that he is. Weel, as long as Jimmy's all right. He's over yonder at the face—ye'd be best tae leave yer motor here an' walk, jist in case.'

Alan didn't like to ask just in case of what; they exited the car and headed across the uneven, puddled quarry floor strewn with fragments of the hard limestone, to where a group of men were busy loading a lorry. Jimmy Benson noticed their approach and walked a few steps towards them, his workmates regarding the visitors with curiosity.

'Whit're ye wantin' noo? Ah telt ye all Ah knew yesterday.'

'Has your son turned up yet, Mr Benson?' asked Alan, trying to keep his tone friendly. Benson shook his head, an expression of worry clouding his dust-covered face.

'Naw, he's no'. Didn'ae come hame last night, Ah dinn'ae ken where the bugger's got tae.'

'Has he any relatives that he might be sta-yin' with?' asked McGinn, his tone more of-ficial. Again Benson shook his head.

'No' really, so tae speak. Ma wife...'Again the cloud passed over Benson's face. 'Weel, she had an older sister doon in Ayrshire, New Cumnock, Ah think it wis where they bid-ed. Her man wis doon the pit, but Ah couldn'ae even tell ye if she's still alive or no'. Last time Ah saw her wis at Jean's funeral an' Ah doubt Billy wid even ken where she stayed.'

It was obvious to the two policeman that Jimmy Ben-son had no idea as to the whereabouts of his son and they took their leave, Benson returning to the inevi-table questioning of his workmates. As they bumped their way back down the road, McGinn gave a sigh.

'Well, yet again that got us nowhere. Any bright ideas where we look next, McInnes?'

Alan scratched his chin thoughtfully.

'Well, sir, what about tryin' the next couple o' stations along the line, see if he got off at one of them.'

*

They drove across the narrow back roads to the little weaving village of Kilmirrin, heading along the main street where the rows of weavers' and mill-workers' houses crowded in on them along either side. Like Barloch, the station sat on a raised island, reached by a long, enclosed ramp. McGinn pulled the Wolseley in to the side of the road and they headed up to the station, a train rattling across the bridge as they did so; steam-hauled, deduced Alan, from the hissing and snorting. A few passengers had alighted and they found the stationmaster still on the platform, engaged in conversation with an elderly gentleman. They waited until the latter had left then approached the uniformed man, who regarded them with curiosity.

'Aye-aye. What can Ah dae for you gentlemen?'

The officers introduced themselves, then McGinn asked, 'We're lookin' for a chap by the name o' Benson—Billy Benson, from Barloch.'

Alan gave a brief description of the young man. The stationmaster shook his head.

'Benson—na, dinn'ae ken anyone o' that name.'

'We think he may have boarded a train from Barloch, last Monday, without a ticket. Just after one o'clock.'

The stationmaster frowned.

'Really? Ach, it happens, Ah suppose.'

'Did anyone of that description get off here—either with or without a ticket?'

The stationmaster rubbed his chin for a moment.

'A couple o' folk alighted, but Ah kent them both. Funny thing though, as the train went by Ah could see in the compartments—they usually use the old suburban carriages durin' the day, ye see—an' the outer door on the very last carriage wis bangin' aboot, as if it had been left open. Ah managed tae get the driver tae stop jist in time an' I got it shut—could ha'e caused a bit o' damage if it had hit somethin'.

Alan and McGinn looked at each other.

'So d'you think that someone might have jumped out of the train?'

'Weel, Ah could'na say for certain but it micht be the case. See, the train wid be slowin' doon tae enter the station, a body could have jumped doon jist along the track there. Mind, it's a fair old jump on tae the track—ye don't realise jist how high up the carriage floor is when it's standin' at the platform. If someone *did* jump, he micht well have hurt himsel'.'

He pointed to where the lines drew back together at the far end of the station. There was light woodland on either side.

'See, he'd be on the ootside o' the train so Ah widn'ae hae seen him.'

The stationmaster shrugged.

'As Ah said, Ah never actually saw anybody, but they could ha'e made off through the trees an' across the fields, mind, afore the train left.'

*

Back in the Wolseley, heading for Barloch, McGinn wound down the window and lit up his ubiquitous Capstan Full Strength.

'Sounds like it might be our man, doesn't it?'

'It does, sir, but I haven't a clue where he'd be headin'.'

'Aye, an' that's the problem. His father says they've no relatives, except for an aunt down in Ayrshire, which is in the opposite direction altogether...'

He threw the cigarette out of the window.

'...which means we're not one bit further ahead. God knows what Nisbet will have to say.'

*

As expected, Inspector Nisbet was none too pleased.

'Well, that's no damned use to anybody, is it? If we think he got off at Kilmirrin, he could be anywhere in the local area. Is there a police office in the village?'

'Yes, sir,' replied Alan. 'We called in and gave them a description. Sergeant Grierson said they'd keep an eye out for him.'

'Huh, keeping an eye out isn't much good. The problem is we've already got extra officers searching for the Campbell girl and the Superintendent is unlikely to be able to spare me any more.'

'What d'you suggest, sir?' asked McGinn, with a sideways glance at Alan, who realised that the sergeant was neatly passing the buck to his superior. Nisbet gave his customary pause.

'As I said, we can't spare the officers for a door-to-door, but I suggest the two of you go back to Kilmirrin and check with the houses nearest the station, see if anyone's noticed a stranger. Bear in mind, from what you've told me, there's a possibility that he's been injured. He shouldn't be hard to spot, especially if he's wearing coal-stained clothes. And check if anyone's had anything stolen.'

'Stolen? Like what, sir?'

Nisbet gave McGinn a disparaging look.

'Use your head, McGinn; a bicycle, for example. Benson could get a good bit further if he stole one. I want you to go back and check; we need to find him, the sooner the better...'

Then, as an afterthought.

'...and Mary Campbell too, for that matter.'

*

It turned out to be a thankless task; there were a number of properties near the Barloch end of Kilmirrin station, although they had little idea of exactly where Benson might have jumped from the train. However, no-one had noticed anything, nor was anyone missing a bicycle. By four-thirty, McGinn reckoned they'd covered most of the adjacent houses.

'We're on a hidin' tae nothin' here, McInnes. If Benson *did* get off here, it looks as if he's made off on foot across the countryside. Might be sleepin' rough, might've made his way further afield. I'm callin' it a day, we'll head back to the office an' give the Inspector the joyful news.'

As they drove back along the narrow country road that led to Barloch, Sergeant McGinn told Alan that Nisbet would be attending his grandmother's funeral the following day.

'That's a bit o' a surprise, Sergeant, I'd have thought he'd have at least come down in the afternoon.'

'So did I, McInnes. I've never known Nisbet tae take a day off, whether it be sickness or even a holiday. Mind, he's only been with us about eight months, but even so, he's just always on duty, come hell or high water.'

'Was he close to his grandmother then?'

McGinn told Alan the story that Nisbet had related.

'I see. You know, I actually feel a wee bit sorry for him.'

McGinn gave a wry laugh.

'Don't waste your emotions, McInnes. The man has no feelings that I can see, he's like a bloody machine most o' the time...right here we are, let's go an' face the music.'

*

The day's search around Barloch had still yielded no positive indication as to either Mary Campbell's or Billy Benson's whereabouts and Inspector Nisbet was far from happy. As he put on his coat, he glared at the two officers.

'Right, McInnes, I take it McGinn has told you that I won't be here tomorrow. The superintendent has been breathing down my neck, wants a quick result, as do I, of course. We've got a murder, a missing girl and a missing suspect and I'd very much like to come back on Friday with information on at least one of them. Don't disappoint me...'

*

It was a grim, sombre-faced man who opened the door and stepped from the sharp, clinical tang of disinfectant present in the tenement stairway to the pervading musty smell of the elderly. He pushed the door shut behind him and walked through the dark, narrow hallway, a skin of dust present on the little table even in the space of ten days. The house was chilled, the fire not having been lit, and he kept his coat on. He entered the small lounge, neat and tidy as always and with a large family bible sitting on the table beside the empty grate. For a long time it had been home; in a way it still was, except the presence that had really made it home was no longer there. He stood for a few moments, the ghosts of his grandmother and grandfather sitting beside the cheerful fire; a passing tram, grinding and clanking its way along Maryhill Road, broke his reverie.

He crossed to the bureau and pulled open a drawer. He knew that this was where Flora Nisbet kept her meagre paperwork and, sure enough, there were several neat bundles of letters and papers, each tied with a piece of string. On the top of the first bundle was an envelope marked "rent", which was empty. Below it was a bulkier brown envelope marked "funeral" and he looked inside. It contained a bundle of notes, mostly one-pound but with a few five-pound ones as well; there certainly looked to be enough to pay for a decent burial. Wrapped around the cash was a neatly-written set of instructions as to the undertaker, the order of service and where the wake was to be held—the local Co-operative Halls, of course! He experienced a pang of guilt and let out a long sigh; too late, the arrangements were already made, he should have come over sooner. He placed the envelope in his pocket, it was too much money to leave lying in an unlocked drawer.

He lifted a second bundle and leafed through the en-velopes; the contents were mostly personal, letters from friends, communications from the Church. At the bottom, he came across a plain white envelope, un-addressed but, unusually, sealed with a large spot of red sealing-wax. He managed a weak smile; he remembered that his grand-father used to seal any important communications with wax, heating the little red stick with a match before letting it drip on to the flap of the envelope then pressing his cygnet ring into it. He could almost remember the smell...

As he looked curiously at the envelope, a voice made him turn; a tiny, wizened old woman, with a bent back and snow-white hair, was standing in the doorway. Without thinking, he placed the envelope in the inside pocket of his suit.

'Mrs Flanigan. How are you?'

'Aye, daein' awa', Gabriel, jist getting auld, ken. Ah wondered when ye micht' be ower.'

Her voice held a slight note of reprimand but Gabriel Nisbet ignored it.

'I've been very busy, Mrs Flanigan, I'm investigating a rather unpleasant murder just now.'

The old woman's eyes seemed to flash for a moment at the thought of a gruesome story and, not for the first time, Nisbet wondered at the appeal amongst the public for the macabre.

'Are ye now?'

It was a question that Nisbet chose not to answer; Mrs Flanigan waited in vain for a few moments before realising that any further information wouldn't be forthcoming.

'Aye, she was richt proud o' ye, Gabriel. She probably never said tae yer face, but she was never done talkin' aboot ye, especially when ye got promoted tae inspector. Ye've done weel, son.'

'Thank you, Mrs Flanigan, that's kind.'

The woman looked at the bundle of papers that Nisbet was holding.

'She'll hae paid the rent—the man wis here jist afore she passed so ye'll hae the use o' the house 'til near the end o' the month. She aye paid a month in advance... some o' us jist dinn'ae hae that kind o' money.'

It was said without reproach; Nisbet wondered if the woman realised that he had given his grandmother the money on the last week-end of every month. Probably not; Flora Nisbet kept her affairs close. Mrs Flanigan continued.

'She was a guid woman, though. Weel liked in the close, aye took her turn on cleanin' the stairs, although she kept her affairs tae hersel'. Quite richt too.'

The two stood for a moment in a silent remembrance of Flora Nisbet, then Mrs Flanigan smiled.

'Will ye come in for a wee cup o' tea afore ye go? Ah've got the kettle on the stove.'

He paused for a moment.

'Em, that would have been nice, Mrs Flanigan, but I'm afraid I need to get back home, it'll be a busy day tomorrow. Thank you very much all the same.'

Mrs Flanigan gave him a watery smile and retreated, leaving Gabriel Nisbet alone with his thoughts...and his ghosts. He knew he wouldn't sleep well that night

*

Alan McInnes, too, was finding sleep elusive. It was his mother's night for giving music lessons and he had waited for her return, which had been only fifteen minutes before his father headed for his night-watchman's shift. They had exchanged a few civil pleasantries, the earlier animosity seemingly forgotten...or ignored. Alan had tried to talk to Isa but she had dismissed him.

'Och, it's nothing for you to be worried about, son, it's just what happens when you've been married as long as your father and I. Just you wait, you'll be no different when you get married.'

She had turned and given her son a knowing smile.

'Speaking of which, when are we going to meet this young lady of yours? You should invite her over some afternoon for tea.'

He looked away briefly.

'Em, that'd be nice, Mother, I'll see when she can manage. She's quite busy, what with work and things.'

He couldn't tell her of his plans for the future; somehow, he couldn't even bring himself to tell her that he had been invited to Nancy's house for dinner on Saturday evening.

As the guilty thoughts tumbled over themselves in his mind, they eventually turned to Nancy, and he smiled in the darkness. He'd maybe see of she was free the following weekend and ask her over as his mother had suggested. Suddenly, his stomach started to churn once more; what if she *did* say no...?

Chapter 9

It was the sound of rain spattering on his window that woke Alan. He stretched and swung himself out of bed; Inspector Nisbet had been emphatic that he was looking for a result of some sort and he was determined to make an impression on that dry, seemingly emotionless man. He liked Gordon McGinn and he suspected the feeling was mutual; after all, they were members of a rather elite brotherhood. He smiled at his vanity, but it would be nice if he could at least add the prefix "detective" to his official title, especially before the New Year.

He headed downstairs, following the tantalising aroma of breakfast cooking. His mother seemed cheerful enough and they chatted easily, as always. Half an hour later, he was heading for the police station, his collar pulled up once more against the driving rain that had appeared overnight. He spared a brief thought for the inspector—it was a miserable day for a funeral.

He opened the door to find Sergeant Tait standing behind the bar, listening to a tirade of grievances from a small, wizened man whom he recognised as Mr Plunkett, Meg Campbell's upstairs neighbour.

'...a' very weel sayin ye'll look intae it, Sergeant, but we cann'ae go on wi' windaes bein' smashed on a regular basis—'

'Ah, Constable McInnes,' interrupted Sergeant Tait, with a look of obvious relief. 'Mr Plunkett's sayin' that

Meg Campbell had another window put in last night...'

'Aye, it wis gone eleven o' the clock
tae. It's ridiculous, so it is...'

Alan interjected in an attempt to stem the flow.

'That's terrible, Mr Plunkett, I'll head up and—'

'An' as for the language, weel, Ah widn'ae like tae re-
peat it, Mrs Campbell's aye yellin' at that lassie...'

Sergeant Tait's voice took on a serious note.

'You realise that Mary Campbell's missing, Mister Plunkett?

The old man paused for a moment, his brows
furrowing as if trying to recall something. Had
he actually forgotten, wondered Alan?

'Aye, weel, that's as may be, but yon mither o' hers wis
screamin' blue murder at her on Tuesday mornin', tryin tae
waken her up—it wis the worst Ah'd heard, Ah can tell ye...'

'But that was the mornin' she discovered her daughter
was missing, Mister Plunkett. The poor woman must have
been beside hersel'. Anyway, why would she be yelling?'

Plunkett paused, catching his breath and Alan began to wonder just how much of what the man said
was the truth and how much was fabrication.

'Aye, weel, she wis likely jist tryin' tae waken the lassie, Ah suppose -...an' it is a shame, richt enough. But
then there wis they twa hard cases that peyed her a
visit yesterday. Ah mean, wan o' them looked like a
boxer! An' the shoutin' that went on that day an' a'...'

Alan was interested now.

'Shouting, Mr Plunkett? What was said, did you hear?'

Plunkett had the grace to look slightly embarrassed.

'Aye, weel, Ah wisn'ae listenin' exactly, but Ah couldn'ae
help but hearin'...aw' aboot that man o' hers owin' them,

Meg Campbell wis shoutin' back, so she wis, effin' an'
blindin' that she had nae money; it wis disgraceful...'

Tait and Alan exchanged a weary glance.

'...then wan o' them shouts on the woman tae "watch her step or she'll be next".'

Plunkett had played his trump card; he gave a
smug smile and folded his arms. Alan frowned.

'Can you be sure o' that, Mr Plunkett?'

The man nodded.

'As sure as Ah'm standin' here. Fair raised his voice,
he did, an' shouted jist whit Ah telt ye. It wis just
afore you an' the mannie in the suit came along.
Jist as weel, there micht hae been violence...'

*

They finally got rid of their vocal visitor, assuring him that
they would investigate. Tait gave Alan a questioning look.

'Aye, you seem tae be gettin' the hang o' this detective work malarkey, constable. Seems that McGinn's
a good influence on ye...oh, speak o' the devil!'

McGinn walked into the office, brushing rain-
drops from his fawn-coloured mackintosh. He
grinned at the two uniformed officers.

'God, what a day. The boys'll no' be happy out
in this. An' what was the "devil" you were talkin'
about—I thought my ears were burning?'

Tait smiled.

'The constable'll tell ye—Ah'll get the kettle on.'

*

Alan related the conversation to Sergeant McGinn as they
drank their tea. McGinn placed the cup back on the desk.

'Interestin'—very interestin'. D'you set much
store by what this man Plunkett says, though?'

'He seemed pretty certain about what
he heard, Sergeant,' replied Alan.

Tait nodded in agreement, adding, 'Although he *is* the local busybody, mind.'

'Is he now—so his word might no' be all that re-
liable. Anyway, first of all, I suggest that McInnes
and I head up to Paisley and have another word
with our friend Penman—he seems tae be cropping up a bit too much for my likin'.'

He looked at Tait.

'If that's okay, Sergeant Tait?'

Tait nodded.

'Aye, that'll be fine, McGinn. Ah'll stay here an' or-
ganise the search teams. Ah'm plannin' on carryin' out
some door-to-door today. We've pretty much searched
everywhere in the immediate area an' Ah don't think it's
likely that the lassie will be found much further afield.'

There was a note in his voice that sounded less than hopeful. Alan gave him a smile
but Tait's expression remained gloomy.

'You never know, Sergeant Tait, hopefully she'll still turn up alive an' well...'

Tait shook his head sadly.

'Ah admire yer optimism, son, but the longer the lassie's missin', the less likely that is.'

He looked at McGinn, who nodded his agreement.

'I'm afraid Sergeant Tait's right, McInnes. It's
no' lookin' too hopeful—c'mon, lets away an'
speak to this Penman character; an' just be thank-
ful we're no' out doin' door to door...'

*

Although situated in Paisley's so called "West End", Well Street was not the most salubrious thoroughfare in that prosperous Renfrewshire town. In keeping with its locale, the premises occupied by "B. Penman, Turf Accountant" appeared drab and dull, grey paint flaking from the stonework and the frosted windows unwashed. Above the shop was a flat that now served as offices, although one single bedroom remained, used occasionally by Penman for his not-infrequent extra-marital liaisons.

Today, however, Bernard "Benny" Penman was seated behind his mahogany desk, puffing rather smugly on a large Cuban cigar. He had just received a phone call that had put a smile on his face—and would undoubtedly add a few digits to his bank balance. A frown briefly flickered across his sly-featured face but he quickly dispelled the thoughts. A few more months and...

The smug smiled returned; he blew a smoke ring across the desk and was considering pouring himself a whisky to celebrate when one of the two telephones on his desk rang. Again with a frown, this time of annoyance, he lifted up the receiver and snapped into the mouthpiece.

'Doris, I told you I wisn'ae tae be disturbed.'

'Ah'm sorry, Mr Penman, but there's two polis here tae see you.'

Penman glared at end of his cigar.

'What the hell do they want?'

Doris didn't reply immediately and Penman had the feeling that the conversation wasn't private.

'Em, they jist said they wanted tae speak tae you, Mr Penman.'

The bookmaker swore under his breath; the previous phone call had set a chain of events in motion that he would have to oversee very carefully and he could do without a surprise visit by the busies. Still, as far as he was aware, everything was in order.

'Damnation! I suppose you'd better send them up, Doris.'

He stubbed out the cigar and put the box back in the top drawer of the desk. If they were lucky, they might get a fag—pretty decent brand too—but they sure as hell weren't getting offered a cigar!

*

'Officers! Come in, come in—have a seat.'

Sergeant McGinn and Constable McInnes sat in front of the desk while Penman walked back around to his own, rather more comfortable chair. Once seated, he reached over and offered them a cigarette from he box that sat on he desk. Alan declined but McGinn took one, accepting a light from Penman's expensive-looking Ronson lighter. He exhaled a cloud of blue smoke as Penman lit his own cigarette. The insincere pleasantries exchanged, Penman leaned back, clasped his hands over his ample belly, and smiled.

'So what can I do for you the day, officers?'

McGinn took the lead.

'It's about Meg Campbell, Mr Penman. The woman you paid a visit to yesterday.'

Penman shook his head, the smile fading to an expression mimicking concern.

'Aye, sad business, losin' her husband like that—anyway, how can I help?'

'Mr Penman, Mrs Campbell had another window smashed last night; would you happen to know anythin' about that?'

Penman shook his head again, the expression of mock benevolence gone.

'Look, I told you already—'

'And her upstairs neighbour clearly heard a threat being uttered at your last visit. Apparently either you or your associate—Tommy, wasn't it—said to Mrs Campbell to "watch her step or she'd be next." Would you care to explain what was meant by that?'

Alan could see the colour rise in Penman's pasty face. The false smile returned, however,

'Och, that wis just big Tommy mouthin' off; he's...well, let's just say Tommy's no' quite the full shillin', if ye get my drift.'

'Mr Penman, it was clearly a threat and what is most concerning is the fact that Tommy warned Mrs Campbell that she'd be next. In my book that implies foreknowledge of what happened to her husband. As his body was only found the day before and as his identity hadn't been made public, can you explain why your associate used that particular phrase?'

For the first time, Penman looked flustered.

'Em, och, it was probably because the woman had just told us her husband had been killed. Like I said, Tommy's no'—'

'Yes, I heard you, Mr Penman. But it's also rather co-incidental that she's had two windows broken and that you've been seen at her house, threatening her, within a couple of days of her husband's death. I have to ask myself if these events are connected somehow.'

There was an uneasy silence, broken by Alan,

who had been primed for the next question.

'Mr Penman, you said that Hugh Campbell owed you money, a gambling debt, I believe. Can you tell us how much that was for?'

Penman glared at the constable.

'That's confidential information, sonny...'

Alan could feel his hackles rise but before he could respond, McGinn interjected.

'Mr Penman, I can easily get a warrant if you refuse to co-operate and that won't look good when your licence comes up for renewal. So, I suggest you answer the constable's question; how much did Campbell owe?'

They could see Penman gritting his teeth, either in anger or frustration.

'Just over two hundred pounds.'

The two officers exchanged an astonished glance before McGinn continued.

'Two hundred pounds! Good God, man, how could you possibly allow a man in Campbell's position to run up a debt of two hundred pounds?'

Penman averted his eyes.

'He said he'd been injured at the steelworks and was due tae get compensation.'

'And you were happy to relieve him of the money?' asked Alan, still in a state of semi-shock at the amount involved. Penman turned on him, immediately on the defensive.

'Look, sonny, it's no' up to me to stand between a fool an' his money...'

'It's Constable, if you don't mind.'

Penman sat with his mouth open for a moment.

'Aye, well "Constable", then; but if Campbell wanted tae blow all his cash in my shop, then that was his business, no' mine. My business is makin' money.'

'Yes, and you seem to do that pretty well, Mr Penman,' replied McGinn.

'What's that supposed to mean, *Sergeant*?'

'Just what I say, Penman. Flash car, flash suits. Never
mind. We'd like a word with Tommy, your associate, now.'

Penman gave a sarcastic laugh.

'Aye, weel, you'll be lucky. Doesn't work for me anymore.'

'What?'

'Just what I said. I had tae let him go, couldn't afford
the wages and, to be honest, I felt myself that he was
a bit threatening with Mrs Campbell, so I gave him
the old heave-ho. Not really my style, intimidation!'

McGinn looked furious.

'And where can we find him?'

Penman shrugged.

'Search me. He was just employed casu-
al-like, I don't have an address or nothin' for
him. I'm really sorry but I can't help.'

'What was his surname?'

Penman shrugged again, his smug expression returning.

'Sorry, he was aye just "Big Tommy". Think he came
from out the East End of Glasgow but I couldn't swear tae
it. Now, if that's all, officers, I've got a business tae run.'

*

Benny Penman crossed to the window, surreptitiously
watching the two officers as they drove up Well Street and
disappeared around the corner.

'Damned bloody polis,' he muttered angrily. He crossed back to the desk and lifted up the
external phone, then dialled a number.

'It's me. Look, I might have a wee problem...no, Ah'm no' discussin' it on the phone...can we meet... no, I can assure you, it's nothin' I cann'ae handle.'

He consulted his expensive Omega watch.

'An hour.... Aye? That'll be fine—the usu- al...? Aye, I'll see you there.'

*

McGinn drove for a few minutes before he spoke; Alan knew that the sergeant was still furious at Penman's evasiveness. Finally, he asked, 'What the hell d'you make o' that, McInnes?'

Alan wasn't used to being asked his opinion in such matters and he paused, considering his words carefully. He wanted to make a good impression but, having had little experience of interviewing what he presumed was now a potential murder suspect, he was unsure of what to say.

'Em, well, it seems very convenient that this "Big Tommy" chap has suddenly disappeared.'

McGinn nodded.

'Aye, doesn't it just; and apparently Penman doesn't even know the bugger's surname! Likely bloody story, if you ask me. You know, I could get a bloody warrant if I needed it but, by that time, you can rest assured that the bugger will have burnt any paperwork relatin' to our friend Tommy. And two hundred bloody pounds! Good God almighty, that's a hell o' an amount o' debt to let Hugh Campbell run up. We'll need to check on this industrial injury that he claims to have had, of course, might have to go along to this steelworks...'

A few moments of silence followed and Alan could see the sergeant's jaw muscles working. Finally, Mc-

Ginn spoke again; his voice had a harsh edge.

'He's a bloody animal, that Penman. Did Nisbet tell you what happened?'

'He just said he'd put Penman's last heavy away for attempted murder. He didn't elaborate.'

'Hm. Well, he was right enough; but what he didn't tell you was that the victim was a good friend of mine, Mick Taylor, a fellow sergeant in the CID. I reckon he got a bit too close to Penman's operation and the bugger sent a certain thug by the name o' Larry Munn to have a word with him. Munn fractured poor Micky's skull, he's in a wheelchair now, bloody pensioned off, poor sod.'

He gave Alan a wry glance, raising an eyebrow.

'Still fancy the CID, McInnes?'

Alan didn't reply; the truth was, he didn't know...finally, he spoke.

'I was thinkin', Sergeant, about Campbell's alleged industrial injury. Could we not just ask the police doctor—you know, the one who does the post-mortems? Surely if there's as an injury of any sort he'd notice it?'

McGinn gave a grim smile.

'Fair point, McInnes, and it might save us some time and effort. But I think I'd like a wee word wi' Campbell's boss down at the steelworks all the same, see if the man had any enemies, get a feel for him, if you know what I mean.'

Alan nodded.

'He wasn't liked in the village, you know, Sergeant.'

McGinn nodded.

'I'd gathered as much. Seems to have been a bit o' a rogue, by all accounts. As I said, best we speak to the powers that be down the road, they might be of a different opinion. But you're right about the Doc, worth askin' the question.'

They drove on for a few more moments, then Alan plucked up the courage to speak again.

'There was something else I noticed, sir.'

McGinn gave him another sideways glance.

'Oh aye? An' what was that?'

'The cigarettes that he offered us...'

'Huh, I'd hardly call them cigarettes, no bloody taste. But what about them?'

'They were State Express 555. It's an expensive brand, in their advertisin' they claim to be the "world's best cigarette", or something along those lines.'

'Aye, well, Penman obviously likes to treat himself. There was a strong whiff o' cigars too but I notice we never got offered one of those. What's your point, McInnes?'

'Well, when we were in Meg Campbell's house, she had a box o' the same cigarettes up on the mantelpiece. I thought at the time that it was an expensive brand for her to be smokin', she looks more like a Craven "A" or even a Woodbine type.'

McGinn frowned.

'You know, you're right enough, although I can't say I noticed what she was smokin'. Might just be coincidence but, now that you mention it, I'd be interested to know where she got hold of them.'

He drove on, reaching the speed limit release outside Johnstone. As he gunned the Wolseley forward, he half-turned to Alan and grinned.

'You're an observant bugger, McInnes...!'

*

Half an hour later they arrived back at Barloch police station.

Sergeant Tait was in his office and Kerr Brodie was standing in front of the fire, trying to dry himself out. McGinn took off his coat and hung it on the peg.

'Right, could do wi' a cuppa. I take it there's no joy wi' the search?'

Brodie shook his head.

'Nothin', sir. We're still on the door-to-door but no-one's seen or heard a thing.'

'Damn. And no word o' Billy Benson either?'

'No, 'fraid not, Sergeant.'

McGinn let out a sigh.

'Nisbet won't be best pleased, especially after to-day—hell o' a day for a funeral, poor bugger. Right, get the kettle on. McInnes, we'll head down to the steelworks after this, try an' get a word with the man-ager. Or, at least, Hugh Campbell's foreman.'

*

Glensherrie steelworks was an enormous industrial sprawl, its chimneys and retorts spewing steam, smoke and noxious fumes into the already heavy atmosphere. Having shown his warrant card to the gate-keeper, McGinn was directed to a large brick-built edifice that housed the works offices. Once parked, they entered the building, where they were greeted by a rather superior-looking lady, her hair in tight curls and a pair of severe, dark spectacles perched on her nose. She gave them a stony look from across her large tidy desk as McGinn introduced himself and asked to speak to Frank Glen, the works manager. The woman replied in a haughty tone.

'I'm afraid Mr Glen is in a meeting just now and can't possibly be disturbed.'

McGinn was having none of it.

'Madam, I'm afraid that it wasn't a request. We're in-vestigatin' the murder o' one o' your employees and it's imperative that I speak to Mr Glen as soon as possible.'

With a decided air of disgruntlement, the wom-an lifted the phone and mumbled a few words, explaining the situation. She placed the receiv-er back down and glared up at McGinn.

'Mr Glen has agreed to see you, but you are greatly inconveniencing him and he can't give you long. Please have a seat.'

The two officers sat down and waited for a few min-utes. Eventually, a harassed-looking man, smart-ly dressed in a grey suit, white shirt and navy tie, appeared from an adjacent door. He peered at them over thick horn-rim spectacles.

'Gentlemen—this way, if you please.'

They were ushered into a bright and spacious of-fice, where Mr Glen indicated that they should sit.

'I must say that this is damned inconve-nient—I have to attend a Directors' meet-ing shortly so can we make this brief?'

He frowned for a moment, then pushed a box of cigarettes towards them, opening the lid.

'Can I offer you a cigarette?'

McGinn glanced knowingly at Alan.

'No, thank you, Mr Glen. State Express—pret-ty high-class smoke, sir. Is that your usual brand?'

Alan noticed a faint colour rise in the manager's cheeks.

'What...oh, em, actually they were a gift... Look, what exactly can I help you with?'

'You are aware that one of your employees, Hugh Campbell, was found murdered last Tuesday?'

'Yes, I had heard. Dreadful business, although from what I gather he won't exactly be missed.'

'Oh,' McGinn responded. 'And why do you say that?'

By his expression, Glen immediately regretted making the comment.

'Em, well, it was just that he wasn't exactly the most popular workman, let's just say.'

'Can I ask, Mr Glen, did Campbell show up for his night shift on Monday?'

'Em...I couldn't say, Sergeant, I don't keep a personal note of the hours that our employees work or of their absences...but give me one moment, please.'

Glen lifted one of several phones on his desk and dialled a number. After a brief conversation, he hung up the receiver.

'I've spoken to our timekeeper and it seems that Campbell didn't clock in for his shift, so presumably he was absent on Monday night, if that's of any assistance.'

McGinn nodded as the manager consulted his expensive-looking watch.

'Look, I have this meeting to attend—I can't give you any more information, naturally I had no personal knowledge of the man—'

McGinn interrupted.

'Would you know if he had made a claim for an industrial injury?'

Glen's eyebrows raised in obvious surprise.

'Well, yes, of course, I would know *that*—it's something that would be dealt with by myself and the directors.'

'Had he?'

'No, absolutely not; there are no pending claims at the moment. Fortunately, Glensherrie has an exemplary safety record.'

'An' you're certain o' that, Mr Glen?'

Frank Glen glared at the sergeant.

'Of course I am. I can assure you that there are
no current claims for any industrial injuries—'

Alan interrupted.

'Mr Glen, you say those cigarettes were a
gift—can I ask who gave them to you?'

For a second they saw a look of slight alarm
register on the other man's features, although
he regained his composure quickly.

'No, you cannot ask, Constable. They
were, as I said, a gift and I don't see that it's
any of your business from whom...'

McGinn cut him off.

'The thing is, Mr Glen, these rather exclusive an' expensive cigarettes seem to be cropping up throughout our investigations. Might just be coincidence, of course, but I'm
no' a great believer in coincidence. So, let me ask the same
question as the constable—who gave you those cigarettes?'

Glen stammered

'Well...em...to be honest, I can't quite recall now.'

McGinn gave the man a long, hard stare; Alan could see
Glen shrinking back in his seat. Finally, McGinn stood up

'Very convenient, eh? Well, if you *do* happen to remember, Mr Glen, I suggest you give me a call. Of course, I
suppose I could apply for a warrant to search your office,
see what else we may find. You might want to mention
that to your Directors, just in case they become alarmed at
the sight of several officers arriving to search the premises.'

Ten minutes after the officers had left, Frank Glen
locked his office door then unlocked one of his cup-

boards. He emptied most of the contents into a large cardboard box then left the office with the intention of paying a visit to the boiler house furnace...

Chapter 10

There was a chill in the shabby Co-operative hall that the wall-mounted gas heaters failed to dispel. It contained a mere eleven souls; despite his undeniable skills as a detective, Gabriel Nisbet had failed to take cognisance of his grandmother's age. Most of her friends and contemporaries, like Flora herself, were deceased and the few mourners that had braved the elements were the neighbours from her tenement, joined by a couple of scruffy individuals who appeared to have tagged along in the hope of a free meal. There was certainly plenty to spare.

Thirty places had been set and, as he chewed on a piece of gristle from his steak and sausage pie, he was almost overwhelmed by a sense of melancholy. He realised that Mrs Flanigan, seated next to him, was talking.

'Sorry, Mrs Flanigan, what were you saying?'

'Och, just how sorry Ah wis that there wisn'ae a better turnout fur Flora. Mrs Syme, her on the top flair, wid have attended but her man, Albert, passed away the other day. Heart attack, they say.'

Nisbet wondered if the day could get any more depressing and his reply was almost mechanical.

'That's a shame—he was the man with the sheepdog, wasn't he?'

Mrs Flanigan took a swallow of her tea.

'Aye, that's the wan—dug's deid too...!'

He almost laughed as Mrs Flanigan continued her melancholy narrative.

'...still that'll be another funeral, Ah suppose, an' another wee lunch—at ma age, that's
about the only socialisin' that Ah get!'

Nisbet looked briefly at his watch; he was tempted
to leave and return to Barloch but thought better of
it. The conventions had to be adhered to, after all. He
speared a bit of pastry; may as well make the best of it.

*

Aldo's Fish Restaurant, sitting on Glasgow's Paisley Road
West and just over the border with Renfrewshire, was
reasonably busy for a Thursday lunchtime. Two mothers,
occupying the window seats and with noisy toddlers in
tow, were nattering over their cigarettes. A few commercial
travellers sat at tables further back, some with notebooks and
papers, others chatting over their fish and chips. Two men
sat at a corner table near the back of the restaurant, deep in
conversation, the remnants of their lunchtime meal pushed to
one side and awaiting collection by the disinterested waitress.
They would barely elicit a glance from a casual observer,
but a closer look would reveal an expression of worry, fear
maybe, on the face of the more smartly-dressed of the two.
He lit a cigarette, puffing the smoke to one side.

'The thing is, Mr Wallace, if yon bloody Hughie
Campbell hadn'ae gone and got himsel' murdered...'

The heavy-set individual seated across from him scowled.

'That's *your* bloody problem, Benny. Ye need
tae take mair care aboot who ye trust.'

'Aye, I know, but—'

'No "buts" Benny—ye ken the game, ye ken the rules.'

Wallace consulted his watch and stood up, throwing a few pound notes onto the table.

'Richt, Ah'm off. Nae mair discussion...' He pointed a beefy finger at the bookmaker as he growled, 'End o' the month, Benny—Ah'm wantin' ma money. An' ye know what happens tae late payers...'

*

Constable McInnes and Sergeant McGinn had driven back to Barloch, where they had just managed to procure two rather cold sausage rolls from the local bakers before it closed for the day. Having eaten them in the car, they sat for a few moments before McGinn lit his customary post-prandial cigarette. The smell of the match, the strong tobacco... suddenly, Alan's memory crystalized. He knew *exactly* where and when he'd smelt that particular combination before. McGinn gave him an odd look.

'Y'okay, McInnes? You had a strange look on your face there.'

Alan decided that he'd keep his thoughts, his sudden flash of what he might call inspiration, to himself. But he had the beginning of an idea...

'Och, nothing, Sergeant, just thinkin' about the case, about Meg Campbell, poor woman's had it pretty rough this last week.'

'Aye, she has that, right enough.'

He drew deeply on his cigarette, his brows furrowed in thought.

'Where d'you think Hugh Campbell would have done his drinkin', McInnes?'

'I've been thinkin' about that myself, Sergeant. I don't go to the local pubs much myself, but it'd probably be the Hole in the Wa' bar, at the top o' Factory street. That's usually where the working men go.'

'Hm. Might be best havin' a wee word an seein' if Campbell was there on Monday night.'

'Mind you, I passed by about ten o'clock that evenin' and I didn't see him, but he might have still been inside. It was a foul night, I wasn't hangin' about an' neither were the drinkers.'

'No, I suppose they wouldn't be. Look, McInnes, could you have a chat wi' the landlord? At least it might help place where the man was before he was murdered. Right, let's get back up to the station and see what's what.'

McGinn started the Wolseley and, a few minutes later, they pulled up outside the police station. Inside, Kerr Brodie and Sergeant Tait were having a somewhat desultory conversation. They looked up as the two officers entered.

'Anythin'?' asked McGinn.

Tait shook his head.

'No, no' a cheep. Seems like we've hit a dead end.'

McGinn looked troubled.

'Damn; Nisbet'll no' be best pleased, I think he was expectin' great things of us all. Right, let's have a cuppa and decide just what the hell we're goin' to do next.'

*

At just after one o'clock Sergeant McGinn was on his second mug of tea since arriving at the office and at least his tenth cigarette of the day. The office phone rang and Constable Brodie lifted the receiver.

'Barloch Police station, Constable Brodie speakin'.'

Alan watched as his colleague's expression changed from one of vague disinterest to one of surprise...then

shock. Brodie hung up and looked across at them, the
expression on his face commanding their full attention.

'That wis Mrs McGeoch, doon at the coal yard.
Says ye need to get doon there—right away'.

Chapter 11

To his obvious irritation, Kerr Brodie was left manning the
bar while McGinn drove Sergeant Tait and Alan down the hill
and up in to the coal yard. The drizzling rain having eased,
Mrs McGeoch was standing outside the office, arms folded,
a cigarette in her mouth and a dark expression on her face.
As the three officers exited the car she nodded across the
yard, simply saying, 'Ower there.'

Alan looked across to where the little shunting engine
had now moved the two empty coal trucks along the siding until it was standing beneath the water-crane. The two
engine-men were leaning against the tower of the crane,
their expressions sombre. As the three officers approached,
they stood up. McGinn immediately took charge.

'Right, lads, what's the story here?'

The engine driver removed a briar pipe and pointed it towards the running-plate at the front of the
jinty, which was still coupled to the wagons.

'Up there, ma freend, an' ye'll see for yersel.'

McGinn nodded at Alan, who stepped forward and
climbed the small steps at the front of the engine. Once
on the level surface of the running-plate, he could feel the
heat from the boiler as the engine hissed gently. He usually
found the smell of smoke, steam and hot oil comforting
but, today, he was filled with a deep sense of foreboding.

'Roon' the front,' the driver called up to him.

Alan made his way gingerly round to the front of

the engine, holding on to the rail on the smoke-box
door as he gazed down into the innards of the filthy
coal wagon. At first, it seemed to be just a pile of dirty
coal sacks but, narrowing his eyes, he could make
out the heel of what looked like a woman's shoe...
and a nylon-clad ankle. He clambered back down.

'What?' asked McGinn.

Alan took a deep breath; he was feeling decidedly queasy.

'Em, I think it might be a body, Sergeant...'

*

The driver moved the engine and the wagons slowly back
to the raised platform that was used to unload the coal. The
two coal yard workers lowered the unloading hatch of the
wagon downwards with a metallic screech, leaving a gap big
enough for someone to enter. McGinn looked at Alan and
raised an eyebrow.

'Sorry, McInnes, but I'm in a suit—don't want to ruin it.'

Alan was left with little choice. He approached the
open hatch and, swallowing hard, got on to his hands
and knees and crawled into the damp, dirty interior as Tait and McGinn looked on. Behind them,
the others formed a rather motley audience.

He stood up, his eyes drawn irrevocably to the pile of
wet sacks. The wagon smelled strongly of coal dust and
rusting metal but there was another pervasive, more
sinister aroma. Alan had seen enough dead and decaying animals in his career; he knew fine well what the
smell was... He crossed to the sacks, confirming that
what he had seen was, indeed, a shoe, high-heeled and
with a skin of dark nylon clothing the dainty foot that it
contained. Gingerly, he leaned over and lifted the sack

furthest from the foot, then turned quickly away, vom-
iting heavily on the coal-grimed floor of the wagon.

*

'Are ye okay, son?' asked Sergeant Tait, as Alan sat beside the
wagon, his head between his knees, How he had managed
to exit the wagon, he didn't know. He took a deep breath.

'Aye, I think so, Sergeant, just a bit o' a shock, seein'...'

He retched again at the memory and McGinn
placed a kindly hand on the young man's shoulder.

'Don't worry, McInnes, we've all been through it at
one time or another. Just take a few deep breaths...'

He looked up at the approach of Mrs McGeoch, who
was clutching three large, steaming mugs. She handed
them to the officers and McGinn gave her a grim smile.

'Just the job, Mrs McGeoch, thanks—drink up
McInnes, that'll help, you're probably in shock.'

Alan gratefully took the hot, sweet tea and swallowed a large mouthful, washing away the taste of
his bile. McGinn waited a moment then asked.

'Was it her right enough—Mary Campbell?'

Alan nodded, then turned his head
and brought up his tea.

*

Doctor Miller was duly summoned and arrived in his shiny
new Land Rover, the ambulance having preceded him by
a few minutes. He parked near the wagon and approached
the officers.

'Good afternoon, gentlemen. I have to
say, I didn't expect to be back here so soon.
Right, what have we got this time?'

McGinn explained the situation and a weary look flickered over the pathologist's refined features. He sighed.

'I see. Right, I suppose we'd better get it over with. I take it I've to manoeuvre myself through there?'

He pointed to the open hatch on the coal wagon.

'I'm afraid so, Doctor.'

McGinn turned to Alan, who was now standing up and swallowing more tea.

'McInnes, I'm sorry, but can you get yourself back in and help the doctor?'

Alan nodded and handed the cup to Sergeant Tait. McGinn approached him, speaking quietly and gently.

'Just do your best, son, an', if you're goin' to be sick again, keep it away from the body.'

Alan swallowed hard and approached the wagon, hauling himself back into the filthy interior. The Doctor followed, Alan giving him a hand as he scrambled through the opening. Dr Miller stood up and looked at the heap of sacks.

'Right, let's have a shufti...'

He lifted the sack that covered the dead girl's face and gave a grimace as he sniffed.

'Mm, not a pretty sight. Been dead for a good few days, I'd say, get a better idea when...'

He looked up at Alan, who was leaning against the side of the wagon.

'Are you okay, Constable?'

Alan gave a nod.

'Aye, I think so.'

Dr Miller turned back to the corpse; he didn't look entirely convinced.

'Good, but if you can try and keep the con-

tents of your stomach to yourself—em, is this the
girl that went missing on Monday night?'

Alan mumbled an affirmative

'I see. Well, I'd say, from the look of her, she's most
likely been dead since about then. I'll get a better idea when I get her on the table, of course.'

He leaned closer, wrinkling his nose in disgust. Even from a few feet away, Alan found the
smell of putrefaction almost overpowering. The
doctor continued, his voice emotionless.

'Right—I'd say the poor girl has been
strangled, by the looks of things.'

He pulled the sack further down but Alan turned away;
he'd seen quite enough of Mary Campbell's remains.

*

After the brief in-situ examination of the body, Dr Miller
summoned the police photographer to record the disturbing
and macabre scene for posterity. The small, wiry man
clambered easily through the gap, cigarette in mouth, and
done his duty without a trace of emotion. Presumably he had
seen it all before, but Alan envied the man's cool, professional
detachment; something that he would need to work on, he
thought. The two ambulance men were then called to remove
the remains and, with a bit of a struggle, they managed to get
the stretcher through the hatchway and place it in the rear of
the ambulance. Dr Miller exchanged a few words with them
before they drove off, then returned to the sombre group.

'Right, gentlemen, I suppose you'll
want me to give this priority?'

McGinn nodded.

'If you could, Doctor. Inspector Nisbet'll

be back tomorrow and I'm sure he'll want to know your findings as soon as possible.'

The doctor looked surprised.

'Tomorrow? Is Nisbet not on duty today?'

'No, it's his grandmother's funeral.'

'Ah, I see. Well, undoubtedly he'll want my findings on this as soon as possible. Oh, by the way, I concluded the post-mortem on Hugh Campbell earlier today...'

He paused for a moment, staring at the ground.

'A rather unfortunate set of circumstances, when you come to think of it, just finished the father, now I'm about to start on the daughter.'

'Actually, Hugh wis only the lassie's step-father,' commented Sergeant Tait.

'Indeed! I see.'

There was a gloomy silence before the Doctor continued.

'Anyway, all pretty much as expected, Campbell senior was killed by a blow to the back of the head, probably from a rock, by the shape of the indentation. Death would have been pretty much instantaneous, there was no sign of water in the lungs.'

'We've been given information suggesting that Campbell may have had an industrial injury of some sort, Doctor. Was there any sign of such an injury?' replied McGinn.

Dr Miller shook his head.

'No, Sergeant, none whatsoever. The man had a few internal issues, advanced cirrhosis of the liver and a few malignant growths on his lungs but, physically, he appeared to be as strong as an ox; as I said, there were no external injuries, recent or otherwise. Oh, and he had been drinking heavily before his death. When I opened him up there was a fair quantity of alcohol—whisky, I'd say—in his stomach.'

Alan could feel sweat break out on his forehead again. McGinn gave him a look and murmured, 'You okay, McInnes?'

Alan managed a nod as McInnes continued.

'So, someone's been lying about the industrial injury, whether it was Penman or Campbell remains to be seen.'

The doctor lifted his examination bag.

'Anyway, I'd best be off, I'll keep you advised as to my findings and I'll forward the full report on Hugh Campbell as soon as my secretary has typed it up.'

Dr Miller walked back towards his Land Rover, leaving behind him a sense of shock... and the lingering smell of death.

*

As the Land Rover lumbered its way back down the slope, Sergeant McGinn lit a cigarette, exhaling heavily. The smell triggered once more the thoughts of Alan's still-unformed plan, temporarily forgotten due to the recent, disturbing discovery. McGinn smoked in silence for a few moments then dropped the cigarette to the ground, crushing it with his heel. He bent down and lifted the remains.

'Best no' leave it, might be mistaken for evidence... Right, McInnes, first and foremost, we need to get the other officers back from their search, now that we've found the body.'

Alan swallowed hard; his constitution was still sensitive and McGinn noticed the expression on the constable's face.

'Look, if you've any aspirations o' joinin' the CID, you'll need to get used to this sort o' thing. Toughen up, son. Oh, an' we'll need to let the poor lassie's mother know as soon as possible. Where's Sergeant Tait?'

'I think he's in the office with Mrs McGeoch.'

'No doubt havin' a fly cuppa! Okay, let's get mov-
in', there's work to be done. Listen, away an' speak to
the crew o' the train an' make sure they don't take
that bloody wagon away. It's a murder scene—an'
if we let it go, Nisbet'll be for murderin' us...'

*

'Ah canna' tell ye how much Ah appreciate this, Isa.'

Isa McInnes bit her lip as she stared straight
ahead. She daren't look at Sergeant Donny Tait.

'Och, I couldn't leave you to do it on your own, Donny.'

'They could hae brought a policewoman doon from Paisley, but that would hae tak-
en ages. Ye ken whit this village is like!'

They walked on in a familiar, companionable silence,
despite the rather morbid circumstances; Isa knew exactly
what Donny meant, it would only have been a matter of
time before someone bore the tragic news to Meg Campbell. Sadly, it would more than likely have been motivat-
ed by malice; the woman was notoriously unpopular.

Tait continued, 'How's Gilbert?'

The question took Isa by surprise, making her feel very slightly awkward.

'Gilbert? Och, he's...'

She paused, unsure of what to say. She sometimes
wondered how much she really knew of her husband these days; his night-shift working meant that
they saw very little of each other but the dour expression on his face when she had told him where, and
with whom, she was going had spoken volumes.

'Em, he's not too bad, Donny. His leg both-
ers him, of course, but...well...'

Another silence ensued.

'He's a guid man, Isa.'

Somehow, Donny Tait's words sounded hollow, false.

Soon, they arrived at Cruicksfield Oval and climbed
the steps to the gloomy facade of Meg Campbell's house.
As usual, the curtains at the window of her upstairs
neighbour twitched and Sergeant Tait gave a wry smile,

'Aye-aye, auld man Plunkett's keepin' watch.'

He knocked on the door then waited for a few moments; unheralded, the door swung inwards and Meg
Campbell looked at their faces. Words were unnecessary; the woman collapsed in a heap on the doorstep.

*

Meg Campbell having been deposited in her grubby easy
chair, Sergeant Tait and Isa McInnes surveyed the room.

'What, in the name o' God, happened here, Isa?'

The room was in disarray; the drawers of the rather dilapidated dresser had been pulled out, their
contents strewn over the threadbare carpet, and the
cupboard, set in to the gable wall, had been emptied. Isa knelt down beside the stricken woman as
she moaned softly, her head buried in her hands.
She placed her hand gently on Meg's shoulder.

'Meg, Meg—can you hear me? Meg,
what on earth happened?'

The woman continued to moan, rocking back
and forth in the chair. Isa stood up once more.

'I'm sure she's in shock, Donny, you'll get
nothing out of her. Listen, I'll away and put

the kettle on, you have a look about.'

Sergeant Tait nodded his assent as Isa disappeared in the direction of the kitchen; she returned within seconds, her expression grim.

'Donny, the kitchen's the same; d'you think somebody's been here, looking for something maybe?'

Donny Tait sighed wearily; he wasn't used
to dealing with situations like this.

'God knows, Isa. Look, you stay here wi' Mrs Campbell,
Ah'll awa' an see if auld Plunkett can tell us anythin'.'

*

Between them, Alan and Sergeant McGinn managed to locate
the officers still engaged on door-to-door enquiries. They
now stood in a silent group, some of them puffing on their
cigarettes as McGinn addressed them, an unfamiliar note of
authority in his voice.

'Right lads, as you know, the search is over, Mary
Campbell's body havin' been located in this coal wagon. Now, we're dealin' wi' a murder scene here so
I want you to go over the ground wi' the proverbial fine tooth comb; an' for those o' you havin' a fly
puff, don't be droppin' yer dog-ends on he ground.'

One of the officers half-heartedly raised
his hand and McGinn nodded.

'Em, whit are we lookin' for, Sarge?'

McGinn glared at him.

'How the hell should I know, Kerrigan? Anythin'—anythin' that shouldn't be here. Someone killed that lassie
and shoved her body in the coal-wagon so they must have
got her up here somehow. Footprints, a track through the
grass where a body might have been dragged, a strand of

material from her skirt, just go over everythin' an' keep yer bloody eyes peeled. An' don't touch that bloody wagon, we'll need to see if there's prints. Right, off you go.'

He turned to Alan.

'Listen, McInnes, your father's the watchman here, isn't he?'

'Aye—well, he alternates week about...'

'But he was here on Monday night?'

Alan nodded; he knew what was coming.

'Right, I'm afraid we need to go an' have a word wi' him, he might've heard somethin'.'

Chapter 12

Bernard Penman chewed angrily on the end of his unlit cigar. By this time on a Thursday he was usually looking forward to Friday, when he usually only worked a half-day ahead of the Saturday rush. A decent lunch, accompanied by a few whiskies then home by three o'clock—unless, of course, he was "entertaining". And therein lay one of the causes of his discontent.

He wasn't a superstitious man, believing that you made your own fortune in life, but he couldn't help but ponder on the oft-repeated tenet of his wife:

"Bad news aye comes in threes..."

'Damned superstitious bitch,' he mumbled under his breath. Marital relations were strained, to say the least.

The first piece of unwelcome news had come first thing that morning. In view of the pressure being applied by Jock Wallace, he had issued Tommy Lumsden with some rather specific instructions. However, Lumsden had called to advise Penman that he had been unable to glean any useful information, which put the bookmaker in a decidedly awkward, and dangerous, situation. He swore again as he continued to chew his cigar; Tommy Lumsden was useless, close to being an imbecile, as far as Penman was concerned.

That was bad enough; but worse was to follow; about an hour after he had spoken to Lumsden, Penman had received a call from Wallace himself and, as he re-

played the terse conversation over in his mind, the
bookmaker felt a frisson of fear run down his spine.

*'But, you'd said the end of the month, Mr Wallace—only just
yesterday...'*

*'Ah ken fine well whit Ah said, Penman, but things change
quick in this game. Ah'm what you might call diversifyin'
ma interests—got tae move wi' the times. Ah've a different
wee shipment comin' in an' Ah'll be needin the cash, so Ah'm
givin' ye until the twenty-fifth—that's three weeks tomorrow.'*

Beads of sweat broke out on Penman's forehead,
just as they had done during the conversation; Jock
Wallace was, most certainly, a man to be feared.

The final call had come through only a few minutes
previously and the implications were almost as serious
as those with Jock Wallace. For about six months, Bernard Penman had been conducting an affair with a young
woman by the name of Betty Mullen; a pretty face, a
curvaceous figure and free with her charms; well, as long
as Penman continued to ply her with gifts such as perfume, jewellery and cigarettes. The spare room adjacent
to his office had proven to be the ideal retreat in which to
sample the undoubted pleasures of Betty's smooth, pale
flesh. He had been careful on several counts, the visits
being conducted "after hours" and the usual intimate
precautions having been taken. However, it appeared that
he hadn't been careful enough; Betty had called to let him
know, in her sweet-as-sugar voice, that she was expecting
a child and that he was, beyond any doubt, the father.

He glowered across at the wall; for all he knew, he was
being set up; maybe the girl wasn't really pregnant at all.
Or maybe she was sleeping with someone else—perhaps it
had all been carefully planned and the phrase "honey-trap"

sprang into his over-active mind. But he could prove none of this and Betty had dropped some barely-veiled threats about what might happen if he didn't come up with sufficient funds to compensate her. Her father was a local "ne'er-do-weel", known to have a short temper and to be quick with his fists. That was bad enough but, if Mrs Penman found out...well, that didn't bear thinking about!

That same shudder of fear ran down his spine; funds were low, due to a combination of high-living, his costly affair and an expensive motor car. Unfortunately, with the opening of another, larger, bookmaker's in the centre of Paisley, business had slumped recently and he felt as if a net were closing around him. As the sweat continued to pour from his forehead, he loosened his tie and un-buttoned his collar then took the cigar out of his mouth, glaring at the soggy end. He threw it into the waste paper basket, noting that it hadn't been emptied for a couple of days. Muttering something about the inefficiency of his staff, he was about to pick up the phone to summon his secretary when he stopped, a vague idea forming in his calculating mind. He stood up, crossed to the cupboard in which his safe was located, then dialled the combination and opened the door. The contents were meagre—a few bundles of one and five-pound notes, totalling just over a hundred and fifty pounds, working capital to back up any larger winning bets and to pay for everyday expenses. A few documents, through which he leafed before removing one. As he started to read, a leer spread across his heavy features; he crossed back to his desk, lifted the phone and dialled on the outside line.

'Lumsden—I've got another wee job for you. Be at the usual place in half an hour...'

*

Alan McInnes had realised that his father was in a foul mood as soon as the man had opened the door. Gilbert McInnes had mumbled a terse "hello" before limping in front of them to the living room and dropping heavily into his armchair. He looked at his son, his brows drawn in a frown.

'Yer mother's awa' out again wi' thon Sergeant Tait. God knows whit she's up to...'

'She's not up to anything, Father. We've found Mary Campbell and she's just gone along to comfort Meg.'

'Comfort *her*? Huh, good luck tae her, the woman hasn'ae a decent bone in her body. Could you no' have got a policewoman?'

'It would have taken too long and we were concerned that she might have heard it from someone else. There's a lot of folk in the village who'd have been happy enough to bring bad news to the woman's door.'

McInnes senior gave a shrug.

'Aye, weel, ye reap whit ye sow.'

McGinn cleared his throat.

'Em, Father, this is Sergeant McGinn, Paisley CID.'

McGinn extended a hand, assuming that Gilbert McInnes belonged to the same fraternity as his son. The older man shook McGinn's hand then glared up at him.

'Ah've nae time for that nonsense. Have a seat, what can I dae for ye?'

McGinn gave Alan a rather surprised look then sat on the sofa.

'I'll come to the point, Mr McInnes. As you already know, we found Mary Campbell's body today, down in the coal yard, where it'd been deposited in an empty coal wagon. There must have been a reasonable amount of effort involved, including opening the door of the wagon.'

McGinn paused and leaned towards the older man.

'Now, I believe that you're the night watchman down at the yard?'

McInnes senior glared across at McGinn.

'Aye, I am—Ah take it you're no' accusin' me o' killin' the lassie?'

'Of course not, Mr McInnes. I just want to know if you heard anythin' or saw anythin' that might have been suspicious. It would have been Monday night, some time after your son visited you.'

Gilbert McInnes rubbed his unshaved chin and gazed distantly in to the fire. Finally he shook his head.

'Naw, nothin', nothin' at a'. It wis a wet night, Ah remember...'

He gave his son an odd look, almost a plea for help, Alan thought.

'...wasn't it, Alan—mind, ye had a cup o' tea an' a wee blether, then ye headed awa'. You never heard anythin', did ye?'

'No, Father, but it would likely have been later. Are you sure there was nothing—a yell, a scream, somebody moving?'

His father's expression changed suddenly.

'Look, Ah telt ye, Ah never heard a thing— are ye suggestin' Ah'm no' tellin the truth?'

McGinn interjected.

'Of course we're not, Mr McInnes, we just have to ask these questions of any potential witnesses, that's all. Don't forget, it's a murder we're investigatin' an' we have to take everything very seriously.'

Gilbert McInnes remained silent; finally, the sergeant stood up.

'Right-oh, we'll leave you in peace, Mr McInnes, but if you do remember anythin', just let your son know.'

'Aye, Ah'll do just that. Ye'll see yersels oot...?'

As they left the living room, Gilbert McInnes called after them.

'An' if ye happen tae see yer mother, Alan, tell her Ah'll be needin' ma tea soon!'

*

The two officers arrived back at Barloch police station, where they found Sergeant Tait and Isa McInnes chatting in lowered tones over cups of tea. Alan was pleased to see his mother, the interview with his father having left a bad taste in his mouth. He introduced her to Sergeant McGinn.

'Pleased to meet you, Sergeant, I hope my lad is proving his worth?'

McGinn smiled warmly.

'Indeed he is, Mrs McInnes—as are you, by all accounts. It's very good of you to help Sergeant Tait out.'

Isa positively beamed.

'Och, Donny...em, Sergeant Tait and I go back more years than either of us cares to remember. Anyway, I'm right worried about that poor woman...'

Sergeant Tait took up the story, relating the state in which they had found Meg Campbell's house. The interview with Mr Plunkett, the upstairs neighbour, had yielded little further information other than hearing "a bit o' commotion" at one point during the previous evening. Plunkett had put this down to yet another argument between his downstairs neighbour and some anonymous caller but, on this occasion, he was unable to provide any visual evidence as to whom that might have been.

'It crossed my mind that old man Plunkett might have been threatened, although he wasn'ae for sayin' anythin' tae that effect. But, if ye were tae ask me, I'd say that the place has been given a good goin' over by somebody, as if they were lookin' for somethin'.'

McGinn and Alan exchanged a glance.

'That's very interestin'' replied McGinn. 'I wonder if it was Penman's lot—they seem to have been showin' a great deal o' interest in the Campbell household.'

'Would it be worth heading up to speak to her again?' asked Alan.

McGinn thought for a moment.

'No, let's leave it an' see what the inspector has to say tomorrow. If Penman an' his thugs *are* lookin' for somethin', then we'd have a better chance o' findin' it if we have a warrant. Inspector Nisbet'll be able to arrange that—I'll mention it to him first thing tomorrow. Speakin' of which, d'you mind if I use your office for a wee while, Sergeant? I just want to make a note of everythin' we've found out today—you know how the Inspector likes it all written down, nice an' clearly!'

Tait nodded and McGinn left the front office. Alan turned to his mother.

'Em...we had to have a word with Father—just in case he'd heard anything on Monday night.'

A look of alarm crossed Isa's face.

'Oh dear—how was he?'

Alan shrugged.

'Och, you know, a wee bit crotchety—I think his leg's botherin' him. Oh, and he said to tell you he'd be needing his tea soon.'

Isa glanced up at the wall clock, a look of dismay now crossing her features.

'Goodness, is that the time—I'd best be away.'

Donny Tait smiled at her.

'Thanks again for bein' such a help, Isa.'

She smiled back, her eyes twinkling.

'Och, it was no trouble, Donny, just let me know anytime if I can be of help. I'll away, then. 'Bye, son, try not to be too late—I'll keep your dinner warm for you.'

Alan stared at his mother's back as she left the station; for some reason, the exchange between Isa and Donny Tait had slightly unsettled him.

*

'That was great, Mother, I fair needed that!'

Isa smiled at her son; he had finally arrived home, well after seven o'clock, but a plate of stewed mutton, potatoes and turnip had been promptly produced and placed in front of him, along with a large glass of milk. He leaned back in his chair, trying to keep the unwanted, unpleasant thoughts and images from the case out of his mind. His mother took the plate away while his father sat in front of the fire, perusing the daily paper as he puffed on his pipe.

'I'll maybe get a wee bit of roast beef for Saturday, son. I hope you're not working?'

He wasn't; well, not officially, at any rate, but he had a plan. Two plans, in fact, neither of which he had spoken of.

'Em, actually, I won't be here for dinner on Saturday, Mother.'

Isa's smile faded and the rustle of the newspaper indicated that Gilbert McInnes had been listening.

'Och, that's a shame. Are you going out with your ladyfriend?'

Alan swallowed hard.

'Well...the thing is... I've been invited over to her house for my tea.'

Isa looked as if she had been slapped. Alan knew
that she had been keen to meet Nancy and the idea
that he had been invited to her parents' house first
had obviously upset her. She turned away quickly.

'That's nice, son. Where does she live?'

'Ralston, in Paisley.'

He was aware of the sound of his father's
newspaper being folded and put aside.

'Ralston, eh? Fancy hooses ower' there—whit does
her father do that they can afford tae live in Ralston?'

Alan had dreaded the question.

'Em...he's a solicitor.'

The silence hung in the air for a moment and Alan
could see his mother's shoulders tense as she awaited
the inevitable response. Gilbert McInnes stood up.

'Whit? Your ladyfriend's father's a bloody lawyer?'

Isa turned round quickly.

'Now Gilbert, there's no need for—'

'Aye there is, woman. Bloody leeches, takin' their
pound o' flesh oot o' what's due tae innocent folk...'

Isa cut him off as Alan looked on in dismay.

'For goodness sake, Gilbert, how many times do we need
to go through this? If it hadn't been for the lawyers, you'd
likely have got no compensation at all after the accident.'

'An' efter whit they bloody took, there was precious little left. Nearly half, Isa—nearly half
was what they took, the thievin' b—'

'Gilbert!' shouted Isa, her cheeks scarlet with anger. 'Don't you dare...here, where d'you think you're off to—you don't start for hours yet?'

Gilbert McInnes had put his pipe and tobacco in his pocket and was heading for the door.

'Ah'm off tae the pub—Ah need a drink tae get this sour taste oot o' ma mooth.'

Chapter 13

It took Alan ages to fall asleep, his exhausted mind unable
to suppress the gruesome images of Mary Campbell, not
to mention the tense atmosphere that had appeared in the
sanctuary of his home. When his mother knocked on his
door, he felt as if he had only just got to sleep.

'Come on, son, I've got your breakfast ready and
I let you sleep a wee bit longer. You don't want to
be late, it'll be a busy day for you, I'd imagine.'

As he swung his long legs out of the bed, he gave
a grim smile; his mother's throwaway comment
was likely be a considerable understatement.

*

A quick jog down School Street ensured that Alan arrived
at the office by nine o'clock, although a glance about showed
that the police Wolseley was absent. The ubiquitous police
van sat outside, the uniformed officers enjoying a bit of late
summer sunshine as they chatted and smoked while awaiting
their orders for the day. Alan nodded to them as he went
inside.

'Morning, Sergeant—Kerr.'

'Mornin.' replied Sergeant Tait, giving Alan a
scrutinising look. 'Did ye sleep all right?'

Alan shrugged.

'Not great, to be honest. It wasn't
the best of days yesterday.'

'No, it wasn'ae. Shame, poor lassie, she certainly didn'ae deserve tae end up in a coal wagon. Brodie, awa' an' get the kettle on—Inspector Nisbet
and Sergeant McGinn won't be down for a wee
while yet, they're making a call on the way...'

*

It was almost ten o'clock before the two CID officers arrived
and one glance at Inspector Nisbet's face indicated that he
wasn't in the best of humours. McGinn followed him in and,
as Alan made to speak, he shook his head. Clearly, Nisbet
was in no mood for idle conversation.

'Right, having had a chat with Sergeant Mc-
Ginn, I decided that we'd pay a visit to Penman and
lean on him a bit, see if he had anything to do with
the situation in the Campbell woman's house.'

His brows furrowed in an angry scowl..

'However, when we arrived at Penman's premises, the fire brigade were still damping down what
appears to have been a major conflagration. There's
nothing left, the entire building is burnt out.'

'Ah hope there were nae casualties,' said
Tait, a note of alarm in his voice.

'Doesn't seem to be,' answered McGinn. 'But
it's a pretty thorough job, by the looks of it.'

'Job?'

'Aye, McInnes. We're workin' on the basis that it was
a deliberate fire, most likely an insurance job. No sign
of Penman, although his staff had all turned up. We're
trackin' down his home address but it's pretty suspicious
that he didn't turn up for work on the very day his place
went up in smoke. The staff say he's always prompt and

never takes any unscheduled time off. They also mentioned that business had been down recently—apparently there's a new place in the centre o' the town that's taken—'

Nisbet cut him off.

'We'll deal with all that at a later date. By the way, I've applied for a warrant to search the Campbell woman's house.'

Sergeant Tait looked troubled at this.

'Has the poor woman no' suffered enough, Inspector? She's just lost her husband and now her daughter...'

Nisbet scowled.

'I'm well aware of that, Sergeant, but we need to find out what Penman was looking for.'

'With all respect, sir, we dinn'ae know that it *was* Penman.'

'Of course it was Penman, surely that much is obvious, Sergeant? McInnes and I witnessed the man coming out of the house with his lackey, she's had two windows smashed and now she's had her house ransacked. Hugh Campbell obviously had something that Penman was looking for—and we're going to find out what it was. Now, we're wasting valuable time here. McGinn, go and tell the men to get back down to the crime scene and continue their search. If that proves to be fruitless, then start another door-to-door—it's now a double murder enquiry, in case you had overlooked that fact.'

Alan could see McGinn gritting his teeth, but his reply was restrained.

'Right, sir.'

'Oh, and once you've done that, I suggest that you and McInnes step up your search for Benson. He's now our number one suspect, on both counts.'

'Both, sir?' asked Alan; suddenly he found himself on the receiving end of Nisbet's scowl.

'That's correct, McInnes, I said both counts. Unless you have any thoughts on the matter?'

Alan decided it would be prudent to remain tight-lipped about his theory.

'No, sir, nothing.'

'Good. Well, what are you standing there for? Tait, I take it your office is free?'

'Aye, sir, it is.'

As Nisbet strode towards the door, Sergeant Tait glanced at Alan and rolled his eyes. While a senior officer's behaviour was, technically, beyond reproach, the Inspector's boorish attitude was severely trying the usually-placid Sergeant's patience!

*

It was just after one o'clock when McInnes and McGinn decided that they were hungry and now they were leaning against the Wolseley, each eating a bag of hot chips while enjoying the welcome sunshine. McGinn took a swig of lemonade from a glass bottle.

'Aah, just the job, cann'ae beat a poke o' chips and some ginger...'

He looked at the label on the bottle, then glanced up at Alan.

"Local brew, eh? It's good.'

'Aye, the factory's just across from the entrance to the coal yard. There's an underground spring that they draw the water from.'

Alan opened his own bottle of limeade and took a long draught of the bright green liquid.

'I never really think about it but you're right, it *is* good!'

They ate in a contented silence for a few minutes, then McGinn scrunched up the chip-paper, looking about for a waste paper bin. Seeing none, he tossed his rubbish into the rear of the car.

'Best get rid o' that before I take Nisbet up the road, mind. He'll moan like God-knows-what if he smells chips in the car! Anyway, McInnes, this hasn't got us very far, has it?'

Alan shook his head in agreement; it hadn't.

Their first port of call had been the Kilmirrin police office, where the sergeant seemed to have forgotten their enquiry of a few days previously. However, no-one had reported any sightings of a stranger, no-one had reported anything missing. They had then called again at the railway station, to be met with a similar lack of information. Other than the open compartment door, there had been no sighting of anyone either alighting from the train or running away from the track.

They had then made their way to the nearby town of Johnstone and had called at Johnstone Lower, the final station on the line before it joined the main route. Once again, no-one answering Billy Benson's description had been seen, either alighting from or joining a train.

'D'you think that, maybe, somethin's happened to him?' asked Alan.

McGinn shook his head, a frown on his face.

'Wouldn't be the first time, unfortunately. Folk like him—well, they're no' exactly hardened criminals and if they end up killin' someone in a fit of temper, sometimes they just can't cope with the guilt.'

A look of horror crossed Alan's face.

'You mean he might have committed suicide?'

147

'Aye—was that not what you meant, McInnes?'

'No, I just wondered if he'd maybe been in an accident or somethin'— remember what the stationmaster said, he might have injured himself if he jumped from the carriage. An' there's lots of ditches and gulleys round the area, with streams at the bottom. He might have fallen an' hurt himself.'

The two men remained silent for a moment; if that *was* the case, then the chances of Benson's survival were poor, to say the least, and it would have been a particularly unpleasant end. McGinn broke the silence.

'Aye, well, in that case, it'll just be a matter of time until some poor soul comes across his remains. Let's stay optimistic, though. Hopefully he's holed up somewhere and, sooner or later, he'll either get found—or give himself up. Cold an' hunger can be very persuasive! '

The sergeant gave Alan a shrewd look.

'What's *your* thoughts on this Benson fellow, McInnes? You've got a good bit of local knowledge—would you put him in the frame for both o' these murders?'

Once again, Alan considered his reply; he felt, somehow, that he was being tested.

'Well, Inspector Nisbet seems to think so.'

'I wasn't asking what the inspector thought, McInnes, I was asking what *you* thought.'

Alan smiled; obviously he wasn't getting off the hook that easily.

'Well, in all honesty, I can't really see him stranglin' Mary Campbell. By all accounts he was right fond of her—and she of him, surprisingly.'

'He seems to be known to you and Sergeant Tait—what's his record?'

'None officially,' Alan replied. 'He's been cautioned a few times—you know, one too many down the pub then making a nuisance of himself, that kind o' thing. He's been in a few scrapes with some of the other local tough nuts but nothing really serious an' he's never been charged with anythin'. He's not the brightest button in the box, mind you, but, he seemed to be settlin' in to the job in the coal yard. It just seems a bit out o' character, if you know what I mean.'

McGinn considered this for a moment.

'An' what about the girl's father—Hugh?' Seems he was a hell o' a lot worse! D'you think Benson might have got into a scrape with *him* over the daughter?'

Alan was tempted to voice his own half-fledged theory but he decided to wait until he managed to prove—or disprove—his suspicions.

'I suppose he might, if Campbell senior tried to warn him off. Of course, I suppose it could have been an accident...'

McGinn shook his head.

'No—a crack on the head is no accident, McInnes. It might not be premeditated but it certainly wasn't a mistake; whoever struck Campbell meant to seriously injure him, if not actually murder him. An' remember, the blow was to the back o' the head—difficult to argue self-defence when your victim's facin' away from you. Would Benson have been capable o' that?'

Alan thought for a moment.

'He had a temper—as did Campbell, of course—so I suppose, given the right circumstances, he might have been. Especially if his girl was involved. But I wouldn't swear to it.'

McGinn grinned.

'Nicely put, McInnes. You think he could possibly have killed Campbell senior but you doubt he'd have harmed the girl. That's certainly a different perspective from Inspector Nisbet, who has the poor bugger down for both deaths.'

'He does seem pretty single-minded about it, Sergeant.'

McGinn's grin was replaced with a frown.

'Aye, he does. I'm just hopin' that his fixation wi' Benny Penman isn'ae cloudin' his judgement.'

'And what do *you* think, Sergeant? D'you reckon Benson's guilty?'

McGinn winked.

'Ah, that *would* be tellin', McInnes. Right, c'mon, we'll look into the Johnstone office and put the word out there, then we'll get down the road and give the Inspector the good news...or lack of it, I suppose!'

*

When they arrived back at the police station, they found Inspector Nisbet with a rather smug look on his face; a look that even the news that their investigations into Benson's whereabouts had yielded no information failed to eradicate.

'Well, we must keep up the search. However, I'm pleased to say that I have the warrant to search the Campbell woman's house, so I suggest we make our way up there right away. I was just waiting for you to return with the car, McGinn—what kept you?'

Alan could sense Sergeant McGinn bristling.

'We had a fair bit o' ground to cover, sir. The various railway stations, then both Kilmirrin and Johnstone police offices. I've given them a full description and they're goin' to circulate it to all duty officers, just in case they make a sightin'. Took a bit longer that anticipated.'

'Very well, I suppose...right, let's be off. Tait, if you hear anything about Benson, send an officer up immediately.'

As he followed the two CID officers out, Alan was aware of Sergeant Tait gritting his teeth as he lifted his pipe and savagely stuffed some tobacco into the bowl.

*

Five minutes later, Nisbet was rapping noisily on Meg Campbell's door. The twitching of the upstairs curtains had, once again, signified that their arrival had not gone unnoticed by the ever-vigilant Mr Plunkett. Having elicited no response, Nisbet banged on the door again, calling out in a loud, officious voice.

'Police, Mrs Campbell, open the door please.'

They heard shuffling footsteps then the door swung open. Meg Campbell looked dreadful; her face was drained of colour, there were dark circles under her red-rimmed eyes and her straggly grey hair was matted. However, her response was laden with anger.

'Whit the hell ur ye wantin' noo? An' why, in the name o' God, dae ye need tae announce it tae the whole bloody street?'

Ignoring the jibe, Nisbet barged in, pushing the woman aside. It was McGinn who spoke as he and Alan entered the narrow hallway.

'I'm sorry, Mrs Campbell, but we have a warrant to search your house.'

Meg Campbell attempted a feeble smile.

'Aye, weel, ye'll be lucky tae find anythin'—thon other bugger didn'ae...'

She stopped herself but the words were already out. Alan spoke, his tone more gentle.

'What other person, Mrs Campbell? Who else searched your house?'

She closed the door with a bang.

'Never you mind.'

As Alan placed a hand on her arm, the woman flinched.

'Mrs Campbell, we're tryin' to help you—please, tell us who it was.'

She seemed to suddenly cave in on herself, her already rounded shoulders slumping further.

'Ach, it wis thon big bastart that came before—Tommy, Ah think he's called. Says that Hughie had somethin' belongin' tae them an' he wis goin' tae find it. Never found a bloody thing though.'

A barking command sounded from inside the house.

'McGinn! McInnes! Can we get started, if it's not too much trouble?'

McGinn sighed.

'Best get on—Mrs Campbell, we'll need to take a statement—'

'The only statement ye'll get oot o' me is tae bugger aff an' leave me in peace. Ah've lost ma lassie an' Ah've lost ma husband, big bastart an' aw' that he wis. Can Ah no' be left tae grieve in peace?'

To Alan's great surprise, tears started to run down her grey, sunken cheeks. For a second, he desperately wished his mother was there.

*

'For goodness' sake, Bernard, can you no' sit at peace? You're fidgetin' like a bloody hen on a hot griddle. An' what the hell's that mark on your cheek? It's gettin' worse as the day goes on.'

Benny price glared at his wife; the love had long since departed their marriage and, for the most part, they lived in an uneasy truce. This afternoon, however, the ceasefire seemed to have terminated.

'God Almighty, Alice, can you no' see that I'm worried sick about the business, what with the fire an everything.. an' for your information, I cut myself shaving this morning.'

She gave him a sceptical look, raising her finely plucked eyebrows..

'Oh, shavin' was it? I see; an' as for the bloody fire? Well, I just hope you're well insured. I've been lookin' at a few brochures and, with winter approachin' I fancy a wee holiday down in the Channel Islands. Jersey looks really nice...'

'For God's sake, woman, my business has just bloody burnt down and you're planning a...a...'

He struggled to control his language as his wife glowered menacingly at him.

'Christ, I need a bloody drink.'

He stormed out of the lounge, leaving Alice Penman glaring at the closed door. He certainly *did* need a drink, after the day's events.

He had arranged to meet Jock Wallace in the usual location, Aldo's fish restaurant, and had arrived to find the burly, well-dressed man already half-way through a plate of egg and chips. Wallace had nodded up at him, masticating a mouthful of beans. Penman had sat down, refusing the offer of food; his appetite had deserted him.

'Ah hear ye had a wee bit o' bad luck, eh Benny?'

Penman had managed a weak smile.

'Aye, well, maybe not so bad, Mr Wallace.'

Wallace pushed his near-empty plate across the table, wiping his mouth with the paper napkin. He took a pack of cigarettes out of his pocket and lit up, greedily sucking in the smoke.

'How so, Benny?'

'You see, I've checked the insurance on the business and the property and it has a rather generous value, if you get my meaning.'

Wallace nodded sagely, exhaling a cloud of tobacco smoke across the table and into Penman's face.

'Very wise, Benny, very wise. Always better tae over-insure that under. Ah'm glad tae hear that, wouldn'ae want ye to be oot o' pocket. Aye, a wise decision richt enough.'

Price realised that Wallace's words had a decidedly insincere ring to them.

'The thing is, Mr Wallace, well, I'm sure you understand...'

Wallace's expression darkened.

'Understand what, Benny?'

'Well, you see, obviously with the fire, I'm not able to carry on my business...'

Wallace tutted.

'...so I may be a bit stretched financially—only in the short term, you understand. But once the insurance pays up...'

'And when micht that be?'

'Well, they've said maybe four to six weeks.'

'Och well, that's no' too bad, Benny. Ah'm sure you'll manage—you'll have put a bit aside for a rainy day, nae doot?'

'Well, things have been a wee bit tight recently, what wi' that new place opening...'

Wallace stubbed out his cigarette in the cheap tin ashtray and placed his beefy hands on the Formica-topped table. He lowered his voice.

'Benny—cut tae the fuckin' chase. What are you tellin' me?'

'Well, it might be a wee bit difficult to settle up by the twenty-fifth...but if you can maybe hold on a few weeks, once I get the insurance money...'

Jock Wallace stood up, favouring Penman with a decidedly menacing grin. He leaned forward, towering over the now cowering bookmaker.

'Benny, Benny, Ah don't know whit tae tell ye...'

He leaned closer.

'But you tell *me*—how old are ye?'

Penman looked up in surprise.

'Eh? How old...what's that got to do wi' anything?'

'Ah'm jist askin'—how old are ye?'

'I'm fifty-seven—but wh...?'

'Fifty-seven? Aye, gettin' on a wee bit. It's just that, the older ye get, the longer it takes fur broken bones tae heal—or so Ah'm told.'

Penman stared up at Wallace like a petrified rabbit. Wallace straightened up and reached across, slapping Penman very gently on the side of the face.

'Ah'm sure ye'll work somethin' oot, Benny. The twenty-fifth, mind.'

As he removed his hand, he closed his thumb and forefinger together, pinching Penman's cheek so hard it brought tears to the bookmaker's eyes.

'An' don't be late. As Ah said, ye know what happens tae late payers.'

It was gone six o'clock and Meg Campbell's house had failed to reveal its secret. Inspector Nisbet had quizzed Mrs Campbell further but she persisted in her denial of any knowledge of what Penman and his lackey had been searching for.

Alan had been making a final search of the small cupboard that sat underneath the access stairs for the upstairs flat inhabited by Mr Plunkett. The dark, dusty space contained little of interest; numerous spiders, a few old and rusty tools, a brush and dustpan, a thread-bare jacket hanging on the back of the door. He made to exit, turning quickly and ducking down to avoid the low door-jamb. As he did so, his foot slid very slightly and, looking down, he could see that the old, cracked piece of linoleum covering the floor had moved by an inch or so. Curious, he crouched down and lifted the corner to find that the floorboards underneath showed fairly fresh saw-cuts. He pulled the lino away com-pletely to reveal what appeared to be a two-foot square trapdoor, secured by four shiny brass screws. Alan stood up and poked his head out of the door-frame.

'Sergeant McGinn—can you come here a minute?'

The sergeant appeared and stood look-ing down at the floor.

'Aye-aye—looks promisin'. Right, we'll need somethin' tae unscrew those...'

Alan reached for a large, wooden-han-dled screwdriver that was hanging by a piece of string from a nail on the back of the door.

'Like this, you mean, Sergeant?'

McGinn grinned.

'Just the thing...handy, that, very handy indeed!'

It took them but a few minutes to remove the screws and to prise the trapdoor open, a damp musty smell emanating from the dark space beneath. The two officers gazed below.

'The house is built on a slope, isn't it, McInnes?'

'Aye, must be about four or five feet up at this point.'

'Right; well, I'm afraid it looks like it's your turn again—sorry...'

Alan grinned.

'I know, Sergeant—the suit...'

Alan took his torch and shone it into the void; beneath the trapdoor they could see a makeshift wooden step and, manoeuvring himself into position, he dropped himself into the space. For a moment, his stomach gave a lurch— what if he found...no, he wouldn't consider that. Swallowing hard, he ducked down, disappearing from view and, as he did so, Nisbet's voice shouted from the hallway.

'McGinn, we may as well give up, we're obviously wasting our time here.'

'Just a minute, Inspector, I think McInnes may be on to somethin'.'

Nisbet appeared in an instant, just in time to hear a low whistle coming from below, followed by Constable McInnes's voice.

'Bloody hell, Sergeant, I think you need to take a look at this...'

Chapter 14

Alan was despatched to the Police Office and returned half an hour later. Having managed to track down two of the uniformed officers, the three had driven back up to the house in the police van. The operation to remove the contents of Meg Campbell's basement was concluded and, while Sergeant McGinn was busily puffing on a cigarette, Inspector Nisbet surveyed their haul with a look of satisfaction on his face. He had listed the contents as they were placed in the van and checked it off with the diligence of a Customs officer.

'McGinn?'

The sergeant dropped his cigarette-end on the ground and approached.

'Right let's check it again—have you got that notebook we found?'

Jammed behind the main gas pipe that ran along the dividing wall of the basement, Alan had discovered a small, stained notebook, annotated with a semi-literate scrawl that appeared to be an inventory of sorts. Nisbet and McGinn proceeded to cross-reference the various items.

'Right—eleven cases of blended whisky, each containing twelve bottles. Except for one, which contains only five bottles.

'Aye—correct.'

'Any indication in there of where the other bottles went, McGinn?'

'Just some initials, sir. FG, BP, WN...'

'BP!' exclaimed Nisbet with a tone akin to excitement. 'Bernard Penman, perhaps?'

'Might be, sir.' McGinn looked at Alan 'An' FG—Frank Glen, the manager o' the steelworks?'

Nisbet's smug look turned to a sneer.

'We can only hope it's Penman...anyway, let's proceed. Three cases of brandy, twelve bottles in two, three in the third. Again, any reference?'

'Just more initials, sir.'

Alan looked on in astonishment as Nisbet continued to list the contents now in the back of the van. Boxes of cigarettes (including two dozen that each contained two hundred State Express 555), Havana cigars, two cases of a fine vintage Port; there was even a box containing a dozen bottles of a rather exclusive perfume. Alan had heard of Chanel Number 5, he seemed to recall a comment attributed to Marilyn Monroe that it was the only thing that she wore to bed. He let out a sigh; if only he could afford a bottle for Nancy... His reverie was interrupted as Nisbet pulled open the lid of the case.

'Twelve bottles—cost a pretty penny, these.'

Alan gazed rather longingly at the white boxes, each adorned with the "twin C" logo of Coco Chanel. As Nisbet made to close the box, Alan stopped him.

'Hang on a minute, Inspector.'

In an uncharacteristic display of humour, Nisbet smiled.

'What, d'you want to know what Chanel smells like, McInnes? Might be your only chance.'

'No sir, it's just...well, look at that box—the one at the end.'

Nisbet stared down, as did Alan and McGinn. The box in question seemed different, somehow.

'I think it's been put in back to front, sir,' said Alan.

McGinn grinned.

'I always said you were an observant bugger, McInnes—an' I think you're bloody well right!'

Alan reached down and lifted out the box, shook it, then looked up.

'It's empty!'

He opened the lid and, indeed, the bottle was absent, although a vague waft of the exotic, expensive scent assailed his nostrils.

'I wonder who took it...hang on...'

He poked his fingers into the small box and removed a scrap of paper, then unfolded it and read the same semi-literate scrawl that had appeared in the inventory. He looked up at Nisbet with an expression of surprise, then handed the note to the Inspector, whose face finally broke into a smile.

'Well, well, well...'

*

McGinn looked at the note, comparing it to the writing in the notebook.

'Aye, the writing's one an' the same, sir, although I daresay it might be best tae get an expert tae confirm it.'

He handed the note back to Nisbet, who re-read it, muttering as he did so.

"One bottle channell perfume took by mister penman 10 augist."

He shook his head.

'Seems that Campbell was barely literate, although it matters not one bit. We've got him...'

He looked up, his eyes blazing.

'...we've got that bastard Penman, at last.'

*

The police van had finally driven away, Nisbet accompanying the two constables to ensure safe delivery and custody of its precious contents. As it turned the corner, McGinn looked up at the house above. The curtains fell quickly back into place.

'Y'know, McInnes, I think we should have a word wi' old Mr Plunkett. That's one hell o' a lot o' stuff that's been unloaded, the man must surely have seen somethin'.'

Alan nodded.

'Aye, he certainly seems to see everythin' else.'

Mr Plunkett was reluctant to allow the two officers to enter his house.

'Whit's this aboot? Ah don't want the neigh-bours thinkin' that Ah'm in trouble, ye ken.'

'Mr Plunkett, we just want a wee chat,' McGinn replied, in a somewhat re-assuring tone that Alan was convinced was false. Once inside, his suspicion was confirmed.

The house was neat and tidy, if rather hazy with pipe smoke. A display of black-and-white photographs on the mantelpiece showed that there had once been a Mrs Plunkett and there were a few others that appeared to be of family. The officers sat on a rather careworn settee.

'So whit d'ye want tae chat aboot?' asked Plunkett, in a hostile tone. 'Have ye found oot who broke the Campbell woman's windaes?'

'Possibly, Mr Plunkett, although that's not spe-cifically why we're here. No doubt you've seen what we took out of the house below?'

Plunkett averted his eyes.

'Aye, weel, ye were makin' that much

noise that Ah looked out the windae jist
tae see what the hell wis goin' on—'

'Indeed, Mr Plunkett,' interrupted McGinn. 'In which
case, you'll no doubt have been aware of the goods in
question bein' taken into the house in the first place.'

Plunkett's eyes widened.

'Here...whit...'

'See, the thing is, Mr Plunkett, we've recovered a considerable amount o' stolen property; cases o' whisky,
brandy, cigarettes, cigars. Now, these must have come
in by the exact same route as we took them out. Probably not all at the same time, I daresay, but surely you
must have been aware of this? After all, the goods
would have been brought by a vehicle of some sort. So,
my question is, Mr Plunkett, over the last few months
were you aware of a car or a van, did you see anyone
taking these goods into Meg Campbell's house?'

Alan watched Plunkett's face redden; his lower lip began to quiver.

'Now see here—Sergeant, wis it?—Ah'm no'
goin' to sit here an' have you accusin' me...'

McGinn's tone became more officious.

'Mr Plunkett, I am *not* accusin' you of anythin'—
well, not yet, at any rate. All I'm askin' is whether or
not you saw any of these stolen goods being taken
in to Mrs Campbell's house. Surely you must—'

'No!'

Plunkett almost yelled the word and Mc-
Ginn stopped mid-sentence, his mouth open.

'What, Mr Plunkett?'

'You bloody heard me—no, I didn'ae see a thing.
Nothing, Ah'm tellin' ye, Ah saw nothin'!'

Alan could see that the old man was on the verge of breaking down; he glanced at McGinn, who nodded, and he took up the questioning, in a much gentler tone.

'Mr Plunkett, I think we all know that you watch what's goin' on around here—an' it's a good thing too, keepin' an eye out for those around you. So, the sergeant an' I are pretty sure that you must have seen somethin'. Tell me, Mr Plunkett, has someone threatened you, by any chance?'

Plunkett lowered his eyes to stare at the worn carpet, his lower lip trembling even more.

'Mr Plunkett?'

The man started to weep, his shoulders heaving.

'Ah mean, Constable McInnes, whit wis Ah tae dae? Look at me, Ah'm jist an auld man, aw' the fight went oot o' me when Catherine passed awa'—no' that there wis ever that much...'

'So you're telling us that some-one *did* threaten you, Mr Plunkett?'

He nodded.

'Aye. Said Ah wis tae keep my eyes an' ears closed—or that they'd dae it for me. Ah had nae choice.'

'You could have come to the police, Mr Plunkett,' said McGinn, in a rather stern tone. Plunkett looked at him.

'Oh aye? An' whit could you have done—watch ower me day an' nicht? Look at whit they did tae Meg Campbell, smashin' her windaes, threaten-in' her. Whit chance would Ah have had?'

It was a fair comment and both officers knew it. With a bit more cajoling, they finally obtained a statement from Mr Plunkett, with an idea of when the deliver-ies had been made. Finally, Alan made the man a cup of tea and they left him sitting on the couch, staring morosely at the pictures on the mantelpiece.

*

McGinn and Alan drove back to the police station and imparted the rather astonishing news to Sergeant Tait over a final cup of tea. The older man shook his head in astonishment.

'God, that's some haul, by the sound o' it. What d'you reckon it's worth?'

'Hard to say,' replied McGinn. 'After all, it's the re-sale value that was important tae Penman, no' the actual value. But it's a fair amount.'

'Where d'you think it would all have come from?' asked Alan. He was still excited by his discovery of he contraband and somewhat elated to have been the one to notice the missing perfume bottle.

'The docks, most likely,' replied McGinn. 'There's that many ships comin' in an' it's easy enough tae divert the odd crate here an' there, I suppose. The City police are doin' their best but, judging by what we found to-day, there's a pretty big organisation behind all this.'

'An' it looks like Penman's a part of it.'

'Aye, McInnes, seems that way. I've nev-er seen Nisbet so excited...'

Sergeant McGinn's voice tailed off and a concerned look crossed his face. Tait put down his mug.

'Whit's botherin' ye, McGinn?'

'Well, it just seems that the Inspector seems to be more concerned about nailin' Penman than he is about trackin' down the murderer—or murderers, for all we know.'

Donny Tait nodded sagely.

'Aye, richt enough. Mind, wi' what you've told me, it

seems the haul ye took frae Meg Campbell's basement micht just be worth murderin' for, if ye get ma drift.'

'You could be right, Tait. Obviously that's what Penman's lackey was lookin' for. Maybe they went after Hugh Campbell an'...well, who knows what happened.'

'Whit did Meg have tae say for hersel'?'

Alan answered.

'She denied any knowledge, Sergeant.'

'Dae ye believe her?'

Alan gave a shrug.

'Aye, I'd say she was telling the truth. Mind you, every time the Inspector questioned her, she looked as if she'd seen a ghost!'

McGinn gave a snort of laughter.

'Huh—he tends tae have that effect on folk—especially ones that are hidin' somethin'. But I'd have tae agree with you, McInnes. I don't honestly think Meg Campbell had anythin' tae do with it.'

'An' how the hell would they get a' that stuff down there without anyone noticin'?' asked Tait. 'Especially thon nosey bugger Plunkett—doesn'ae miss a trick, that fellow.'

'We questioned him,' replied McGinn. 'He *did* see an' hear the stuff goin' in but he says he was threatened, told tae keep quiet, most likely by that big bugger, Tommy. The inspector'll be keen tae get his hands on him, I'd imagine; if we can find him, that is. He put a call through to the City police but, if the bugger's gone to ground somewhere in the East End, well...'

He shrugged his shoulders.

'So what'll happen now?' asked Alan.

'Well, I think Inspector Nisbet'll be gettin' Penman into the Paisley office as soon as he can. At the very least he'll be implicated in the handling of stolen goods...'

He gave Alan a dark look

'...an' possibly as an accessory tae murder.'

*

The three officers chatted about the case for a while longer and it was past eight o'clock before Alan lifted his coat and made to leave. He asked Sergeant McGinn if his presence was required over the weekend, but he said no.

'I'll leave my telephone number with Sergeant Tait—if you get any word about Benson, let me know. Otherwise, have the weekend off, you deserve it—been a tough week for you.'

'Thanks Sergeant. Right, I'll see you on Monday.'

'You will.'

As Alan opened the door, McGinn called after him.

'McInnes—you did well, might make a detective o' you yet!'

The smile remained on the constable's face all the way home.

*

As usual, Isa McInnes had his dinner ready for him and he tucked in with gusto as he told her of the day's proceedings. She sat quietly, shaking her head rather sorrowfully.

'Goodness, poor Meg, what an awful carry on after losing her husband and her daughter.'

'Aye, Mother, just shows you never know what's goin' on. Who'd have thought it though, in a quiet wee place like Barloch.'

'Aye, but there's maybe a lot more goes on than you'd realise, son. Anyway, away you an put your

166

feet up in front of the television. Your father's away for a drink, that's him off for a week now.'

'Em, Mother...?'

'Yes, Alan?'

'Is everythin' okay with the two o' you?'

Isa gave her son an odd look.

'What d'you mean, son?'

He wasn't exactly sure himself.

'Och, nothin' really, it's just that you seem to be arguin' a lot these days, that's all.'

She looked away.

'Aye, well, when you've been married as long as we have, there's wee stresses and strains that appear now and again. It's nothing to worry yourself about—away through and see what's on, I'll be through once I've cleared up. I think you should probably get an early night, you must be tired and you want to be well-slept if you're meeting your ladyfriend's parents tomorrow.'

Was there a note of reproach in her voice, he wondered, as she placed the dishes in the sink. A wave of guilt swept over him as he walked through to the lounge, flopped down on the comfortable settee and switched on the television.

Five minutes later, he was fast asleep.

Chapter 15

Saturday morning dawned clear and bright, almost as if
summer had returned, and Alan was wakened by the sun
streaming through a crack in his curtains. After a shave
(rather more carefully than usual) and a wash, he dressed
in his best white shirt, neatly pressed grey flannels and
his prized, black-and-white checked sports jacket. As an
afterthought, he placed a striped tie in one pocket and his
warrant card in the other...just in case.

His mother was already busy, the smell of baking emanating from the cooking-range oven, bacon and eggs sizzling in the pan on top.

'You look smart, son. I pressed your flannels last night.'

'Thanks, Mother.'

On an impulse, he leaned down and
kissed her on the cheek. She smiled.

'Och, away with you, Alan McInnes! Sit down and
have your breakfast. Where are you off to this early, I thought you'd be having a wee bit of a lie-in?'

'Em, well, I'm not exactly sure...'

He told her of his rather vague idea and she gave him
a worried look, the sort that only a mother can bestow.

'Oh Alan, are you sure you should be going off
on your own like this? Would you not be best to
speak to that sergeant... Mr McGinn, isn't it?'

'It is; no, don't you worry, Mother, it's just a, well,
what is it the Yanks say in the films—a hunch, I sup-

pose. No, I'll just do a wee bit of diggin' by myself an' if nothin' comes of it, well, there's no harm done.'

He set to on the bacon and eggs, washed down with two cups of tea. Half an hour later, he was ready to leave and his mother saw him to the door.

'Your father's having a lie-in. I think his leg's bothering him but you know what he's like—stoic to the last! Listen, son, don't make too much of a thing about Nancy's father being a lawyer—you know what he's like once he gets started.'

'I won't, Mother. Look, I don't know when I'll be home tonight so don't wait up.'

'Well, as long as you don't miss the last train. I hope you have a nice time tonight; and don't you be intimidated—you're a fine-looking lad and a good policeman, you should be very proud of yourself. Don't let any fancy lawyer try and do you down!'

He grinned.

'Don't worry, Mother, I won't; and even if I don't get a train to the village, I can get a later one to Lochside and walk the rest of the way.'

'Oh, that's an awfully dark road at night. You be careful, Alan McInnes.'

She was about to close the door behind him when, as an afterthought, she said, 'And don't you be getting ideas above your station today, mind. You don't want to be blotting your copybook with Sergeant McGinn and that inspector who seems to be such a horrid man.'

He laughed.

'Don't you worry yourself, Mother, I'll be a good laddie! And I'll be careful too, I promise. Bye.'

Just for good measure—and because he was

still feeling rather guilty—he leaned back in
and kissed her cheek for a second time.

*

Alan was in buoyant mood as he set off down School Street
but, as he crossed Barloch's main road, his mind began to
fill with misgivings. He had no clear plan as to what he
was about to do, just a vague idea. Then, as he approached
the ramp to Barloch Station, he almost turned back—he
suddenly realised that his idea wasn't even vague; frankly,
he hadn't the faintest idea how to proceed with his own little
investigation! His shoulders slumped slightly as he turned
into the entrance and walked up the ramp.

There were a few morning travellers standing on the
platform, awaiting the arrival of the early train for a
day's shopping in Paisley or Glasgow. He entered the
ticket-office, where Bert Oliphant, the stationmaster, was handing out a ticket to an elderly lady. Once
the woman had left, he approached the window.

'Mornin' Alan, you're up wi' the lark this mornin'!'

'Aye, Mr Oliphant, just got a wee bit o' business
to attend to—listen, can I ask you somethin'?'

'Aye, of course, but the train'll be here in...' he
turned and consulted the large wall-clock behind him '...just under six minutes.'

'Oh—well, can I have a return to...em, actually...'

Bert Oliphant narrowed his eyes.

'D'ye no' know where you're headed?'

Alan could feel the colour rise in his
cheeks; was he on a fool's errand?

'Well, not really, to be honest. Listen, Mr Oliphant, last Monday night, about ten o'clock, did anybody

170

get off a train and, well, hang about, I suppose?'

Mr Oliphant gave him a shrewd look.

'Is this part o' yer enquiries, like?'

'In a way—I'm just following something up, really.'

The stationmaster rubbed his magnificent beard.

'Well, now ye come tae mention it, there *was* a fellow got off the down train at ten minutes to the hour.
He stood at the far end ramp—if ye mind, it was a
foul night—an' smoked a couple o' cigarettes.'

Alan could feel the hairs on the
back of his neck bristling.

'Did he say where he'd come from, by any chance?'

'Aye, as a matter o' fact he did! He was carryin'
one o thae kit-bags that sailors have an' I asked if
he was a seaman. He told me he was, an' that his
ship was laid up in Greenock wi' engine trouble.'

'Greenock?'

'Aye, son, that's whit he said. He wis along there, shel-
terin' frae the rain inside the canopy, for aboot fifteen
minutes. Next time I looked he wis gone—don't know
where. I wondered if he maybe had family in the village.'

'Did you see him again—I mean, did he
catch a train over the next few days?'

Bert Oliphant shook his head.

'Naw, lad, no' as far as I know. Mind, I'm no' always here so I suppose he could have. You could
ask my assistant, he'll be in this afternoon...'

A sharp whistle interrupted him, heralding the approach
of the train. Alan quickly purchased a return ticket to
Paisley Gilmour Street station, thanked the stationmaster
and rushed outside, where a soot-begrimed standard tank
engine was drawing its train of grubby maroon coaches

into the station. He opened the door of a non-smoking compartment, stepped inside and slammed the door shut behind him. As he sat down, he looked up at the sign above the dirt-streaked window; with careful use of a pen, some wag had changed "Please do not lean out of the window" to "Please do not clean soot off the window!" He smiled; his day had already gone better than planned, although he couldn't help wondering just how much of detective work rested on simple, plain good luck!

*

Alan changed trains at Gilmour Street, catching the next one that headed towards the coastal town of Greenock, lying on the River Clyde's so-called "tail-o'-the-bank". He was enjoying the journey down the coast; it had been a long time since he had visited the busy industrial town and, even though he was on what he considered to be semi-official business, he was looking forward to a change of scene after what had been a rather fraught and disturbing week. As he watched the world speeding by, accompanied by the comforting, hypnotic "clickety-clack" of the carriage wheels, he felt his eyes start to close. Fortunately, his carriage was populated by a number of good-natured football supporters, wearing the black and white colours of Paisley's St Mirren football club. No doubt en route to play against Greenock's Morton, their occasional bursts into song served to keep him from dozing off. He wondered if they would be as good natured on the return journey; that very much depended on the result, as well as the quantity of alcohol consumed.

As the train clanked its way through the urban sprawl of Port Glasgow, Alan's earlier good humour once again started to dissipate. The quaysides that lay adjacent to the many yards held many ships and he felt as if he was about to search for a needle in a haystack. Undeterred, he alighted at Greenock Central station and made his way down Bogle Street, towards Rue End Street, the main thoroughfare through the town. A few minutes later, he was standing at the quayside of the East India dock, staring at the array of moored craft, as well as a number of pugnacious little tugboats. A crew member stepped off one of these, clad in a set of oily overalls and wiping his hands on a dirty rag. Alan approached him.

'Excuse me?'

'Aye, son?'

'Is there a harbour master's office hereabouts?'

'Aye, along the other end—see thon brick building...?'

Alan nodded, his gaze follow-

ing the man's outstretched arm.

'...but if ye're efter the harbour-mais-

ter, he's no' there the noo.'

Alan let out an inward groan.

'Oh—d'you know where he is, by any chance?'

The crew-man consulted a wristwatch.

'He'll be up in the wee cafe ha'ein' his breakfast. Should be feenished in aboot fifteen minutes so, if ye gang al-ang the noo, you'll likely catch him as he comes back.'

Alan thanked the man for the information and made his way along the busy dockside. It was a fascinating scene, with ships loading and unloading, even on a Saturday. Several of the little tugboats were scurrying towards the entrance to the dock, their tall funnels belch-ing black smoke. As he neared the brick building, its faded wooden sign proclaiming it as the offices of the harbour master, a burly, bearded man wearing a naval hat and a dark blue pullover crossed the road and, with the rolling gait of the seafarer, walked towards the building. Alan called out as the man opened the door.

'Excuse me!'

The man turned, a vaguely suspicious look on his face.

'Aye?'

'Are you the harbour master?'

The older man stared at Alan for a moment, as if sizing him up.

'Depends who's askin'!'

Alan didn't know how to respond to this and the man obviously took pity on him. He gave the constable a wink.

'Ah'm just pullin' yer leg, son, Ah'm the harbour master.'

Alan had the feeling that his proposed interview might not be as straightforward as he'd hoped.

'Could I have a word with you, please?'

The burly man pushed the door open, answering Alan over his shoulder.

'Whit aboot?'

'Em, I'm lookin' for someone.'

The man stopped and turned.

'Are you the polis?'

Was he that obvious, Alan wondered. He took his warrant card from his pocket and showed it to the rather surly individual.

'Aye, but this isn't exactly an official enquiry.'

Then, as an afterthought, he added, 'Yet.'

The man regarded the card then looked up warily.

'Ye'd best come in then.'

The office walls were lined with charts and plans of the docks, noticeboards with various announcements and schedules. There was a large, rather cluttered desk beside the window that overlooked the harbour. The harbour master sat down and lifted a disreputable pipe, stuffing tobacco into it from a worn leather pouch. He looked up at Alan for a moment, once again as if assessing the young constable's worth. He seemed to reach a decision

'By the way, it's Nicol Watson—captain, retired.'

'Constable McInnes—I'm down from Barloch.'

Watson lit his pipe.

'Barloch, eh? Ye're a bit oot o' yer territory here, then, are ye no'? Here, were there no' a couple o' murders there last week—has this got anythin' to do wi' they?'

Alan had hoped that the man hadn't heard of the two deaths, but obviously the news had spread; after all, it had been widely reported in the newspapers.

'In a way, Mr Watson but, as I said, this is unoffi-cial at the moment. I'm just trying to trace a mem-ber of the family, he's a merchant seaman.'

'I see. Any idea whit ship he's on? That'll be the place tae start.'

Alan shook his head and let out a sigh.

'That's the thing, Mr Watson, I don't.'

The man puffed out a cloud of blue to-bacco smoke and gave a chuckle.

'Weel, as ye can see, we've got a hell o' a lot o' ships here. If ye don't know which one he wis on, then ye've got a pretty impossible task ahead o' ye!'

'All I know is that the ship came in last Monday—that'd be the thirty-first.'

'Weel, that narrows it doon a bit, I suppose...'

Clamping his pipe firmly between his teeth, Wat-son lifted a huge ledger and opened the pages.

'Anythin' else ye can tell me?'

'Yes, apparently the ship's being repaired—seems it had a problem with its engines.'

Watson scanned down the register with a beefy finger, then tapped the page.

'Weel, in that case, ye're in luck! I can tell ye that the boat ye're after is the *Crown o' Cordova*—it's up in one o' Scott's yards havin' its boiler repaired, I believe. Due to sail oot again on Tuesday next—that'll be the eighth o' September.'

He closed the large ledger with a heavy thump.

'So that's yer ship, Mr McInnes. But, as tae yer man—weel, he could be anywhere, I suppose.'

Alan could feel the vague cloud of despair forming once more.

'Would the crew not stay on board?'

Watson shook his head as he emitted another cloud of fragrant tobacco smoke.

'Naw, no' if it's in a yard gettin' repaired. But if the crew didn'ae go home, they'd likely book in tae the Sailors' hostel doon' the road.'

Alan's little cloud of despair dispelled.

'The Sailors' hostel?'

'Aye—weel, the British Sailors' Society, tae gie it its full title— it's a place where seafarers can bide if their ship's oot o' commission, or if they just want a bit o' time ashore. Ye'll see the building back along Rue End Street, a big square, brick-built place. That's where I'd try if I were you.'

Alan thanked the harbour master and was about to leave when Watson called after him.

'Are ye after this man for those killin's?'

Alan shook his head and smiled.

'No, Mr Watson, as I said, he's just a family member we're tryin' to track down. Thanks again for your assistance.'

*

The Sailors' Society building was easy enough to locate—a long, brick-built edifice with a flat roof, sitting on the seaward side of Rue End Street. Alan climbed up the steps and entered the hallway, his nostrils assailed by a mixture of disinfectant and stale tobacco smoke. There was a sliding glass window on one side and he approached, knocking gently on the glass. A thin, rather severe man approached, looking questioningly at Alan over the top of a pair of half-moon spectacles. He slid the glass panel open.

'Good morning—can I help you?'

Alan hesitated, unsure whether to make his request informal or official; he decided on the latter and fished his warrant card from his jacket pocket. The bespectacled man scrutinised it and looked back up at Alan.

'Yes, I hope so, I'm trying to trace the whereabouts of a crew member of the ship, *Crown of Cordova*, it docked last Monday.'

*

The Saturday morning shoppers were already filling the streets and shops of the town; no-one took any particular notice of the swarthy, sullen-looking man leaning against a lamp-post, his peaked cap pulled down almost over his eyes. He removed a packet of Capstan full strength from his pockets, his scowl deepening as he realised he was down to his last fag. He took it out then screwed the packet up before nonchalantly tossing it onto the pavement. He had planned on returning to the hostel for a couple of hours, during which he'd have a look at the racing pages of the daily newspaper, have forty winks, then head to the nearest book-maker's shop, where he'd spend the afternoon—as well as the bulk of his wages! A fish supper, followed by a trip to an adjacent public house, would nicely round off his Saturday night before heading back to the austerity of the hostel. Unless, of course, he met a lady who might just have a place of her own, who might be interested in some male company—for a small fee...

As he struck a match, his eyes registered a movement at the door of the Sailors' Society; a tall, dark-haired young man had just exited, a rather smug smile on his face. It was the short haircut and the somewhat erect stance that caused the man to be suspicious of the younger man's profession. The sullen stranger lit his cigarette and watched the well-dressed individual as he crossed the road, heading in his direction. Pulling his hat lower, he drew heavily on his cigarette and took the daily paper from his pocket, scanning the headlines; he could wait a few minutes more before heading back to his accommodation. The young man passed within a few feet, seemingly oblivious to the stranger's scrutiny, then stopped and entered a cafe. The stranger threw his cigarette into the gutter, shoved his hands in his pockets and walked purposefully towards the bleak facade of the hostel. Had anyone been observing him closely, they would have noticed the expression on his face had changed from one of disdainful disinterest to one of consternation.

Chapter 16

'That was a lovely dinner, Mrs Wright, thank you very much.'

Helen Wright beamed at what she considered to be the rather handsome young man seated at the dining table next to Nancy, her noticeably radiant daughter. Well-mannered too—indeed, although she'd perhaps hoped for better than a policeman for her only child, Alan McInnes seemed, on the whole, to be a pleasant, intelligent and engaging young man. She glanced briefly at her husband; his daughter was well and truly placed on a pedestal and, in Andrew Wright's eyes, Nancy could do no wrong. Would *any* man really be good enough for her, she wondered? Mind you, he looked to be in a reasonably benevolent mood, always a good sign; especially today when, on a beautiful late-summer's morning, he had been forced to forego his customary golf four-ball, instead being summoned to Paisley's police station by a prospective client.

'Oh, you're most welcome, Alan, I'm so glad you enjoyed it—no greater compliment to a cook than a clean plate!'

If truth be told, Alan had struggled slightly with the rich, heavy dinner, running to four courses. His palate was more used to his mother's plain, simple cooking. Nancy smiled at him.

'You certainly seem to have worked up a good appetite, Alan McInnes—what were *you* up to today?'

'Now now,' interrupted Nancy's father, 'a man's entitled to his privacy—and to pursue his own activities...even if mine *were* so rudely interrupted this morning. Right, Alan, let's you and me retire to my study, leave the girls to clear up.'

Andrew Wright rose, leaving Alan feeling both slightly nervous and slightly guilty—at home, he would, at the very least, have helped to carry the dishes to the kitchen. He turned to Nancy

'Em, are you sure that's alright...?

She smiled back.

'Och, away you go, Mummy and I can have a nice wee chat over the dishes whilst you and Daddy get to know one another.'

Alan felt his stomach lurch slightly; would this be an opportune moment to discuss his future plans with Nancy's father?

*

'So, Alan, could I tempt you with a wee brandy?'

Andrew Wright had already uncorked a crystal decanter and was pouring generous measures into two brandy balloons.

'Em, oh, well...'

Mr Wright gave him a curious look.

'Never had brandy before?'

'Actually, no, I haven't, I'm normally a beer man.'

Alan was already feeling the effects of several glasses of an extremely pleasant red wine, another drink new to his palate. Andrew handed him the glass and it seemed churlish to refuse. His host smiled pleasantly

'Well, there's a first time for everything—here you are, Alan. Just sip it, mind, it's not beer, you know. Have a seat.'

Clutching his glass carefully, Alan sat down on a large, leather settee. Andrew Wright's study was like no room

Alan had ever seen. Callanish, the Wright family home
in Paisley's rather exclusive suburb of Ralston, was a
large, detached sandstone villa, set in beautifully tended
grounds. The study sat at the rear of the property, with
French windows opening on to the large back garden,
its multitude of flowers and shrubs currently bathed in a
late evening glow. Wood-panelled, the room smelled of
leather and cigar-smoke; in the middle sat a large, solid
mahogany desk, with an ornate brass lamp. There were
numerous bookshelves set around the walls, laden with an
astounding array of books, from old and leather-bound
to recent, gaudy-covered novels. Andrew lifted a cigar
box from the desk, opening it and offering it to Alan.

'Oh, no, thanks, I don't smoke.'

Andrew smiled and selected a cigar from himself, running it briefly under his nose.

'Good for you—Helen doesn't really approve of me
smoking and I'm only allowed to do so in here. So
much for a man being master of his own house, eh?'

He sat down on the large leather chair behind his
desk then, after a bit of a palaver, he finally got his cigar lit. The aroma of the smoke was extremely pleasant
and, for a moment, Alan was tempted. Andrew leaned
back, took a second puff then took a sip of brandy.

'Ah, that's good—life's little pleasures, eh? So,
Alan, how are you enjoying the police?'

The directness of he question took Alan by surprise.

'Oh—well, it's fine thanks, Mr Wright...'

Andrew Wright chuckled.

'Oh, for goodness sake call me Andrew, my boy,
let's not stand on formality. Anyway, I always think
that "Mr Wright" always sounds a bit silly—es-

pecially from my daughter's young man!'

Again, Alan was taken by surprise.

'Oh, yes, well, I see what you mean. But, as I said... Andrew, I'm really enjoying it, actually. I'm hoping that, one day, I might be able to transfer to the CID...'

He paused for a moment, asking himself if that was, indeed, still the case.

'...but this week's been, well, a bit difficult.'

'Ah yes, these murders. Unpleasant business—I take it you've been involved in the investigations?'

Alan briefly outlined his part in the discovery of both victims. As he described the circumstances of finding Mary Campbell's body, his host frowned.

'Oh God—that must have been dreadful for you.'

'Yes, it was pretty bad—you see, I knew the girl, she was local...'

He could feel the blood drain from his face at the memory; Andrew Wright leaned across the desk.

'Try not to dwell on it, Alan, I know it's difficult but you need to remain detached. The thing is, if you ever have to go to court, you'll need to be able to recount such incidents with clarity and composure. You can't be seen to—well, go to pieces, I suppose, in the witness box. The prosecution won't thank you for that!'

He gave a chuckle; Alan could feel the brandy going to his head, although he was finding it extremely pleasant and easy to drink.

'Em, can I ask...Andrew, what type of law do you specialise in?'

Andrew Wright gave him a broad smile.

'Ah, I wondered if you'd ask...actually, I'm a criminal defence lawyer.'

Alan wasn't quite sure how to respond to this and Andrew continued to smile at him.

'You see, you're probably thinking that we're on opposite sides of the fence but, in reality, that's not the case. Let me explain—I take it you're familiar with *Habeas Corpus*...?'

*

It was almost an hour and three brandies later before Alan and Andrew Wright joined Nancy and her mother in Callanish's comfortable lounge. Alan couldn't remember the last time he had felt so pleasantly inebriated—the customary "bagged-up" feeling after five or six pints of beer was absent, replaced by a pleasant glow of bonhomie. Andrew Wright, too, seemed to be in a decidedly relaxed frame of mind and, over the rather delicious coffee and shortbread, the conversation had flowed easily. Finally, it was time for Alan to take his leave, although he was aware that he was unlikely to be in time for the last train from Paisley to Barloch town station. Nancy had said that she would walk him to the bus stop and, the final round of thanks and hand-shaking complete, they had strolled, arm-in-arm, along the quiet, suburban avenue towards the main thoroughfare of Glasgow Road. Once out of sight of Callanish, Nancy stopped, turning to face him with a conspiratorial grin.

'Alan McInnes, you're drunk!'

'I am not!'

'You are so—did Daddy ply you with brandy?'

He couldn't deny it; his head was spinning!

'Oh, for goodness sake, how many did you have?'

'Em...two—or three...I think!'

Nancy giggled appealingly.

'Well, I suppose that's a good sign. Hardly anybody gets into Daddy's inner sanctum, you know.'

'His what?'

'His study, silly! You know, I think he
likes you—Mummy certainly does.'

Then, before he could reply, her arms were
around his neck, their lips met, his arms were
around her waist, her hips pressed against his...

Alan McInnes wasn't sure that he believed in the concept
of heaven but, if it *did* exist, then this must be pretty close!
As he finally boarded the late-night Young's bus that would
take him to Paisley Gilmour Street station (hopefully in
time for the last train to Barloch) he realised that, at some
stage, he would have to ask Andrew Wright for his daughter's hand in marriage— always assuming Nancy said yes!

*

Brian McGrory drained the dregs of his teacup and stood
up, trying his best to ignore the stiffness in his knees. The
kitchen, the heart of Laverock Farm, was warm and cosy
and, for a moment, he considered staying put and having a
second cup of tea. He shook his head, dismissing the thought
as quickly as it arrived.

'Paddy! Bess!'

The two black and white collies, already watching him
intently, jumped up and eagerly followed their master
to the kitchen door, tails wagging in anticipation. Brian
pulled on his heavy overcoat and placed his deerstalker hat on his head; the morning was bright but, already,
there was a hint of autumn in the air. Despite this, however, his long years of experience as a farmer told him

that there might be a storm brewing before long. He glanced at the grandfather clock, ticking comfortingly in the corner. Six forty-five—plenty of time to walk the dogs, check the cattle and the horses, then have a peaceful perambulation around the policies of his farm before he was dragged, rather unwillingly, to Kilmirrin church for the obligatory, and interminably boring, Sunday morning service. Once in the hallway, he unlocked the small cupboard next to the outer door and took out his shotgun, along with half a dozen cartridges. If he was lucky, he might just bag a couple of rabbits, or maybe a pigeon or two, for the pot. It always pleased Elsie, his wife, to have fresh game to bring to the table; with three hungry teenage mouths to feed, God knew they needed it!

He walked across the farm close, his shotgun crooked safely across his arm as the two dogs nipped at each other's tails. A beautiful, crisp morning, he thought; he enjoyed being out in the fresh air and he could really do without today's church service. There always seemed to be too many odd little jobs to be done, with too little time to complete them!

Brian passed the silage pit and approached the hay shed that held the winter feed for the several horses that the farm possessed. Fortunately, the days of horse-drawn ploughing had passed, the work now carried out by a powerful, grey Ferguson tractor, but he still indulged his passion for his two magnificent Clydesdale horses. As he neared the hay shed, the dogs started to growl as they approached the door.

'Whit's the matter? Paddy—Bess, whit is it?'

The dogs turned, understanding the questioning tone in their master's voice, but their growling persisted. As Brian opened the barn door, he paused and placed two cartridges in the shotgun, snapping the barrels shut...just in case.

'Hello? A' body there?'

His question was greeted by silence, but Paddy and Bess, now growling ferociously, dived ahead, crossing to the far corner of the barn. Brian followed, raising the shotgun.

'Hello—if ye're there, ye'd best come oot, else Ah'll set the dogs on ye!'

The growling intensified further; Brian looked towards the dark corner where the two dogs were standing, their hackles on end. They started to bark furiously and the farmer peered into the gloom, where he could just make out what seemed to be a pile of sacks. However, as he moved closer, he could see that, from below the sacks, a pair of booted feet were protruding.

*

Someone was calling his name; the voice seemed distant, familiar—was it Nancy? He felt a faint glow of pleasure. Nancy...!

'Alan! ALAN—oh, for goodness sake...'

He was being shaken now, rather violently. He opened his eyes but swiftly closed them again. His bedroom seemed to be spinning, his head was pounding—surely Nancy wouldn't...

'Alan—for goodness sake! Son, are you all right?'

He identified the voice as belonging to his mother and half-opened his eyes again, wincing as the light seared his retinas. She was sitting on the bed now, a look of concern on her face.

'Alan, will you waken up—that's Sergeant Tait on the phone.'

Finally, an extremely hungover Alan McInnes was awake; he raised himself up on one elbow.

'Sorry, Mother, I was...'

She looked down at him with an accusatory expression.

'Alan McInnes—how much did you have to drink last night?'

He shook his head; it felt like his brain was detached from his skull. He had missed the train to Barloch town, instead catching the last one that stopped at Lochside station, about a mile from the village. He must have walked home, but he couldn't remember; nor could he remember arriving at his house, getting into bed...

'I don't know, Mother—Nancy's father gave me a few brandies.'

'Brandy! In heaven's name, son, what were you doing drinking brandy? That's a toff's drink.'

Alan didn't answer; he felt as if he was going to be sick. Isa continued, her voice softening.

'Anyway, Donny...Sergeant Tait wants to speak to you.'

'What? But...but it's Sunday, Mother. What does he want?'

Isa McInnes shook her head—she had never seen her son with a hangover and she wasn't sure whether to be angry or amused. It would certainly teach him a lesson!

'Well, he says he needs you go down to the station right away.'

Alan groaned as he flopped back down on the bed.

'Why—did he say why?'

'Yes, he thinks Billy Benson's been found.'

*

Coffee wasn't the beverage of choice in the McInnes

household but, somehow, Isa had managed to produce a small jar of instant from the depths of her larder; she boiled some milk and Alan had gratefully sipped the warm, comforting brew. And a second. Finally, he deemed himself fit to get dressed and walk down to the police station, having decided that, under the circumstances, he had best wear his uniform. Every step down the hill seemed to cause a thumping inside his head and he was filled with a sense of dread in case he had disgraced himself the previous night. Nancy would never forgive him. Then, fortunately, he remembered *that* kiss; he supposed that their relationship must still be sound.

He opened the door of the station, where Sergeant Tait took one look at him and smiled.

'Good God Almighty, McInnes, you look bloody awful! What the hell were you up to last night?'

Alan explained, Tait nodding sagely as he puffed on his pipe.

'Brandy, eh? Aye, that's a wicked drink if ye're no' used tae it. A toff's drink.'

'That's what my mother said!'

Donny Tait's eyes twinkled briefly.

'Aye, weel, she'd know.'

Before Alan could ask for an explanation of this enigmatic remark, the door opened and Sergeant McGinn came in, casually attired in a rather worn tweed sports jacket and brown cavalry-twill trousers.

'Aye-aye—Christ, McInnes, you look bloody awful...'

'That's jist what Ah've told him, McGinn!' chuckled Tait. 'Are you sure you're fit for duty?'

Alan nodded, grimacing as his head pounded once more. 'I'll be fine'

'Tait, have you any aspirin?'

'Aye, Ah'll get some.'

As Tait disappeared into his office, McGinn gave Alan an affectionate pat on the shoulder..

'Don't worry, son, we've all been through it— what the hell were you drinkin' anyway?'

'Brandy; Nancy's father kept them coming and I didn't like to refuse.'

'Nancy? Oh, aye, your girl! Brandy though, that's a fancy nip! What does her father do for a livin'?'

'Andrew? He's a lawyer.'

McGinn let out a laugh

'A lawyer, eh? And you're on first-name terms already! Well done, you've got your feet firmly under the table there, son. Jings, "Andrew" on the first night! It was about six months before I got to call my father-in-law by his first name!'

'Well, he got fed up with me calling him Mr Wright. I suppose it *does* sound a bit daft...'

Suddenly, McGinn gaped, looking at Alan as if he'd had slapped him.

'Wait—his name's Andrew Wright and he's a bloody lawyer? No' a criminal defence lawyer, by any chance?'

Alan's throat tightened.

'Em...yes, d'you know him?'

McGinn's face started to redden, his fists clenching by his sides.

'Know him? Good God almighty, McInnes, he's bloody representin' Benny Penman—Nisbet and I spent nearly two hours yesterday mornin' in the company o' Penman and his bloody brief. Christ, you didn't discuss Penman with him at all, I hope?'

Alan shook his head but the truth was, he couldn't remember. McGinn started to pace up and down across the small office.

'For God's sake keep this to yourself, McInnes. If Inspector Nisbet gets to hear of it, he'll have your bloody guts for garters! And I suggest you rack those brains of yours and recall every-bloody-thing that the two of you spoke about, just in case you've inadvertently given anythin' away. We've got a great case against Penman, if it all goes sour because Wright's got hold of any inside information, well...'

*

The two officers were in the Wolseley, heading towards the village of Kilmirrin. They hadn't spoken a word since they had left Barloch. Alan was sitting in the passenger seat with his eyes closed, wishing McGinn would drive more slowly. They bumped along the back road from Barloch, then, finally, McGinn asked, in a calmer tone, 'So, where's this farm, McInnes?'

Alan opened his eyes briefly; they had nearly reached Kilmirrin.

'Up through the village, over the hill. Laverock farm, about a mile up the hill on the left,' he mumbled.

They drove on, passing through the quaint little weaving village. A church bell was chiming, summoning the locals to the morning service. McGinn spoke again.

'So, Sergeant Tait tells me that this farmer—Brian McGrory—was out for an early mornin' walk and came across someone sleepin' rough in his hay shed. By the description, it sounds like it's Benson, but we'll find out when we get there.'

Alan didn't reply.

'An' if he's been on the run since Monday, he'll
be fit for nothin'. Cold, hungry, the bugger'll probably be happy enough to spend a night in the
jail...McInnes, are you bloody sleepin'?'

Chapter 17

Sergeant McGinn knocked on the door of Laverock farm, a traditional, solid two-storey building with a row of out-buildings adjoining one side and a milking-parlour on the other. Immediately, the sound of barking emanated from inside and, a few moments later, the door was opened by a round-faced woman with twinkling blue eyes, her greying-red hair tied in a neat bun.

'Mrs McGrory—I'm Detective Sergeant McGinn, this is Constable McInnes. I believe you called the local police station regarding a man found in one of your sheds?'

Mrs McGrory smiled.

'Aye, ye'd best come in—we're a' ben the kitchen.'

They followed in her wake as she bustled through the hallway and into the spacious, cosy farm kitchen. A large, square table, covered with an oilcloth, sat in the middle, with eight chairs set around it. On one of these sat a mis-erable-looking figure, his hair matted and with six days of dark stubble on his face. He was sitting with his back to a large cooking-range and, although he was wrapped in a thick woollen blanket, he appeared to be shivering. McGinn glanced at Alan and whispered, 'Is that him?'

Alan nodded; the man was barely recognisable but there was no doubt that they were looking at Billy Ben-son. An empty plate sat in front of him and he was clutching a large white mug in one hand. In the corner of the room stood a watchful Brian McGrory, the shotgun still crooked over his arm; the farmer was obviously taking no chances. Mrs McGrory crossed over to the range and placed her hand gently on Benson's shoulder.

'How're you feelin' now, son—a wee bittie better?'

Benson nodded and mumbled his thanks.

'Guid, guid; Brian, for heaven's sake will ye pit that gun awa'—he's goin' naewhere...'

She cast a glance at the two officers.

'...well, except maybe wi' these twa.'

As the farmer removed the cartridges from the shotgun and snapped the barrels shut, his wife bent down and opened the oven door, removing a large baking tray on which sat a dozen enormous scones.

'Right, Ah'm sure ye'll ha'e room for ane o' these.'

'Mrs McGrory, I'm afraid we'll need to be taking—'

She interrupted Sergeant McGinn, giving him a stern look.

'Ye'll be takin' naeb'dy naewhere, Sergeant, until the body's got a decent meal inside o' him. The puir cratur's hauf-starved and chilled tae the bone. Jist let him get another cuppie an' a scone or twa then ye can be oan yer way.'

She gave Alan a scrutinising look.

'Ah'm thinkin' that you could maybe be dae'in wi' somethin' yersel', laddie, ye look right peaky tae me—are ye awricht?'

McGinn gave the woman the ghost of a wink.

'The constable wasn't expectin' to be on duty this mornin', Mrs McGrory.'

She smiled knowingly.

'Ah see! Weel, sit yersels' doon an' Ah'll make a fresh pot...'

The door to the kitchen burst open suddenly and a tall,

tousle-haired young man, clad in striped pyjamas, bound-
ed into the room. He was a younger image of his father.

'Maw, is that fresh scones? Ah'm starvin'...'

The youth's eyes opened wide as he took in the scene;
three strangers, one a uniformed policeman, with his
father apparently standing guard, still with the unloaded shotgun clutched in one hand. Mrs McGrory crossed over quickly and took her son's arm.

'Come awa' ben the parlour an' Ah'll explain, Hamish...'

*

Half an hour later, and suitably refreshed, McGinn, Alan and
Benson departed the farmhouse, the latter still draped in the
woollen blanket but with his hands securely handcuffed in
front of him, despite Mrs McGrory's remonstrations.

'Oh for guidness sake, the laddie's no gaun' tae gie' ye any
trouble—look at him, there's nae fecht left inside o' him.'

But McGinn had insisted—he wasn't taking any risks.

Alan was feeling marginally better, having been plied
with two scones, laden with butter and home-made
bramble jam, and a large mug of hot milk. Mrs Mc-
Grory clearly knew how to treat a hangover! As they
stepped out into the farm close, they were watched
by Hamish and his siblings, the sombre expression
on their faces belied by the sparkle of excitement in
their eyes. McGinn opened the rear door of the Wolseley and guided Benson inside, then turned to Alan.

'Best get in the back wi' him, just in case.'

As Alan climbed in beside the prisoner, Mrs McGrory called out.

'Ye'll bring back the blanket once ye're done?'

'We will, don't worry.'

'An' dinn'ae ye be bad tae the boy—
he's jist a poor sowel, so he is.'

'Don't worry, Mrs McGrory, we'll take care o' him'
replied McGinn. 'An' thanks again for your hospi-
tality—I think the constable's feelin' a bit better.'

Mrs McGrory beamed—had Alan been looking, he would have recognised the expression
of maternal pride from his own mother.

*

By the time the trio arrived back at Barloch police station,
Alan was, indeed, beginning to recover, although the journey
in the rear of the Wolseley, especially over the narrow,
twisting back-road from Kilmirrin, had caused him a few
anxious and nauseous moments. Billy Benson remained
silent throughout, his head slumped dejectedly on his chest.
McGinn had warned Alan against talking to him as, in such
circumstances, anything Benson said would be inadmissible
as evidence.

McGinn opened the rear door and ushered Benson out; Mrs McGrory had been correct, there was
no fight left in the man. His shoulders were slumped,
his head downcast—and he stank to high heaven! The
three entered the station, McGinn leading the way
and Alan bringing up the rear, although he very much
doubted that Benson would attempt to make a run
for it. They found Sergeant Tait standing at the bar.

'So ye got yer man—Christ, Benson, ye're a
bloody mess, ye should never have run off like
that. What the hell were ye thinkin', man?'

Benson appeared to mutter an apology.

'Richt, through ye come—I'll bring ye

some water an' ye can have a wash, but I'm
afraid I cann'ae let ye have a razor...'

He looked knowingly at the other two and McGinn
nodded his agreement. It suddenly dawned on Alan why.

'You don't think he'd...'

McGinn raised a hand.

'Just a precaution, McInnes, we'll be takin' his bootlaces as well.'

The outer door opened and Isa McInnes walked in,
clutching a hen-basket covered with a checked dish-cloth.

'Mother! What are you doin' here?'

She smiled at her son—then turned towards Donny Tait.

'Och, well, I though that if you'd found Billy, you'd
be needing to feed him. I've brought you some sandwiches, we had a roast yesterday and there was a
bit left over, just being Gilbert and myself...'

Was there another touch of reproach
in her voice, Alan wondered?

'...and I've made a wee apple and bramble crum-
ble—the Bramleys were just ready to pick and
there's been a great crop of brambles this year.
I'll bring you a pot of jam when it's made.'

Donny Tait's eyes twinkled.

'Och, ye're an angel, Isa, so ye are. Just let us get
Benson comfortable an' I'll come back through.'

Even in his hungover condition, Alan sensed a
vague, unspoken connection between his superi-
or and his mother. It disturbed him very slightly and, as Tait followed McGinn and their prisoner
out of the front office, he turned and looked at Isa,
whose expression was the picture of innocence.

'Mother, there was no need to bring anything down, Sergeant Tait can—'

She interrupted, giving her son a rather stern look.

'No, Alan, he can't. There would have been a time, when his dear wife was alive, when she would have provided for any prisoners held here, but Donny's on his own now. He can barely fend for himself, by all accounts—how on earth is he going to manage to feed a prisoner, especially one who appears to have been sleeping rough for nearly a week? No, Donny and I go back a long way and I would never see him stuck.'

She folded her arms, discouraging any further discussion on the matter; anyway, Alan hadn't the energy to argue.

'All right, Mother, I can see your point...'

McGinn returned.

'Right, McInnes, I think you should get yoursel' up the road and get some rest. Listen, you've been a big help today, I appreciate you comin' in when you were supposed to be off duty...'

He winked across at Isa

'...especially in the condition you were in!'

Isa looked slightly embarrassed.

'I'm really sorry about Alan, Sergeant, he doesn't usually find himself in such a state.'

'No need to apologise, Mrs McInnes, no need at all— we've all been guilty of a hangover at one time or another.'

Alan felt as if he was invisible; he interrupted.

'What'll happen now, Sergeant?'

'Eh? Oh, well, I spoke to Inspector Nisbet earlier this mornin' and he's going to leave questionin' Benson until tomorrow; says a night in the cells'll soften him up.'

Isa McInnes turned on the sergeant.

'Soften him up! Are you intending to force a confession from the poor lad when he's cold, tired, hungry and been sleeping rough for a week? Have you never heard of *Habeas Corpus*?'

Both Sergeant McGinn and Constable McInnes turned to stare at the petite, grey-haired woman who appeared to be quoting a basic principle of human rights. McGinn grinned.

'Indeed I have, Mrs McInnes, but we have the right to hold Benson as a suspect for the murder of Mary Campbell—an' possibly Hugh Campbell as well.'

Her eyes widened in anger.

'What? Well, you'll make bloody fools of yourselves if you think that! Benson may be a bit of a rough diamond but he certainly didn't kill Mary Campbell—he loved that lassie dearly and he wouldn't have harmed a hair on her head.'

'Mother!'

'No, Alan, this is just wrong, but I suppose you're not going to listen to anything I have to say.'

'On the contrary, Mrs McInnes,' interrupted McGinn. 'Your opinion *is* important and I, personally, value it highly. However, it's up to Inspector Nisbet and he's ordered that Benson be detained until he interviews him personally tomorrow morning. And I can assure you that there will be no "forced confessions" being elicited.'

'And will he have a solicitor present?'

McGinn cast a sideways glance at Alan, raising an eyebrow.

'If he requests one, a solicitor will be provided.'

'Good; well, that's fine, as long as justice is done. But remember, Sergeant McGinn, innocent until proven guilty.'

She turned to go but McGinn had the last word.

'Mrs McInnes.'

She turned to face him.

'Yes, Sergeant?'

He smiled at her.

'You've missed your vocation, ma'am—
you should have been a lawyer!'

As she turned away once more, Alan could see
a smile of satisfaction on his mother's face.

'Best away up wi' her, McInnes, get some rest; and
make sure you're down sharp and fresh tomorrow,
the inspector might even let you attend the interview
wi' Benson—it'll be a good experience for you.'

Alan breathed a sigh of relief.

'Thanks, Sergeant. I'll see you in the mornin'.'

As he headed for the door, McGinn called
out, 'She's quite a woman, your mother!'

Alan smiled.

'Aye, she is that!'

But as Alan left, Sergeant Mc-
Ginn muttered, half to himself

'An' no bloody wonder Tait's got a soft spot for her.'

*

Alan quickly caught up with his mother, walking with his
usual courtesy on the outside of the pavement. She smiled
up at her handsome son. She placed her arm through his.

'You seem to have made a bit of an impression on Sergeant McGinn, son.'

He chuckled

'Aye, an' so have you, Mother!'

She, too, laughed.

'Och, well, I don't like to see people being treated un-

199

fairly. That poor Benson boy, he's had a right hard time, losing his mother and living up in that lonely cottage with only his father for company. It's such a shame, he was settling down and he seemed fond of the poor Campbell girl. If you have anything to do with it, you make sure they don't force him to confess to anything he didn't do.'

'I won't, Mother.' he replied, without conviction; he very much doubted if he *would* have anything to do with it.

They walked on slowly—Alan felt like he could sleep for days.

'Mother—how d'you know about *Habeas Corpus*?'

She smiled again; she was thoroughly enjoying being escorted home by her son.

'Ah, there's a lot I know that might surprise you, Alan McInnes; and I hope *you've* learned not to drink too much brandy in future!'

'Aye, I've learned my lesson—here, it's funny, Sergeant Tait said the same as you, that it was a toff's drink. He made some comment about you knowing...'

Her eyes twinkled for a moment.

'Like I said, son, there's a lot I know.'

To Alan's relief, they were approaching their front door.

'Listen, away you up to your bed and have a wee sleep; I'll waken you in a few hours, you should have recovered your appetite by then.'

He kissed her cheek and they stepped inside. Wearily, he climbed the stairs but, as he opened his bedroom door, it suddenly dawned on him that he had completely forgotten to mention his expedition to Greenock, not to mention the discovery he had made, to Sergeant McGinn. He yawned, kicked off his boots and lay on his bed; it would just have to wait until the morning.

201

Chapter 18

The police Wolseley was already parked outside the police station when Alan arrived at eight forty-five the following morning. He felt fully recovered, having slept for about ten hours. Following his afternoon nap, his mother had made him a light meal, at which he had, fortunately, managed to avoid an argument with his father, ignoring the pointed, and rather cruel, remarks about "bloody lawyers" and "not being able to handle his drink." Apart from the fact that he hadn't the energy, his mother's pleading looks had dissuaded him from rising to the bait.

On his walk down School Street, he rehearsed what he was going to say to Sergeant McGinn regarding his visit to Greenock but, in the cold light of day, he wondered just how the CID officer might respond. He found McGinn leaning on the wall beside the main door, smoking his habitual Capstan full-strength. However, he dropped it on the ground as Alan approached, giving the young constable a conspiratorial wink.

'Feelin' better the day, McInnes?'

'Aye, Sergeant. Slept like a log last night an' I'm fine now. I'm really sorry about yesterday!.'

'Forget it—we've all suffered from an excess the night before—anyway, you didn't expect to be on duty so there's no blame. Right, let's get on.'

'Actually, Sergeant, if you've got a minute...'

But McGinn appeared to ignore him; detaching himself from the wall, he took Alan's elbow and guided him back down the pathway.

'Now, son, let's you an' me have a wee talk—away from any curious listeners.'

Alan's heart started to pound; this wasn't exactly what he'd planned. They walked a short way down the road, McGinn stopping as they reached the grounds of the little village hall. His usual friendly manner was exchanged for a stern, official tone and Alan's heart sank.

'Look here, McInnes, now that your head's clear o' brandy fumes, I want to know what the hell you an' Andrew Wright discussed on Saturday night; and don't be omitting anything either—I need to know what was said, every last damn word.'

Alan took a deep breath.

'I've been thinking about it, Sergeant, and I'm certain that Penman wasn't mentioned. Mr Wright spoke a lot about the law, about how he wasn't really on the opposite side from us. It was more about how justice needed to be done an' that there could be no room for doubt in a guilty verdict, especially if it was a capital crime. He asked a few things about the murders, nothin' really important though, just casual conversation. But Penman definitely wasn't discussed.'

McGinn stared at him for a moment; Alan could feel beads of perspiration break out on his brow.

'You're absolutely certain, McInnes?'

'Yes, Sergeant, I am.'

The sergeant gave a long sigh of relief.

'Thank God for that.'

McGinn sat down on the low wall that surrounded the hall and lit another cigarette.

'See, we've got Penman fair and square; actually, I'm convinced he was actually almost relieved when we turned up. Our suspicion is that the bugger's in a lot of debt and that someone further up the chain was breathin' down his neck for payment. Hence the mysterious fire at his bookmaker's premises—an insurance job if ever I saw one.'

He took a deep draw on his cigarette.

'So, it seems that Hugh Campbell was storin' most, if not all, of Penman's contraband but the man suspects that Campbell was also sellin' his stuff on the side. Anyway, he eventually tried to collect the money that Campbell owed as well as the goods, but it seems that Campbell refused to say where they were bein' kept.'

'That's why they ransacked the house, then?'

'Indeed it is, but they never found anything, obviously. He had it well hidden—an' if it hadn't been for you, McInnes, it might *still* be hidden.'

Alan's spirits rose slightly as this compliment. McGinn continued.

'Anyway, Penman's sayin' nothin' about who he's in debt to an' I'm thinkin' that he feels he'll be safer in jail that at the mercy of some nasty bugger up in Glasgow...'

He stared at the glowing end of his cigarette for a moment.

'...but it'd be good if we could get hold o' Penman's boss too, although it's unlikely he'll tell us. After all, they can get to a man in jail if they really want to.'

'So d'you think Penman might have killed Campbell—or had him killed?'

McGinn drew on his cigarette, shaking his head.

'No, I don't—neither does Inspector Nisbet. He was happy enough to threaten violence towards Meg Campbell but I don't think he killed her husband. Seems Campbell was quite an important part of their organisation; livin' in a scruffy house in a quiet wee village like this, no-one would be likely to suspect him o' bein' the quartermaster for a criminal gang dealin' in tobacco, spirits, an' the like. There's also the point that, if they had done away wi him, how would they track down the missin' goods? It's often the way though, like many petty criminals, he got ideas above his station; and got caught out in the end.'

'That'd certainly explain Meg Campbell's fancy cigarettes, wouldn't it?'

McGinn grinned.

'Aye, you're an observant bugger right enough, McInnes. An' of course, there's also our friend, the manager down at Glensherrie steelworks. Campbell probably had a great wee network goin' down there, selling booze an' fags.'

'And did Campbell have a gambling debt right enough?'

'Aye, but just about thirty quid or so. There was never any industrial injury, as we already know, that was just a cover story. No, the bulk of Campbell's debt was for goods he'd sold and never given Penman the money. Penman was lookin' for his cash an' also wanted his goods back—he suspected Campbell was skimming—'

He was interrupted by a shout from further up the street.

'McGinn—where the hell are you?'

'Comin', sir' he called back. 'Right, McInnes, let's get back up an' see what the mornin' brings.'

Alan felt he had missed his opportunity; hopefully there'd be another one before it was too late.

*

To the local sergeant's obvious annoyance, Donald Tait's office desk had been completely cleared and the room was now serving as an interview room. Nisbet sat behind the desk, looking for all the world like a stern, Victorian schoolmaster. Billy Benson, washed and—under the close supervision of Tait—shaved, sat across from him, a picture of abject misery. McGinn stood immediately next to the prisoner while Alan, who had been invited to observe, was standing with his back to the door, blocking any attempt by Benson to escape. One look at the young man, however, indicated this to be an extremely unlikely scenario.

Nisbet studied a set of handwritten notes through a pair of black NHS spectacles. Finally, he took them off and regarded Benson for a moment.

'Right, let's get started. Your name is William Benson, commonly known as Billy; is that correct?'

Benson nodded.

'Speak up, man, we need to hear your response.'

'Aye.'

'Aye what?'

'Aye, ma name's Billy Benson.'

'And you live with your father at number one Shielhill Cottages?'

'Aye, Ah do.'

'Benson, what is your date of birth?'

Benson finally looked up, a frown on his heavy features.

'Ma whit?'

'Your date of birth?'

Benson shook his head; Alan managed to catch Nisbet's attention.

'What, McInnes—I told you to remain silent.'

'If I could just have a word, sir...'

Uninvited, Alan stepped forward and Benson looked up at him, the ghost of a smile appearing at the sight of a familiar, friendly face.

'Billy, when's your birthday?'

'Ma birthday—em, it's the ninth o' January, Ah think.'

'Good—now, what year were you born in?'

Benson's brows knitted together again.

'Em, Ma faither said it wis the year afore the war started...'

'So that would be nineteen thirty-eight?'

Benson nodded enthusiastically.

'Aye, that's richt, that's it...nineteen...whit ye just said...'

The inspector nodded and wrote down the information, then indicated to Alan to step away once more. McGinn winked at him, mouthing "well done."

'Right, Benson, can you account for your movements on the night of Monday the thirty-first of August?'

Benson gave the inspector another blank look.

'Oh, for God's sake, man, last Monday— what were you doing last Monday night?'

Benson scratched his chin.

'Weel, ah had ma denner, then Ah went doon the village an' met Mary...'

His lower lip started to tremble but he managed to maintain his composure and continue.

'We went a wee walk, had a wee chat an' a smoke, then—'

'Constable McInnes said he caught you and Mary Campbell up Braid's close and that you appeared to be...fornicating. Is that correct?'

Again, Benson stared blankly at the Inspector.

'We wis *whit*?'

'Fornicating—you were having...sex.'

The last worded seemed to spill reluctantly from

the inspector's mouth, as if he had difficulty in saying it. Benson's head dropped down once more.

'We micht have been.'

'Were you or were you not?'

Benson nodded

'Aye, we were.'

'And when the constable accosted you, you both ran off?'

'Aye.'

'Where did you go after that?'

Benson shrugged.

'Naewhere in particular—the notion had kin-
da worn off. We sheltered under the railway bridge an' then Mary went hame.'

'You didn't escort your ladyfriend to her house, then?'

Benson shook his head.

'Where did you go afterwards?'

'Ah jist walked aboot a bit, then Ah went hame ma'sel.'

'Can anyone corroborate this?'

Another blank look.

'Oh, for God's sake—did anyone see you, Benson, can anyone confirm your statement?'

Benson shook his head.

'Naw, there wis naeb'dy aboot, it wis pourin' wi' rain.'

'And why didn't you have the common de-
cency to escort Mary Campbell home?'

'Ah wis feart Ah met her faither.'

'And why was that?'

Benson snorted.

'He wis a violent bastard...'

'Watch your language, Benson.'

'Aye, weel, he wis! Ah wis never good enough for Mary
even though he wisn'ae really her proper faither. Ah

sometimes wondered if he wanted her for himsel'...'

Nisbet looked surprised; this thought clearly hadn't occurred to him.

'Was there any indication that Hugh Campbell *had* assaulted his step-daughter? Did she ever make any such accusation?'

'Naw, she never said. Ah think her...well, her brother Colin had warned him off in the past, but he's been awa' for years noo. Anyroads, Mary could handle hersel' weel enough.'

Nisbet paused, putting on his spectacles and consulting his notes once more, although Alan was certain this was just a ploy. He looked up again.

'You didn't like Hugh Campbell, did you?'

'Naeb'dy liked the man, he wis a ba... a bloody animal, once he'd a drink in him. Used tae beat Mary's maw, she often had a keeker, or bruises oan her arms—ask anyb'dy in the village.'

Nisbet looked across at Alan, who nodded his agreement.

'I see.'

He placed the notes down and leaned back in Sergeant Tait's chair, glaring at Benson over the spectacles.

'Benson, did you kill Hugh Campbell?'

Benson sat bolt upright.

'Whit? Me...Ah...Ah...naw, Ah never killed naeb'dy! Here, you cann'ae pin that oan me, Ah, never—'

Nisbet interrupted the protestations, leaning forward once more. His tone was louder now, more severe.

'You see, Benson, you had the motive—by your own statement, you were never good enough for Mary and you had a strong dislike for Hugh Campbell. You had the opportunity—once you'd left Mary, you can't account for your movements and you have no alibi. You certainly have the ability—you're a strong, well-built young man. We know that Campbell senior had been drinking in the Hole in the Wa' until ten o'clock, the last time he was seen alive—well, except by his killer. Did you hang about, Benson, waiting to meet him? Did you get into a fight, in which you hit him with a rock? Did he goad you, tell you that you weren't good enough?'

Alan was aghast; Nisbet was putting words into Benson's mouth, words that he believed to be untrue. He bit his cheeks, his fists clenching with suppressed anger. Benson's mouth was opening and closing like a fish, he seemed unable to form any words. Nisbet was relentless.

'And why did you run, Benson? When Hugh Campbell's body was discovered the next day you ran. You jumped on a train without a ticket, you jumped off again just before Kilmirrin, you lived rough for almost a week, didn't you Benson? You ran from the scene of the crime—why?' Because you were *guilty*, Benson, that's why...'

Nisbet punctuated these last few words by thumping his fist on the desk. Benson jumped to his feet but McGinn pushed him back down into the chair. Benson shouted, his spittle flying across the desk.

'Naw! Naw! Ah never...Ah never killed Campbell, Ah swear...'

Nisbet shouted back, a manic gleam in the man's eyes.

'No? Then why did you run, Benson? Like a bloody coward! Tell me—why, if you didn't kill Campbell?'

Benson deflated once more.

'Because Ah though it wis Mary ye'd found.'

Again, Nisbet looked surprised.

'Mary? But we didn't know she had been murdered at that point. Why would you think it was her?'

Benson began to snuffle.

'Because...because Ah heard wan o' the women doon at the loch side sayin' that Mary had disappeared, then when you found the body, Ah thocht it must be her. Ah knew that Mr McInnes had seen us the nicht afore, Ah knew Ah'd get the blame...'

'Rubbish! If you were innocent, there was no need to run. Why would you get the blame, Benson?'

The man broke down completely, his shoulders heaving, his head buried in his beefy hands. Between sobs, he blurted out.

"Cos Ah always get the bloody blame...it's aye the same, it wis big...big, stupit Billy whit done it... but Ah never killed naeb'dy an' that the God's own truth...'

*

In a near-insensible state, Benson was led back to his small, bleak cell; they could get no more out him. Nisbet appeared satisfied, however.

'That's softened him up; give him a couple of hours to think over what we've asked him and we'll see what he has to say later. Right, I've a few notes to make...'

Summarily dismissed, Alan and McGinn stepped outside into the welcome brightness of another fine, morning, having ignored Sergeant Tait and Constable Brodie's enquiring glances. Once outside, McGinn lit up.

'Well, McInnes—you're no' lookin' too happy about the proceedings back there!'

If he was being honest with himself, Alan was horrified at the way Nisbet had bullied Benson, making suggestions, putting words into the young man's mouth. He didn't reply..

'Look, son, don't take the inspector's approach too seriously. If Benson *is* innocent, he'll stick to his story. If he's makin' the whole thing up, then Nisbet'll get the truth out o' him. Don't worry, this is just what an interrogation is all about, makin' sure the suspect is really tellin' you the truth. Aye, it's harsh at times but you'd be surprised just how much people can lie to get themselves out o' trouble.'

'It just seemed really unfair—I mean, Benson's obviously upset over Mary's death, the poor bugger's...well, defeated, is the best way I can put it.'

'An' that's exactly what the Inspector wants! If he sticks to his story when he's at rock-bottom, then we can pretty much reckon that it's true. Look, if you don't want to be involved...'

'No, I do, Sergeant, it's just, well, it's the first time I've witnessed an interview like that.'

McGinn gave a grim smile.

'Aye, well, if you've a notion to join the CID, it won't be the last. Right, let's get back...'

'Em, Sergeant?'

'Aye, McInnes?'

'Actually, there was somethin' that I was wantin' to talk to you about...'

*

It took Alan about ten minutes to recount the story of his trip to Greenock. Despite his earlier rehearsal, he felt that he had rather blurted out the narrative rather than giving a concise summary of the day's events. Once he had finished, McGinn remained silent, puffing on the dregs of his cigarette.

Finally, he dropped the butt on the ground and looked Alan in the eye.

'Right, McInnes, first of all, there's little doubt that you exceeded your authority. You were in plain clothes but you're not a detective, you're a uniformed constable. That's misdemeanour number one.'

'But—'

McGinn raised his hand.

'Don't interrupt me, son. You produced a warrant card—on two occasions, by your own admission—when you were off-duty and not authorised to do so. Number two.'

Alan remained silent.

'Number three, why the hell didn't you say somethin'? If you'd told me about your so-called "hunch" last week, we could have investigated it. Instead, you went off on your own, with no authority to do so, no-one to watch your back, and with some half-bloody-baked plan! What the hell were you thinkin', McInnes?'

Alan hung his head disconsolately.

'I just thought I'd check it out, Sergeant, if the whole thing turned out to be a waste of time then I'd have said nothin', but if not, well...'

McGinn shook his head.

'Thing is, this might actually be somethin' right enough, although I don't quite know what to make o' it yet. The problem now is...'

He paused, a grim expression on his face.

'...we've no choice but to tell Inspector Nisbet, an' God knows what *he'll* have to say to you...!'

*

As they opened the door to the police station, they met

Inspector Nisbet coming out.

'There you are.'

Somehow, the statement carried a note of re-proach; Nisbet closed the station door behind him, lowering his voice as he continued.

'I've just had Dr Miller on the phone; he's con-cluded Mary Campbell's port-mortem.'

There was a strange gleam in the Inspector's eyes.

'She died by strangulation of course...'

McGinn and Alan waited expectantly.

'...but it turns out that the girl was with child. Dr Miller estimates that she was about fourteen weeks pregnant.'

Chapter 19

The three officers returned to Sergeant Tait's office. Inspector Nisbet, as usual, occupied the seat behind the desk, with McGinn sitting opposite. Alan stood beside the sergeant and Nisbet was in full flow, the light of victory in his eyes.

'So I suggest we let Benson stew for an hour or so, then confront him with this latest piece of evidence. My thoughts are that, having discovered that he was about to be a father, he got into an argument with the girl and strangled her. The man's obviously weak-willed, there's no way he would be able to take on the responsibility of fatherhood.'

'But what about Hugh Campbell, sir?' asked McGinn, a worried look on his face. 'Is Benson still in the frame for that as well?'

'When you've killed once, McGinn, it's always easier to kill again to cover your tracks. Campbell senior most likely caught the two of them arguing, Benson attacked and killed him then turned his attention to the girl—or vice-versa. Either way, he's our man, I'm convinced of it.'

'But the scratches on Hugh Campbell's face— that wouldn't have been Benson, surely?'

Nisbet swept McGinn's objection aside with a wave of his hand.

'Trivial details, McGinn, maybe the two of them had an altercation, we may never discover what actually happened.'

'Em, Inspector?'

Nisbet glared at Alan.

'What is it, McInnes?'

'I don't really believe that Benson is capable of murder, sir, I think he really loved the girl...'

'Oh, for God's sake, McInnes, forget your damned romantic notions, the man's half-witted, surely you can see that? Once provoked, he would be capable of anything, in my opinion. He's a brute of a man, no doubt as handy with his fists as Hugh Campbell was. No, I believe—'

McGinn interrupted, much to Nisbet's annoyance, judging by the expression on his pinched features..

'Inspector, McInnes has a piece o' information that may have some relevance.'

Nisbet turned his glare towards the sergeant.

'Really? Very well, McInnes, let's hear it.'

'You see, sir, I'd spoken to the Barloch stationmaster, Mr Oliphant, and he told me that, on Monday night, about ten o'clock, a chap had arrived on a late train from Paisley. He told Mr Oliphant that he'd come off a boat at Greenock and that it was laid up due to engine trouble. Seems he hung about for about ten minutes or so, standin' at the end of the platform, smoking...'

Nisbet interrupted impatiently.

'And the relevance of this, McInnes?'

'Well, I happened to be in Greenock on Saturday and I thought I'd make a few enquiries around the docks, just in case—'

'In case what, McInnes? This sounds like you're acting on a whim—what's your bloody point?'

Alan swallowed.

'Well, I asked about, as I said. I spoke to the harbour

master and then I asked in the British Sailors' Society...'

'Under what authority?'

'Em, well, I showed my warrant card...'

'Were you in uniform?'

'Em...no, sir, but...'

Nisbet stood up, almost knock-ing over the chair behind him.

'What? You went about under the pretext of be-ing a plain-clothes officer when, in fact, you were simply an off-duty uniformed constable, you then showed your warrant card and started asking ques-tions? What the hell were you playing at, McInnes?'

'Sir,' interrupted McGinn. 'I've already spoken to Constable McInnes regardin' his behaviour, but I think that you should hear what he has to say.'

Nisbet's face had turned scarlet.

'Very well. What did you find out—and this had better be good!'

'Well, sir, I just had this idea...you see, it seems that Meg Campbell's son, Colin, is a crew member on the *Crown of Cordova*, the boat that's laid up. I think he's the man that Mr Oliphant saw in the station on Monday night. Although he's been staying at this Sailors' Society hostel down in Greenock, he checked out late on Mon-day afternoon and didn't return until the Tuesday.'

Nisbet continued to glare at the constable for a moment, then sat back down, steepling his hands and leaning them against his forehead, his brows wrinkled in thought. Alan spoke again.

'Oh, an' one more thing, Inspector, it seems that his boat, the *Cordova*, is due to sail again tomorrow.'

Nisbet mumbled something under his breath; Alan

wasn't sure if the man was swearing. He looked up again, his face white with rage, then spoke through gritted teeth.

'McInnes, step outside for a moment.'

Alan did as the inspector asked; Sergeant Tait, who was leaning on the Bar, gave him a shrewd glance.

'Gettin' a bit o' a dressin' down there, lad?'

Alan nodded. His face was red with embarrassment and he was beginning to wish that he'd never set foot on the train to Greenock.

'Would'na worry yersel' too much, though. Thon Nisbet's no' an easy man tae please, Ah'd imagine it'd take a lot tae pit a smile on his face.'

Alan waited anxiously for a few more minutes, then the office door opened once more.

'McInnes!' barked McGinn.

Once inside, Nisbet appeared to have calmed down somewhat, although his face was set in a scowl.

'Right, McInnes, your information does cast a new light on matters, although you were well out of line taking the action that you did. Anyway, I'll deal with that later. I've discussed the matter with Sergeant McGinn and I've decided that we should head down to Greenock immediately and bring Colin Campbell in for questioning. I'll phone ahead and arrange for some local uniformed officers to attend—McGinn, get the car ready, we'll head down right away. McInnes, you may as well come with us, at least you can tell us where to go.'

Alan presumed that the Inspector didn't mean literally—he was sorely tempted! As he turned to leave, Nisbet asked, 'What the devil made you think of all this, McInnes?'

He turned back, glancing at an equally curious McGinn.

'Well, it was actually the sergeant's cigarettes—the Capstan full-strength.'

'Hm, a particularly foul brand.'

Alan looked at McGinn but the sergeant remained stony-faced.

'But how the hell did that lead you to look for Campbell?'

'Well, sir, Sergeant McGinn's brand has quite a distinctive, strong smell and he'd told me that he'd picked up the habit in the Merchant Navy; seems that Capstan is a common smoke among sailors. When I passed by the ramp to the station last Monday night, I smelled the same smell, along with that of a freshly-struck match. It seemed a bit odd, lookin' back—I mean, there hadn't been a train for a while an' I got the impression that someone was just hangin' about, if you see what I mean. Then, when Sergeant McGinn lit up, the smell reminded me... took me a wee while to make the connection but, when I did, I remembered that Colin Campbell was also in the Merchant Navy. I knew that he had no great likin' for his step-father and it just set me thinkin', had he been hangin' about, waitin' for Campbell? Then, when I asked Mr Oliphant, it seemed to confirm my suspicions...sir.'

Nisbet considered this for a moment.

'Hm. Well, as I said, your approach was unorthodox to say the least, but I have to say it was a good enough piece of deduction, McInnes. Right, let's get on...'

*

The narrow, twisting hill road that ran across the moors from Barloch to Greenock had taken its toll on Alan McInnes. McGinn was a competent driver but Nisbet had urged that he make haste and the Wolseley had swayed and lurched its way over the numerous bumps and around the many bends.

By the time they crested the hills, the magnificent vista of the Clyde estuary coming into view, he was white as a sheet and fighting to contain his nausea. They descended the steep hill that led down through Port Glasgow until, finally, they were on the level stretch of main road that would take them to their destination. Once they had passed the docks, Nisbet pointed.

'There's the uniformed officers—stop here, McGinn.'

The sergeant obliged and Nisbet exited the car, discussing the situation with the two uniformed constables. After a minute, he came back over.

'Right, leave the car here, McGinn. They say that no-one has entered or left the building for the last forty-five minutes. I've sent them round the back, presumably there'll be a fire exit or rear access that they can keep an eye on. Right, let's go.'

Glad of his release from the rear of the vehicle, Alan followed McGinn and Nisbet across the road and up the steps of the Sailors' Society building. Once inside, Nisbet marched across to the glass-fronted office, rapping officiously on the closed window. A different member of staff from the one Alan had spoken to approached, sliding the glass open.

'Here, what's your hurry, ma friend, nae need tae knock the bloody glass out—'

Nisbet held up his warrant card, stopping the man mid-sentence.

'We're looking for a man by the name of Colin Campbell—I understand that he's staying here.'

The man scrutinised Nisbet's identity then consulted a ledger, running his finger slowly down the entries.

'Campbell...Campbell, aye, here we are.'

He looked up.

'Room twenty-seven, jist up those stairs over yonder.'

'Is he in at the moment?' asked McGinn.

The man closed the ledger and shrugged.

'Couldn'a tell ye. He's no' checked oot, if that's any help, but they dinn'ae always. See, if they're jist nippin' oot for a pack o' fags or the like, then they usually dinn'ae bother. Jist makes a lot more work for us.'

'How long have you been on duty today?' asked a frustrated-looking Inspector Nisbet.

'Since eight this mornin'.'

'And would you have recognised Campbell if he'd passed by?'

The man considered the question.

'Aye, like as no' I would—a sullen fellow, no' much tae say, but polite enough. Naw, as far as Ah'm aware, Campbell hasn'ae gone oot the day.'

'Good. Do you have a master-key?'

The man behind the window frowned.

'Aye, but Ah'm no' sure—'

McGinn cut him off.

'If you'd rather we batter the door down, then that's fine...'

The man glowered at the sergeant then reached up, taking a key from a row of wall-hooks. He handed it to McGinn.

'Room twenty-seven, mind—that's a master key...'

As McGinn took the key, Nisbet was already striding towards the stairs. He grinned at the man as he followed.

'Twenty-seven it is, don't you worry!'

As Nisbet reached the stairway, he turned and barked across.

'McInnes, you stay here, just in case. Be ready

to stop him if he tries to make a run for it.'

Nisbet and McGinn took the stairs two at a time, leaving Alan standing at the bottom and feeling rather left out; still, he probably deserved it, he thought. He heard a sharp knocking followed by Nisbet's dulcet tones..

'Police, Mr Campbell; open up!'

Silence; more knocking, louder this time.

'Police—open the door, Campbell, we know you're in there.'

Silence once more; Alan heard the faint sound of the door being opened, followed by Nisbet's voice, very slightly muffled as, presumably, he entered Campbell's room. Alan readied himself, just in case. A few minutes passed, then Nisbet stormed back down the stairs, heading straight for Alan. He stopped in front of him, his face scarlet with rage.

'You bloody fool, McInnes, Campbell's gone, his room's empty. No doubt he became aware of your amateurish enquiries and now he's flown the damned coop! God all mighty, I'm tempted to have you suspended from duty!'

McGinn had descended the stairs and was approaching; Alan looked at him in desperation, vainly hoping that Nisbet was mistaken, but the sergeant shook his head.

'I'm afraid he's away right enough, McInnes, all that's left is an old pair o' socks an' a newspaper.'

He turned to the inspector

'But, to be fair, sir, Campbell may have been intendin' to leave anyway. We don't actually know if this *was* a consequence o' McInnes's actions.'

Nisbet appeared to ponder on this for a moment, then turned back towards the man in the office, who was watching the proceedings with interest.

'Have you any idea where Campbell was going?'

The man shook his head.

'No' me—like Ah telt ye, Ah wisn'ae even aware that he'd left! Anyway, Ah've been aff since Friday, it wis one o' the other chaps that's been on duty over the weekend. He'll be back on Thursday, if ye want tae have a word.'

'No, that's no bloody use, Campbell's ship is due to leave tomorrow.'

'Excuse me, sir.'

'What, McInnes? Have you something useful to add to this debacle?'

Alan cringed slightly.

'Well, I wondered if, maybe, Campbell's gone back to his ship. If we went along and spoke to the harbour master, he could tell us if the repairs to the *Crown of Cordova* have been completed...'

'McInnes is right,' interrupted McGinn. 'Presumably there's a charge for stayin' here—if his ship's ready, then he'd save himself a bob or two by goin' back aboard. Worth a try, sir, surely?'

Nisbet considered this suggestion.

'Oh, very well, I suppose it is. McInnes, I presume you know where we're going?'

'Yes sir.'

'Thank God—at least you're of some damned use. McGinn, get round the back and tell those uniformed officers to follow us along; better to be safe than sorry.'

*

Nicol Watson, the harbour master, favoured Inspector Nisbet with the same distrusting look that he had given Alan.

'Yer man here's been doon already, In-

223

spector. Whit are ye wantin' noo?'

'I want to know if the boat, the *Crown of Cordova*, has completed its repairs.'

Watson consulted the same, heavy ledger as before, running his finger slowly down the columns in what appeared to be a characteristic maritime fashion. It occurred to Alan that, maybe they were all simply being obstructive of the police investigations, for some reason. Eventually, Watson found the relevant entry.

'Aye, here we are...richt enough, the tugs brought her in earlier this mornin', she's probably gettin' steam up by now.'

'Would any of the crew have stayed aboard the vessel?'

Watson closed the ledger and ponderously shook his head.

'Ah explained tae yer constable here that naebody would stay on board when she wis in for repair. The captain'll be aboard today for sure, the engineer an' the stoker an' all if she's gettin' steam up; as tae the ithers, it depends. They micht be, if she's leaving tomorrow. Ah doubt she's no' got her cargo on board yet, mind.'

'Where can I find this vessel?' barked McGinn, clearly impatient at the man's procrastination. Again, Watson took his time in replying.

'Aye, weel, you'll find her doon at the foot o' the dock yonder...'

He pointed in the general direction of the dock.

'...jist tae the starboard side o' the entrance there. See, the wan wi' the black smoke comin' oot her funnel.'

Nisbet responded with a curt "thank you" and the three officers exited the cramped office. Once outside, Nisbet headed apace towards the rather shabby-looking merchant vessel that was moored next to the dock entrance. It was what Alan would have termed a "tramp steamer", an elderly craft with a tall, old-fashioned smoke stack, her hull painted black and her superstructure a rust-streaked white. As they approached, he could see the name written on her bow. A narrow gangway led up onto the deck, where a young deckhand was busy scrubbing the wooden planks. Nisbet led the way on board, the deckhand looking curiously at the new arrivals.

'I'm looking for the captain.'

'He's up on the bridge, ma freend' said the young man, leaning on his brush. 'Alang there an' up that wee stair. Best tae knock afore ye go in, mind, he doesn'a welcome un-announced veesitors on the bridge...'

*

Nisbet knocked on the varnished wooden door, complete with a brass-ringed porthole. A deep, booming voice responded.

'Aye, who's there?'

'This is Inspector Nisbet, Paisley CID. Could I have a word with you, please?'

The door opened and they were confronted by an enormous, powerfully-built individual, with a bushy red beard and clad in a black officer's uniform with a white-topped cap.

'Aye, aye, ye'd best come awa' in.'

They followed the captain into the bridge, a small, spotless place adorned with brass and wood; a large table sat against the rear bulkhead, covered with an enormous nautical chart. The captain spoke again, his accent clearly identifying his highland origins.

'Captain Duncan MacTavish at your service, gentlemen. What can I be doin' for yourselves?'

'We're looking for a member of your crew—a Colin Campbell.'

MacTavish raised a hairy eyebrow, considering this for a moment.

'I see; an' just what is it that Meester Campbell is supposed to have done?'

'We just want to talk to him, Mr MacTavish.'

The man frowned at Nisbet.

'It's Captain MacTavish, if you please...'

Nisbet looked slightly taken aback, unused to having his authority questioned.

'Em, sorry, Captain MacTavish. We wish to speak to Mr Campbell in relation to an ongoing enquiry.'

'An enquiry, is it? Aye, must be quite an enquiry to warrant three officers on the job, if you were to ask me.'

Nisbet was becoming increasingly impatient.

'Look, Mist...Captain MacTavish, I must ask if you've seen Campbell recently. He was staying in the British Sailors' Society hostel but he checked out of there, sometime after Saturday, and I wondered if he was staying on board the ship.'

MacTavish gave Nisbet a disparaging look, shaking his head slowly.

'On board *my* ship?' the captain corrected. 'Och, no, no, nobody stays on board when there's repairs bein' done. Noo that they're done, it's just ma'sel', the engine room boys gettin' steam up an' the deck-boy gettin' her shipshape. No, if he's not in the hostel then you would be best to look elsewhere. He's certainly not aboard the *Crown*.'

'You're quite sure of that, Captain MacTavish?'

The disparaging look changed in an instant to one of annoyance, anger even.

'Are you questionin' my word, Inspector Nisbet? I'm master of this vessel and proud to be so. My word is good, you can ask any of my crew. I'm a fair and honest man and I do not take kindly to any implications that I'm tellin' lies. So, I'll say it once more so that there's no doubt—Meester Campbell is not aboard this vessel and I'm not expectin' him until tomorrow mornin', as we are due to sail in the afternoon.'

'And you've no idea where he might be?'

Captain MacTavish took a step closer, looming over Nisbet. The Inspector took a step back, realising he was up against a more forceful authority.

'It is none of my business what my crew gets up to when they're off duty, sir. Colin Campbell has been on the *Crown* for a number o' years and he's a good man; quiet, mind, keeps himself to himself, but he's a hard worker and he respects the chain of command, which is more than can be said for some.'

He walked towards the door; as far as Captain MacTavish was concerned, the interview was terminated. Nisbet, however, had different ideas.

'Captain MacTavish, you must understand that this is a very serious business, very serious indeed. We are investigating the murder of both Mr Campbell's sister and his step-father. His mother has lost a husband and a daughter so if you have any idea as to the whereabouts of Campbell, then you are obliged to tell us. Otherwise, if the man turns up, it is imperative that you tell him to contact us immediately. Do I make myself clear?

MacTavish rubbed his beard thoughtfully for a moment, although his bushy eyebrows remained set in a frown.

'Aye, aye, that's clear enough, Inspector.'

Finally, the captain opened the door.

'Now, gentlemen, if you have no further business, I have a great deal to attend to before we set sail.'

Chapter 20

Alan trailed along miserably behind Nisbet and McGinn as they headed back up the dock-side to where the Wolseley was parked. Nisbet had instructed the two local constables to keep watch for Campbell at the harbour entrance and to detain him should he arrive; although their faces registered their displeasure, Nisbet's tone had brooked any vocal objection. He had called back in to speak to the harbour master, issuing the same instructions, although Watson's response appeared to have done little to improve the inspector's humour. Alan heard the harbour master state, "Ah'm no' one o' yer lackeys" before Nisbet came out of the office, his face contorted in anger.

As they reached the car, Alan was struck by one last, desperate thought. As McGinn reached for the driver's door, he half-whispered, afraid that Nisbet would hear him.

'Sergeant?'

McGinn turned, the bonhomie that had developed between the two officers over the previous week apparently vanished.

'What, McInnes?'

'Em, look I'm really sorry...'

'Save it, son. The damage is done, let's just get on, eh?'

'Well, that's what I was goin' to say—you said there was a newspaper in Campbell's room—did you notice what day's it was, by any chance?'

McGinn's brow furrowed slightly.

'Saturday's, I think...'

His eyes widened.

'Hang on—wait, that'd be the day that Mary Campbell's death would have been reported in the paper, wouldn't it? We didn't release the details until Friday afternoon...'

'...so you're thinkin' that Campbell might only have found out about his sister's death on the Saturday...'

'...and he might just have gone down to Barloch to see his mother.'

McGinn opened the door and slid into the seat, speaking hurriedly to Nisbet; a few moments later, he called out to Alan.

'Get in, McInnes, we're off to Meg Campbell's house. We'll pick up constable Brodie on the way, just in case!'

*

If anything, the journey back to Barloch was worse than the outward trip had been; McGinn seemed to be in an even greater hurry and, by the time they arrived outside the police station, Alan was, yet again, as white as a sheet. Thankfully, he got out of the car and walked up to the station, aware that the atmosphere had become humid and still. He glanced briefly up at the hills behind the village, where dark clouds were beginning to gather; somehow, it all seemed to match his mood, he thought. He opened the door and went inside to find Sergeant Tait and Kerr Brodie engaged in conversation.

'Kerr.'

'Hullo, Alan—God, ye look bloody aw-ful—whit's the matter wi' ye?'

'Been in the back o' the car, comin' up from Greenock. McGinn's a hell of a fast driver...listen, you need to come with us, right away.'

230

Brodie immediately looked interested; his involvement with the investigation to date had mostly been trudging about in the muddy shoreline of the Bar Loch.

'Aye? Where're we goin'?'

'Up to Meg Campbell's house.'

Sergeant Tait gave Alan an enquiring look.

'An' what are ye wantin' tae go up there for? Ah thought that, efter the other day, we'd concluded oor business at the hoose. An' have we no' done wi' Meg—no' that Ah've got a lot o' time for the woman, but surely the poor biddy's had enough?'

Alan shook his head.

'We think that her son, Colin, might be there.'

Tait looked decidedly sceptical.

'Colin? Naw, he's no' been back for ages...but whit if he is? Efter all, the man's lost his sister an' his mother's grievin' for her daughter, no' tae mention that good-for-nothin' husband o' hers. Surely he's a right tae—'

'Aye, but the thing is, Sergeant, I think that Colin was here on Monday night as well.'

Tait's expression changed to one of surprise.

'Whit? Here on Monday? How d'you make that oot?'

'Mr Oliphant thinks he saw him. I went down to Greenock on Saturday an 'they said that Campbell should have been stayin' at the sailor's hostel on Monday night but that he left an' didn't come back until Tuesday.'

Tait and Brodie remained silent, digesting the information as Alan continued

'So, if Campbell *was* here on Monday, the night...'

'...the nicht that Hugh Campbell wis murdered... God Almighty, laddie, this is gettin' mair complicated by the minute. Right, Brodie, aff ye go, an' mind what ye're aboot, Ah don't want ye lettin' the side doon'.

As Alan turned to leave, he though that Sergeant Tait's exhortation had, perhaps, come a bit too late.

· *

A few minutes later, the Wolseley drew up outside the Campbell household, the air of neglect seemingly heightened since the previous Friday's activities. As they exited the car, Alan looked up, but Mr Plunkett's curtains remained static; either the man had learned his lesson, or he was simply not at home. Nisbet hissed his orders.

'Right, McGinn, you and Brodie head round the back and wait until we gain entry at the front. McInnes, you come with me but keep your mouth shut, let me handle the Campbell woman. Just be prepared—by all accounts, Campbell may well be capable of violence.'

Alan wasn't sure to which accounts Nisbet referred, but he certainly wasn't going to pass comment! As McGinn and Brodie headed off round the side of the house, he followed Nisbet up the steps. The inspector didn't stand on ceremony; with his clenched fist, he battered loudly on the front door,.

'Police, Mrs Campbell, open up!'

His command was greeted by silence; he banged once more.

'Mrs Campbell, open up. This is Inspector Nisbet...'

Alan thought that he heard whispered words from inside, then the door opened. Meg Campbell was barely recognisable; clad in the same disreputable clothes as the previous week, she had black circles beneath her eyes and her hair was even more matted. Nisbet made to push past her but she stood her ground.

'Here, huv ye a bloody warrant this time?'

Nisbet roughly pushed the frail woman aside.

'I don't need one, woman, get out of my
way—is your son, Colin, here?'

With an astonishing display of strength, Meg Campbell grabbed at his arm as he passed, pulling him round
until he was looking down at her. She glared up at him.

'You leave ma boy oot o' this— huv ye no' caused
this bloody family enough trouble? Can ye no'
jist leave us be, we've suffered enough...'

A shout came from along the hallway, followed by a
scream of pain. Nisbet shrugged off the woman's grip,
pushed her to the ground then ran along the hallway;
Alan followed, glancing down at the woman, who
was now sobbing into the folds of her filthy apron.

Nisbet exited the back door first, Alan close on
his heels, where he took in the situation at a glance.
Kerr Brodie was kneeling on the ground, his hands
in front of his face, blood pouring from between his
fingers; he was mumbling semi-coherently, something to the effect of "bastard's broken ma nose!"

McGinn was kneeling on the back of a burly figure that was writhing, face down, in an attempt to
break free of the sergeant's grip. McGinn pushed
the figure's arm further up his back as he yelled.

'Shut it, sonny boy, or I'll break ye'r bloody arm.'

He turned to Alan.

'For Christ's sake, McInnes, will you get
your bloody handcuffs on this bastard...'

*

Sergeant McGinn drove back down to Barloch police station

with Kerr Brodie seated beside him, a bloody handkerchief clutched to his face. In the rear seat, Colin Campbell sat morosely next to Inspector Nisbet, still with his hands securely cuffed behind his back. Alan had been left behind to keep an eye on a near-hysterical Meg Campbell, with instructions to search for any fresh evidence relating to her son if the opportunity arose; Alan very much doubted if it would. Meg was sitting on the couch, rocking back and forth, her near-skeletal arms wrapped around her frail body. She appeared to be mumbling "ma boy...ma boy..." and Alan was afraid to leave the stricken woman by herself. About five minutes after the others had left, there was a knock on the door; Alan crossed to the open living-room door and called out.

'Aye—who is it?'

'Eh, hullo? It's Plunkett frae upstairs.
Is that you, Constable McInnes?'

'Aye—come in, Mr Plunkett.'

The man came timidly along the hall and entered the untidy, odorous living room.

'God Almighty, whit's happened tae her—Ah saw a man bein' lifted jist there—who wis that?'

Nosey as ever, Alan thought.

'I'm sorry, Mr Plunkett, it's an ongoing enquiry, I can't reveal...'

Meg Campbell continued with her feeble mantra and Plunkett looked across at her, watching her lips.

'Here—wis it that boy o' hers, by any chance?'

'As I said, Mr Plunkett, I'm not at liberty to say...'

He had an idea.

'...but you could help me out.'

Plunkett looked at Alan with an eager expression.

'Aye, whit can Ah dae?'

'Could you make Mrs Campbell a cup of tea—plenty o' sugar, I think she's in shock an' I don't want to leave her.'

'Aye, aye, certainly.'

Plunkett tottered out but returned a few seconds later, a look of disgust on his face.

'Ah'll maybe awa' upstairs tae ma ain hoose an' make it, if that's all richt? Would ye like one yersel', Constable McInnes?'

'That would be grand, Mr Plunkett—I could murder a cuppa, thanks.'

*

McGinn, having ascertained that the station possessed a second prison cell, returned to the car, opening the back door. Campbell ignored him, staring morosely at the floor.

'They just need to clear it out, sir, apparently it's being used as a storeroom.'

Nisbet gave a grunt of annoyance.

'Damn!'

The inspector pulled the door shut and McGinn leaned against the car, lighting a welcome cigarette. It was proving to be a very interesting day. As he smoked, he was aware of a figure approaching and realised that it was Isa McInnes.

'Good afternoon, Mrs McInnes.'

She smiled.

'Hello, Sergeant McGinn. I've made a fresh batch of pancakes and I brought you some down for you to have with your tea.'

McGinn returned the smile; he liked the woman.

'That's very kind of you.'

She looked at the hunched, handcuffed figure inside the car.

'Oh my...here, is that Colin Campbell, Meg's boy?'

'It is indeed, Mrs McInnes, we just want to ask him a few questions.'

Isa seemed at a loss as to what to say next; McGinn realised that she had probably never seen a man in handcuffs.

'Em, oh...well, I'll away in and give these to Donny.'

McGinn watched her slim personage as she walked up the path to the station, curious about the relationship that appeared to exist between Isa and his fellow sergeant. He couldn't quite fathom it. Having finished his cigarette, he folded his arms, enjoying the brief respite from the day's events. He realised that he was very warm and, pulling his tie down, he unbuttoned his shirt button; no doubt Nisbet would have something to say.... his thoughts were interrupted by the inspector rapping loudly on the window and McGinn opened the door.

'This is wasting time, McGinn. Take us back up to Mrs Campbell's house and we'll see what McInnes has managed to turn up—if anything. Brodie, get yourself inside and cleaned up, I don't want blood all over the car!'

Still clutching the bloody handkerchief, Kerr Brodie opened the door and made his way up to the station.

McGinn jumped into the car; as he pulled away, he caught Campbell's malevolent stare in the rear-view mirror; the man looked as if he was still spoiling for a fight.

*

It took Tait almost fifteen minutes to remove the bulk of the accumulated unclaimed lost-property, boxes of paperwork and general detritus of a village police station from Barloch's second prison cell. He had forbidden Isa to assist but had grumbled incessantly as he moved the miscellany of innumerable years to the front office. Having deposited a punctured bicycle wheel beside the door, he brushed his hands on his trousers and gave a long sigh.

'Can he no' take the man tae Paisley—this is puttin' us under a lot o' strain. Ah cann'ae even mind the last time we had anyone in the first cell, far less the second one.'

'Och, I wish you'd let me help, Don-ny, you're not as young as you once were.'

He straightened his aching back and smiled.

'Aye, weel, neither are you, Isa, al-though ye don't look a day...'

She blushed noticeably.

'Away with you, Donald Tait, you know that's not true.'

The door burst open and Kerr Brodie walked in, the bloody handkerchief still pressed to his face. Isa stared at him for a moment before her mater-nal instincts immediately came to the fore.

'Oh, Kerr, son, what's happened to you?'

'Ah was punched od de dose, Mrs Mciddes...'

'Oh, you poor lad. Here...'

'No, id's okay, Ah'll away to the...to the...'

He disappeared hastily, leaving Tait and Isa looking at each other in astonishment.

*

Brodie was still in the toilet when the door opened and Alan McInnes strode in with an air of urgency.

'Is the cell ready, Sergeant, the Inspector wants... Mother—what on earth are you doin' here?'

Isa McInnes's cheeks reddened again.

'Och, I'd made some pancakes and I'd brought

you some down to have with your tea.'

Before he could respond, the door opened once more; Colin Campbell was being led by Nisbet, with McGinn bringing up the rear, his hand firmly on the prisoner's shoulder. As they entered, McGinn nodded at Alan's mother.

'Mrs McInnes—listen, constable Brodie's been injured, would you maybe...'

'Yes, I know, he's in the toilet. I'll see what I can do when he comes back.'

'Thank you.'

'What happened to him?' asked Isa. McGinn nodded in the direction of the prisoner.

'This one decided to turn violent.'

He leaned towards the silent, sullen prisoner.

'Aye, assaultin' a police officer, Campbell—an' that's just for starters...'

Campbell turned to glare at McGinn.

'Awa' an' fuck yersel, copper...aahhh, ya bastard.'

McGinn had punched Campbell hard in the stomach; the man doubled over in pain, falling to his knees.

'Watch yer mouth, Campbell, there's a lady present.'

As Nisbet attempted to drag the man back on to his feet, Kerr Brodie appeared, his nose still dripping blood. Alan looked at his colleague, then at his mother. She looked horrified, although whether at the blood, the language or McGinn's use of force, Alan wasn't sure. Suddenly, Isa turned towards Sergeant Tait.

'Donny, can I have the keys of your house please?'

Tait frowned.

'Ma hoose? Em, what for, Isa?'

'I need to get that poor lad cleaned up and

it would be as well in there as in here. I've
seen quite enough violence for one day.'

Isa glared in the direction of Sergeant McGinn.

'Oh, and do you have a first-aid kit, by any chance?'

'Eh? Oh, aye, Ah think there's one...'

He reached under the counter and lifted out
a white tin box with a red cross on it.

'...aye, here ye are. Oh, an' the keys...'

He delved into his trouser pocket and handed Isa a bunch of keys.

'The silver one there, look.'

He held up a large mortice key; Alan somehow had the impression that his mother briefly
brushed the back of his hand as she took them.

'Thanks, Donny.'

As McGinn and Nisbet ushered the prisoner through to the cells, Isa called out, her tone
harking back to her days in the classroom.

'Sergeant McGinn?'

The sergeant turned, a look of slight surprise on his face.

'Yes, Mrs McInnes?'

'That was quite unnecessary, you know. I'm not
some silly wee lassie, I've heard worse in my time.
Keep your hands off that man from now on—if I
hear of any further use of gratuitous violence, then
rest assured I'll be taking the matter further.'

She turned and led Kerr Brodie out of the door,
leaving behind a speechless McGinn and a half-smil-
ing Tait. As for her son, he had never been proud-
er of the slight figure that was Isa McInnes.

*

'Oh, goodness, Kerr, your poor nose is in some mess.'

The constable winced as Isa dabbed at the bloody appendage with a damp cloth.

'Id id broken, d'you think?'

'Och, I'm not sure, maybe it's just what we used to call a "jeelly nose." Here, hold the cloth against it, I'll see if the Sergeant has any disinfectant kicking about. Needless to say, there was none in the first-aid kit!'

She left Kerr seated on Tait's threadbare couch, head back and holding the cloth against his face. She looked around with a feeling of despair as she headed towards the kitchenette; while Donny Tait no doubt tried his best, the house was untidy and could do with a good clean. The grate of the coal fire hadn't been cleaned out, the surfaces were dusty and the corners of the room hadn't seen a sweeper for weeks, by the look of them. As she entered the kitchen her heart sank; dirty dishes sat on the counter, a half-eaten slice of bread and butter—was that all Donny had for his breakfast, she wondered? She opened a few cupboards, all of which were near-empty and grubby. Finally, she looked under the sink and retrieved a half-empty bottle of TCP disinfectant. She wondered briefly how long it had been there but, as far as she was aware, it probably didn't go "off". She went back to the living room.

'Right, Kerr, let's get a wee bit disinfectant on that...'

'Oww!'

'Oh, come on now, don't be a baby...there. Right, I'll see if the first aid kit has any Elastoplast...good, it has. I'll just put a few wee strips where the skin has split.'

She ministered to her moaning patient for a few more minutes then, once done, she kissed her finger and placed it gently on Kerr's nose. He managed a smile at this small, fundamental maternal act.

'Right, that'll do for now, Kerr. I'll away and make us a cup of tea.'

Kerr made to get up.

'I'd best be gedding back, Mrs Mciddes...'

She pushed him gently back down.

'You'll do no such thing—you've had a nasty punch there and you might well be in shock. Sit where you are, I'll get the kettle on...'

As she walked back to the kitchenette, she silently added.

'...and give the kitchen a wee bit of a clean. That'll have to do...for now.'

*

Campbell was safely locked in the hastily-cleared second cell; McGinn and Nisbet were ensconced in Tait's office, while Tait and Alan were engaged in conversation, the latter having related the chain of events leading up to Campbell's arrest.

'You should'na have gone off on yer ain like that, though, lad. Whit if ye'd met Campbell—the man's a bit o' a thug, from whit Ah've seen today, God knows what micht have happened.'

'Aye, I realise that now, Sergeant, I just thought it might be an idea...'

'Aye, an idea above yer station. Listen, it's fine tae set yer heart on bein' a detective, but ye need tae dae it the richt way. None o' this goin' off on yer ain, riskin trouble—an' riskin' losin' the bloody prisoner, goin' by whit ye've told me.'

Alan hung his head slightly; although the outcome had been satisfactory, he knew that his own behaviour most certainly hadn't. Tait placed a kindly hand on Alan's shoulder.

'Ah'll have a wee word wi' McGinn on the quiet—he seems a decent enough fellow an', of course, he's one o the brotherhood. Dinn'ae worry, McInnes, Ah'm sure it'll all work out.'

Alan didn't share Tait's optimism, remembering Nisbet's comment about "dealing with him later." Finally, the office door opened and the two CID men came out, Nisbet leading the way.

'Right, we'll have another go at Benson, see what he has to say about Mary Campbell expecting his child. Bring him through, Tait; McInnes, you can attend, cover the door as before and keep your damned mouth shut, you've caused us enough trouble today already.'

*

Alan was shocked by Billy Benson's appearance; dark circles under his eyes indicated that he hadn't slept much, the stubble on his face suggesting that, once again, he hadn't been allowed to shave. McGinn pushed him roughly into the seat across from Nisbet.

'So, Benson, have you anything further to say?'

Benson shook his head.

'Naw.'

'I see.'

He paused, leaning back in the chair.

'Tell me, Benson, how long had you been seeing Mary Campbell?'

Benson appeared to make a calculation.

'No' sure—we started courtin' no' long efter ma birthday'

'So about seven months then?'

'If you say so.'

'I do, Benson. Shame about her, mind you.'

Alan could see Benson's body tensing.

'Whit d'ye mean?'

'I mean it's a shame that she died, especially when she was carrying your child.'

Benson's hands grabbed the arms of the chair but McGinn placed a warning hand on his shoulder.

'Steady, Benson, you just stay where you are.'

'Who telt ye that?'

'The police surgeon—and Dr Miller doesn't usually make mistakes about that sort of thing. Apparently poor Mary was about fourteen weeks pregnant when she died.'

Benson remained silent.

'So, I suppose you could say it's a double murder.'

Alan could see Benson's broad shoulders begin to heave and he realised that the man was crying. Nisbet, unmoved, continued his interrogation.

'So you may as well tell us what happened, Benson. Did she tell you, is that it? Did she tell you she was expecting and you couldn't cope with the responsibility? I mean, you're a young man, all your life ahead of you, you wouldn't want to be tied down to marriage, fatherhood, as such an early age...'

Benson sobbed.

'Ah did'na know, she never said...'

'Oh, I think she did, Benson. I think she told you that night—or did she tell you that she was expecting but that the child wasn't yours? Maybe that's it—maybe she goaded you, told you someone else was the father, you couldn't take it, you put your hands around that pretty neck of hers—'

Without warning, Benson leapt to his feet, brushing McGinn's hand away. He dived across the desk and punched Inspector Nisbet full on the jaw, sending both him and the chair clattering backwards on to the floor.

'Bastart—Mary never...she wis *ma* girl...'

Benson tried to scramble across the table towards the prone Nisbet but, this time, McGinn caught him, forcing his arm up his back.

'Enough, Benson!' he shouted. 'Assaultin' a police officer's a serious offence—mind you, maybe you've got worse offences tae worry about.'

Benson subsided back into the chair, now sobbing uncontrollably.

'Ah never knew, honest Ah never, Mary never said anythin' aboot...weel, she never said. Ah wid never have hurt ma wee Mary, Ah loved her...'

Alan looked pleadingly at McGinn; in his opinion, Benson was clearly innocent. Nisbet had righted the chair and sat back down, rubbing his already-swelling jaw; Alan felt not one ounce of sympathy for the man.

'Get him out of my sight, McGinn. We'll let him sleep on it.'

As McGinn hauled Benson to his feet, Nisbet made a parting comment.

'You'll tell us sooner or later, Benson. Why prolong your misery, you'll feel better once you get it off your chest. You may as well get it over with.'

Benson turned towards the inspector as if ready to renew the attack, but McGinn's grasp was strong; between sobs, the young man managed to blurt out

'Ah loved ma Mary...an' if ye think...Ah killed her then... ye're bloody stupider than ye look...Mister Inspector.'

Chapter 20

Much to Alan's chagrin, he had been excluded from the meeting now taking place in Sergeant Tait's cramped office-cum-interview room. Nisbet was seated in his usual place, his notepad and a pencil at the ready

'Well, McGinn. What d'you make of it?'

The sergeant was seated opposite Nisbet, his heel tapping restlessly on the floor; he was desperately in need of a smoke. He shook his head.

'To be honest, sir, I think Benson's tellin' the truth. I don't think he knew that Mary was expectin' an' I really don't think he killed her. I think his feelin's for her are...were genuine.'

Nisbet considered this for a moment.

'I am inclined to agree with you, McGinn; in fact, I don't actually think that the man has the intelligence to lie. However, I'm not so sure about the death of Campbell senior; if the two had an argument over Mary, given Benson's obvious feelings for the girl I think he'd have been perfectly capable of killing Campbell. No, I think we'll hold on to him for another night at least. Certainly until we've questioned Colin Campbell. What d'you make of *him*?'

'Well, he's a violent, strong bugger, for a start! Made a fair mess o' Brodie's nose an' it took me all my time to hold him down when we caught him. An' he's got a foul mouth, of course...'

'Yes, I do appreciate that, McGinn, but your use of force was probably unnecessary.'

'But he shouldn't have used language like that in front o' Mrs McInnes.'

'No, but equally you shouldn't have punched him in front of a civilian witness. You need to watch your temper, McGinn.'

The sergeant gritted his teeth but remained silent. He felt that Campbell had deserved all he got, particularly in view of the injury sustained by Kerr Brodie but, as always where Inspector Nisbet was concerned, there seemed little point in trying to defend his actions. Nisbet continued.

'And there was nothing of interest in the kit-bag we recovered from his mother's house?'

McGinn shook his head.

'Just clothes, some money, two bottles o' beer an' a few old family photos. I think they were of him wi' his sister when they were kids; on the seafront at Rothesay, probably taken by a street photographer—they had a stamp and a number on the back. I recognised it, use tae go there when—'

Nisbet cut him off.

'But nothing of significance?'

McGinn sniffed back his irritation and shook his head.

'No, sir, nothin'.'

Nisbet made a few further notes in his neat, regimented handwriting, then placed his pencil on the desk.

'Right, I suggest we leave Campbell and Benson in the tender care of Sergeant Tait for another night; we'll come back first thing tomorrow and see what they have to say for themselves.'

*

The two CID men departed, Nisbet having a brief chat with Sergeant Tait on their way out.

'And don't be overly kind to them, Tait, it's not a hotel you're running. Just the basics for those two until they decide to talk to us.'

Sergeant Tait had merely nodded his acquiescence in the general direction of Nisbet's back as he walked out. Alan got the distinct feeling that he was still out of favour as neither officer had addressed him directly.

Kerr Brodie had been sent home, Sergeant Tait deeming him unfit to continue on duty that day despite Isa McInnes's ministrations; she had returned to the office, where she was chatting to Tait and to her son.

'Right, Donny, I'm going up the road and I'll get some food prepared for you and your guests.'

'Isa, there's really nae need...'

She gave him a look that immediately silenced him.

'Donny, for goodness sake, judging by the state of your house you're barely managing to feed yourself—how on earth are you going to feed those two big lads that you've got in the cells? Unless you still offer your prisoners a diet of bread and water?'

Alan smiled; when his mother got a bee in her bonnet about something, there was really little point in arguing. Tait also appeared to realise this, giving a long, weary sigh.

'Och, well, if ye really dinn'a mind, Isa, it wid be a great help. But Ah'll reimburse ye'r expenses, ye cann'a be feedin' a' an sundry...'

She smiled.

'Yes, that'll be fine, Donny, a contribution would

be most welcome. Right, I'll get off and pay a
wee visit to the Co-operative, there's a few clean-
ing things that I'll need for your house as well.'

'Isa...'

She looked at Tait, silencing him a second time.

'Just a few bits and pieces. Alan, will
you be home for your dinner?'

Alan looked at Sergeant Tait.

'If ye can just stay an' cover the rest of Brodie's shift that'll
be fine, Let's just hope tae God that we've seen an end
tae oor troubles, Ah'm gettin' too bluidy old for a' this..'

*

To Sergeant Tait's and Constable McInnes's great relief, the
remainder of the Monday shift passed without incident;
during his routine foot patrol, Alan had felt that the little
village of Barloch seemed hushed somehow, even the
children playing in the street seemed to be making less
noise than usual. Maybe it was the dark clouds that now lay
overhead, harbingers of a late-summer thunderstorm. The
locals that he encountered had all nodded and bid him a
good afternoon, but there was no attempt to engage in the
customary conversation, none of the expected questions. He
concluded that they simply didn't want to know; maybe they,
too, had had enough of murder and mayhem.

He tried to retain an optimistic outlook but his heart was
heavy; Nisbet appeared to have given up on Alan altogether and even the normally ebullient Sergeant McGinn was
giving him the cold-shoulder. Alan realised that he deserved a certain amount of discipline but, after all, surely
his actions had, ultimately, led to Colin Campbell's arrest?
He hoped that Sergeant Tait would remember to have a

favourable word with McGinn. As he arrived at his front door, he realised that, since he had first joined the force, this was the weariest and most worn out he had ever felt and he had never been so glad to arrive home. He was hot, tired and hungry but, as he took out his key, opened the door and stepped inside, he stopped in his tracks at the sound of raised voices coming from the living-room.

'...think I don't bloody know, Isa...'

'Gilbert, there's no need for language...'

'Ach, you an' you're bloody hoity-toity ways, can a man no' even swear in his ain hoose if he wants...'

'Gilbert...'

'...naw, you jist listen tae me—Ah've suspected for a long time, Isa McInnes, an' Ah've kept ma ain counsel, but...'

'You known *nothing*, Gilbert McInnes, nothing at all...'

'...ach awa' wi' ye, it's bloody obvious. D'ye think Ah haven'ae seen ye, the way the two o' ye...'

Alan slammed the front door shut and the raised voices ceased instantly. Within seconds, his mother was in the hallway, wearing her coat and carrying what seemed like a very well-laden hen-basket. Her face was flushed and Alan suspected that she'd been crying but, as always, she greeted him with a smile. It seemed rather strained on this occasion, however.

'Alan—you're home early, son.'

'Aye, Mother, the sergeant let me away a bit early, on account of what's been happening. Mother, what were the two o' you shoutin' about?'

'Och, nothing, Alan, just a wee disagreement.'

Suddenly, Gilbert stormed out of the living room, grabbing his jacket from the peg in the narrow hallway as he pushed past mother and son.

'Ah'm awa' oot fur a bit o' fresh air...'

He looked at his son, his expression unreadable.

'...an' if ye're lookin' for yer tea, Alan, it'll be late—ye'r mither's goin' awa' doon tae see her "friend," Donny Tait—*again*! Seems he's mair important than we are...'

*

Three men slept uneasily in Barloch that night, waiting for the inevitable storm to come. The humidity had increased and the village was silent and still, awaiting the first flash of lightning, the first crack of thunder. Colin Campbell and Billy Benson lay on their hard, narrow beds in the prison cells, alone with their fears and their thoughts; but, although Alan McInnes lay in a more comfortable bed, it was doubtful if his thoughts were any less disturbed...

*

Alan awoke with a start as the bright flash illuminated his small bedroom. The thunder came only a few seconds later, indicating that the storm was nearby. Another flash, another crash of thunder that sounded more like an explosion. He found it thrilling somehow but, after a few minutes he heard another, fainter sound coming from below. He swung his long legs out of the bed, searching for his slippers, then padded downstairs. His mother was sitting in the darkness of the living room, her arms clutched around her slight body. She was sobbing gently as he entered, standing unseen for a few moments until the next bright flash illuminated the room in an unearthly glare. She jumped in alarm.

'Oh, son, you gave me a fright, I didn't hear you coming down.'

He sat on the arm of the chair and placed a hand on her shoulder; he could feel her trembling.

'Mother, are you all right?'

'Och, I just hate all this flashing and banging, it...'

'What, mother?'

She shuddered.

'...it reminds me of the war, the Clydebank Blitz, all those poor people...'

Another flash...another crump of thunder; Alan shuddered himself. It *did* sound like a bomb exploding.

'It's okay, Mother, I'll stay with you.'

'Och, don't be daft, away back to your bed, I'll be fine.'

He knew that wasn't the case; he took her hand and led her to the couch, then sat beside her, placing an arm around her slight shoulders. She didn't resist.

'Mother?'

'Yes, Alan?'

'What were you and father arguing about earlier?'

She didn't answer.

'Mother?'

Another flash...another explosion. She started to cry again.

'Oh, Alan, it...oh God forgive me, son, I—'

This time, the flash and the thunderclap seemed instantaneous, immediately followed by another searing flash, another explosive rumble that shook the very fabric of their house. Isa started to cry uncontrollably and Alan held her tightly in his arms. A few minutes later, her head buried in his shoulder, Isa McInnes finally made her confession.

The storm eventually passed about seven in the morning; Isa was sound asleep, still cradled in her son's strong, loving arms. Alan, however, was staring at the mantelpiece, still trying to come to terms with what his mother had told him.

*

In Glasgow, too, the violent storm brought back painful memories for the citizens. Many recalled the terror of that dreadful bombing raid, the horrific recollections still raw in their minds; many grieved for those who perished in those dark days and even darker nights. There were many who, at the height of the storm, wished for the safety of an Anderson shelter, half-buried but safe from the maelstrom that raged overhead. Some sheltered under their beds, some pulled up the covers, hands over their ears. Few slept.

Yet some remained abroad, even as the rain lashed in torrents on the cobbles, reflecting the stark, white glare of the lightning. A perfect night to conceal their nefarious activities, their sounds concealed, their identities hidden. Unusually, their overseer was in attendance; he trusted few but recent events had left him ever more wary of those who carried out his bidding in exchange for an envelope stuffed with a few notes. An unbidden visit from this powerful and fearsome presence would act as a timely reminder as to whom, ultimately, they worked for.

The evening's activities complete, Jock Wallace stared briefly down at the mighty, swollen River Clyde, its waters churned by the deluge. A flash illuminated its surface momentarily and, through a brief mist of rage, he imagined a body floating away in the night, a body whose identity he knew all too well.

He turned away and walked along the quayside, his collar pulled up futilely against the incessant downpour. Bernard Penman might believe that he'd be safe in prison but Wallace's reach was long. He smiled

evilly in the dark; had Penman but known, he might
have chosen the dark, deep waters of the Clyde...

Chapter 22

'Damn it all, McGinn, I want to get back down to Barloch
and question Colin Campbell. It'll just need to wait.'

'I'm sorry, sir, but Penman's insisting—'

'Penman's in no bloody position to insist on anything.'

'Aye, I know, but it's that damned solicitor o'
his, Andrew Wright. He's in court all day, apparently, an' this is the only time he can spare.'

Inspector Nisbet pursed his lips angrily; Campbell's forthcoming interrogation was already
planned and he could well have done without this interruption. He reached a decision.

'Oh, very well then, I suppose we'd better hear
what the man has to say. Half an hour, mind.
I'm not giving him one minute longer...'

*

The streets of Barloch appeared to have been scoured clean
by the previous night's deluge; the torrent had washed the
accumulated debris from the gulleys and drains, the foliage
on the bushes and trees appeared verdant in the bright
morning sunshine that so often followed such a violent
storm. But, although a weight seemed to have been lifted
from the little village, Constable Alan McInnes felt that it
now rested squarely on his own shoulders. Exhausted and
bleary-eyed, he made his way down School Street, dreading
the morning that lay ahead. As he approached the police

station he glanced at his watch; eight-fifty. He would have expected the CID officers to have arrived early to begin what he presumed would be their ruthless and relentless questioning of Colin Campbell, but the police Wolseley was conspicuous by its absence. With a heavy heart, he turned and walked up the path to the office door; their presence would, at least, have spared him the pain of the next few minutes.

*

Gordon McGinn neither liked nor trusted Andrew Wright; like many detectives, he had an inbuilt wariness of those involved in the defence of the criminal fraternity. Judging by the expression of distaste on his face, Inspector Nisbet shared his feelings. Wright, smartly dressed in a crisp white shirt, a plain grey tie with a gold pin and a navy pin-striped suit, had opened the conversation.

'Officers, my client has asked me to place a proposal before you.'

Nisbet glared at Wright, who appeared smug, self-confident and completely at ease. Penman, on the other hand, gave the impression of a frightened rabbit; dishevelled, his thinning grey hair uncombed, he sat in a despondent silence beside his solicitor. Nisbet's reply was terse.

'And that is?'

Wright smiled, revealing even, white teeth; it gave him an expression rather like a shark, McGinn thought.

'Mr Penman has been the unfortunate victim of circumstances—'

'Rubbish. Your client has been involved in the sale, and quite probably the theft, of stolen goods.'

'Come now, Inspector, innocent until proven

255

guilty, remember! Now, if you would be so good as to let me finish. You see, my client is willing to provide you with certain pieces of information...'

He let the sentence dangle in mid-air; Nisbet took the bait.

'I'm listening.'

'Ah, but before my client divulges said information, there would need to be certain guarantees in place...'

*

Sergeant McGinn turned the Wolseley into Barloch Main Street, relieved to be nearing the end of their journey. Since they had left Paisley, he had been subjected to an incessant tirade from his superior officer.

'I mean, who the hell does he think he is—and as for that smarmy lawyer! I don't know how these people sleep at night, I honestly don't...'

Finally, McGinn managed to interject.

'But is it no' worth considerin', sir? After all, we're pretty certain that Penman's just a player, albeit a fairly important one. If he was prepared to give us information that led us to an arrest higher up the chain...'

'And what guarantee do we have that the man would be telling us the truth, McGinn? I wouldn't trust a word that comes out of his mouth. No, I'm not prepared to negotiate.'

McGinn had had enough of Inspector Nisbet's apparent one-man vendetta against Penman. The bookmaker was crooked, for sure, but the sergeant's superior officer appeared fixated by the man. He played his trump card.

'The thing is, sir, we're presumin' that Hugh Campbell owed Penman money—that, and the stolen goods he was storin' must surely have been the motivation for the subsequent harassment of the widow. It follows, does it not, that Penman in turn owed money to someone higher up? What if *they're* the killer—it might no' be Campbell junior, Penman *or* Benson that killed Hugh Campbell. We're obviously dealin' with a highly-organised criminal gang here an' they have a great deal at stake. I don't think they'd stop at murder if someone was double-crossin' them, do you...sir?'

Nisbet remained silent as the car drew up outside Barloch police station; as they got out, he half-mumbled, 'Let's see what Campbell has to say—I'll reserve judgement until then.'

McGinn smiled to himself as they walked up the path; the inspector was never inclined to admit that he might be wrong.

*

With barely a glance at Tait and McInnes, Nisbet strode purposefully towards the Sergeant's office. As he passed the bar desk, he barked, 'Bring Campbell through in ten minutes and make sure he's cuffed. McInnes, you can guard the door as before.'

Sergeant McGinn waited until his superior office banged the office door shut; he was aware that the atmosphere in the small front office could have been cut with a knife. He looked from Constable McInnes to Sergeant Tait and grinned.

'Somethin' the matter, lads? You've got faces like a wet Fair weekend!'

Tait was staring at the floor with what McGinn suspected was a look akin to shame. Alan McInnes appeared angry, his cheeks flushed, his fists balled. Neither man replied to McGinn's light-hearted question and the tension between the two men remained palpable. The sergeant's smile faded.

'Look, whatever the hell it is, I suggest you put it to one side. The Inspector's in one hell o' a mood an' the last thing we need are any personal issues gettin' in the way o' the investigation. So, let's try and put the smile back on our faces an' concentrate on the job in hand, eh?'

Tait nodded slowly but his expression remained sorrowful. McGinn beckoned to Alan.

'A word, McInnes.'

They exited the station and McGinn lit a cigarette, inhaling deeply.

'We were held up by that bugger Penman—he's wantin' to try an' make some sort o' a deal in exchange for information about who's behind the supply of the stolen fags and booze.'

Alan replied, rather unenthusiastically, 'Is that why the inspector's in a mood?'

'Aye—that an' the fact that your ladyfriend's father, Andrew Wright, was in attendance, layin' down the terms and conditions, so to speak.'

McGinn turned to Alan, his eyes seeming to bore into the young constable's skull. Alan cast his eyes down, unable to hold McGinn's gaze.

'Look, McInnes, you're a good policeman but you should have never gone off an' done your own investigatin' the way you did.'

'I realise that now, Sergeant, I was...well...'

'You were just tryin to impress us?'

Alan nodded.

'Aye, I suppose I was. I'm really sorry.'

'Well, I'm not so sure about the Inspector, but your

reasonin' has impressed *me*. But what I really wanted to speak t'you about was your friend, Andrew Wright.'

Alan tensed, wondering what the solicitor might have said.

'Don't worry, son, I managed a quick word with Wright an' it seems that he holds you in pretty high regard. He assured me that you didn't give away any sensitive information regardin' either Penman or the murders an' I'm quite prepared to accept that at face value. No matter what I think o' the man, I don't believe him to be a liar.'

Alan breathed out a long sigh.

'Thanks, Sergeant, that's a great relief...'

McGinn frowned.

'A relief? Why, did you think that you *might* have told him somethin' after he plied you with brandy?'

'No—no, that's not what I meant, it's just a relief that you believe me, that's all.'

McGinn grinned; he extended his hand and the two men exchanged their hidden understanding.

'Right, we'll put it all behind us, you've learned your lesson. Let's get back in an' see what Nisbet has to say—an' can you and Sergeant Tait try no' to look so bloody miserable, whatever it may be that's happened...'

Of that, Alan wasn't quite so sure and, as he opened the door, McGinn noticed the constable's shoulders droop. He had his suspicions—after all, he *was* a detective...

*

Colin Campbell was unshaven, unkempt and seemingly uncaring. Alan and McGinn escorted him, duly handcuffed, from the cells to Tait's small office and seated him in the customary position, across the desk from Inspector Nisbet with McGinn standing behind him. Alan had locked the office door and was standing with his back against it, strongly resisting the urge to lean back and close his eyes. Nisbet made the usual pretence of consulting his notes, although Alan was sure that the inspector already knew exactly how the interview was going to proceed; finally, he looked up, Campbell staring back and truculently holding the officer's gaze as Nisbet began.

'You are Colin Campbell?'

'Aye.'

'Date of birth?'

'Ye've already got it there.'

Nisbet scowled across at the prisoner.

'I'm asking you to confirm it, Campbell.'

Campbell sneered.

'Nae need, if you've already got it in front o' ye.'

McGinn put a firm hand on Campbell's shoulder.

'Just answer the bloody question, son-ny-boy. No need for smart back-chat.'

With some reluctance, Campbell confirmed his date of birth; Nisbet made a show of making a note of some sort then placed his pencil on the table.

'Campbell, first of all, you will be charged with assaulting a police officer...'

'He started it.'

Nisbet slapped the table and raised his voice noticeably.

'You resisted arrest, Campbell. You assaulted one of my officers—it's likely that you've broken the man's nose.'

'Serves the bastart right.'

McGinn dug his fingers hard into Campbell's shoulder and the man let out a gasp of pain

'Oww! Here, that wis sair...'

'Aye, well, mind your language an' answer the inspector's questions, or there'll be worse—don't forget I'm missin' a bloody tooth on your account.'

Campbell turned and leered up at McGinn.

'Aye, here we go, try an' beat a confession oot o' me, Ah know the drill. Weel, guid luck tae ye, it'll no' be any worse than Ah've had in Marseilles or Dublin. Ye think ye're a hard man but Ah've met a good many that wid have ye on the floor in a minute.'

'Just answer the question, Campbell, and we can get this over and done with,' interjected Nisbet.

'Whit was the question again...Sir?'

Nisbet leaned back in Tait's chair, which creaked alarmingly.

'You didn't like Hugh Campbell, did you?'

Alan could see the prisoner's shoulders tensing.

'He wis a rotten bastart; it's only a coward that hits women. Deserved all he got...'

'And what *did* he get, Campbell? Enlighten me.'

'Got himsel' bloody killed, didn't he? Couldn'ae hae happened tae a nicer chap!'

Nisbet paused, then leaned forward.

'And did *you* kill him, Campbell? What did you kill him with—a knife? Did you hit him with a crowbar?'

Colin Campbell snorted.

'Huh, ye think Ah'm gonn'ae fall intae that trap, eh? Weel, Ah'm sayin nothin', Ah want a lawyer. But Ah'll tell ye this, if Ah *had* killed him, it wid have been wi' ma bare hands. Hughie Campbell did'nae scare me.'

He clammed up suddenly. Nisbet gave a wry smile.

'With your bare hands, eh? A likely tale, if you ask me. And you're wanting a lawyer? Usually a sign of guilt, isn't it, McGinn?'

'It is that, sir. Are you admit-
tin' that you're guilty, Campbell?'

'Like Ah said, Ah'm sayin' nothin' more until—'

'Yes, you'll get your lawyer, all in due course. So what happened, Campbell? Did the two of you get into an argument? Had he beaten your mother again, was that it? Did you end up having a fight? Were you waiting for him when he came out of the pub? You were seen hanging about in the station entrance in Factory Street...'

Campbell sat up.

'Who telt ye that? Ye cann'ae prove nothin'.'

'We can, Campbell, and we will. The stationmaster saw you, he spoke to you and I'm sure he'll be able to identify you in a parade. The constable here also saw you in the station passageway while he was on his night-ly round—isn't that correct, Constable McInnes?'

Alan froze; the inspector appeared to be asking him to tell a blatant lie.

'Em, well...'

'So, you see, we have you placed near the crime scene, at the time of Hugh Campbell's murder. We know that you booked out of the sailor's hostel in Greenock on the Monday night and we know that you didn't return until the Tuesday. Can you ac-count for your movements during that time?'

'Ah'm sayin' nothin until...'

McGinn dug his fingers into Campbell's shoul-der once more as he leant forward and growled.

'Aye we know, until you've seen a bloody lawyer. Well, you're goin' to need one, that's a certainty.'

Nisbet continued.

'Campbell, why did you run when we appeared at your mother's house?'

Campbell gave another derisive snort.

'Because Ah knew ye'd bloody try tae frame me—which is exactly whit ye're dae'in' the now, is it no?'

Nisbet gave a cold smile.

'No, Campbell, we're not trying to frame you. We don't need to—you see, we already have enough evidence to take you to court. It might go better for you if you just admit to the killing. Did Campbell provoke you, is that it? You could even argue self-defence, you might get off with a life sentence rather than the rope.'

Campbell laughed out loud.

'The bloody rope, eh? Christ, ye must be desperate tae get a conviction if ye're startin' tae threaten me wi' hangin'! Weel, Ah can assure ye that Ah'm no' gonn'ae hang—an' Ah'm no' sayin' anither bloody word until Ah've spoken tae a lawyer.'

Campbell sat back and folded his arms defiantly across his barrel chest; true to his word, and try as they might, he refused to utter another syllable or acknowledge any of the inspector's questions. Finally, once McGinn had dragged him to his feet, Colin Campbell was escorted back to his cell.

*

Alan accompanied McGinn back outside, where the latter lit up once again, blowing a cloud of blue smoke into the clear air as he leaned his head back against the wall. Alan reckoned that the sergeant must be at least a forty-a-day man.

'I don't know what to make o' this bugger Campbell—what's your thoughts?'

Alan considered the question. Although he was becoming rather accustomed to being asked for his opinion, he still had the vague feeling that he was being tested.

'Not sure, Sergeant. D'you really reckon that a man's guilty if he asks for a lawyer?'

McGinn chuckled.

'No, no' always. Some folk just know their rights, but it doesn't do any harm to make them *think* that we believe them to be guilty. If they are, it makes them less sure o' themselves. If they're innocent—well, they've nothin' to fear.'

He turned and gave Alan piercing stare, his blue eyes twinkling.

'An' what do *you* say, McInnes—d'you think Campbell's innocent or guilty?'

'Em...I'm inclined towards guilty, Sergeant. He seems to have been in the area at the time Hughie was murdered, he can't—or won't—account for his movements and he ran off from his mother's house when we arrived. An' he's a big lad, he'd certainly have been a match for Hughie Campbell.'

McGinn nodded.

'Aye, that's all well an' good but it's all circumstantial, isn't it? We don't have a murder weapon and we're no' likely to get one either, according to Dr Miller. The loch will be full o' damned stones. A jury's no' goin' to return a guilty verdict on him just bein' in the area at the time o' the murder.'

'So what do we do now?'

McGinn threw away his cigarette butt.

'Well, we can try and find some more evidence, which won't be easy, or we can wait until he cracks. Might be a while before he does that, though—seems he's a man o' few words! Right, I suppose we should

get back in an' see what's happenin'. I think the inspector's wantin' to have another go at Benson.'

As Alan turned towards the door, Mc-
Ginn placed a hand on his shoulder.

'Just before we go in...'

Alan had an inkling of what was coming; he had been dreading it.

'Aye, Sergeant?'

'What the hell's up with you and Sergeant Tait? In
the time that I've been here, the two of you have got on
like the proverbial house on fire. But, when we came
in this mornin', it looked as if you were about to have a
crack at his jaw. Now, it's maybe none o' my business but
I   'd say somethin' pretty serious has happened.'

Alan stared at the door; he couldn't
bring himself to face McGinn.

'Och, it was nothin'.'

'Nothin' my arse, McInnes. C'mon, whatever it is, it'll go no further, I promise.'

Alan could feel his eyes pricking and he remained facing away from the sergeant.

'It's my mother, you see, she...'

McGinn's grip tightened, a look of concern appearing on his face—not that Alan could see.

'Wait—is there somethin' wrong with her?'

Alan shook his head.

'No, nothin' like that, it's just...well, she
told me last night that...that...'

He bit his lip; he refused to break down in front
of a superior officer. McGinn's grip relaxed.

'She told you that Donny Tait's your father?'

Alan continued to stare at the door.

'Wh...how the hell d'you know?'

'Because I'm a bloody detective, son, and a good one at that. I've seen the way the two o' them look at each other.'

'But they're just friends, they went to school together...'

'Aye, an' the rest. I'm no' stupid, McInnes. Even the way your father spoke to you, I'd imagine that he knows—or suspects.'

Alan could feel a lump rise in his throat.

'I don't know...'

'Well, I'd say that he probably does! You know, McInnes, I've suspected for a few days, just by the way you all interact. You look nothin' like your father but there's a distinct family resemblance to Tait. Even the way he treats you, he's softer on you than any local sergeant I've ever come across.'

Alan's head dropped and McGinn squeezed his shoulder.

'Look, son, you can't help what's happened, none o' this is your doin'. Life can take some strange twists and turns and we just have to make the best o' it. Tait's a decent man, you're mother's a lovely woman. Your father? Well, he is what he is but he's raised you to become a good, honest young man, a good policeman, an' you should be grateful for that. Aye, I know it must have come as a hell o' a shock but none o' us can know what goes on in other people's minds, none of us can be responsible for other people's actions. Take those two in there—whatever they've done, and for whatever reasons, the responsibility lies with them and them alone. So, just give yourself a wee bit time to come to terms with it—life'll go on.'

Finally, Alan turned around; to his credit, he had managed to control his emotions

'Listen, Sergeant, I really appreci-

266

ate your understanding...'

'Och, don't bloody go all soft on me, McInnes. And, like I said, this'll go no further. Right, let's get back in...'

As he reached for the door, he winked.

'Just think, it could have been worse.'

Alan looked surprised.

'Worse? How?'

'Imagine if it'd been Inspector Nisbet!'

*

Sergeant Tait looked up as they entered; his face was flushed but he managed a rather weak smile. Alan took a deep breath and nodded; it was a start, at least. But, before either man could speak, the office door burst open and Nisbet strode out, an angry look on his face.

'Where the hell were you?'

He didn't wait for a reply.

'I want to have another go at Benson—I'm still reasonably certain that he's responsible for the girl's murder and he's had enough time to reflect on his sins. Bring him through in a couple of minutes.'

He turned and walked back towards Tait's office, leaving the three officers staring at his retreating back. McGinn shook his head and mumbled something vaguely derogatory while Tait and Alan exchanged a rather conspiratorial glance.

Suddenly, the front door to the police office banged open and the three officers turned as one towards the slight figure responsible. Meg Campbell stood in the entrance, looking even more grubby and dishevelled than ever. Her eyes were wide and staring, the dark circles below them now resembling bruises. She looked on the verge of a breakdown, Alan thought, as he spoke.

'Mrs Campbell—what can we—'

'Where is he?'

McGinn crossed towards the highly agitated woman.

'Your son is being held on suspicion—'

'No ma bloody son; where's that bastart Nisbet?'

'Now, Mrs Campbell, there's no need for language like that. Inspector Nisbet is busy in the office...'

Without a further word, Meg Campbell barged past McGinn and scurried towards the closed office door. The sergeant tried to grab her arm but she managed to shrug off his grip. Before he could stop her, she had entered the small room, slamming the door behind her; they heard the key turn in the lock. McGinn strode across and tried the handle but to no avail. He rapped loudly on the door.

'Mrs Campbell, open this door immediately.'

There was no response; this time, he battered his fist against the unyielding, solid barrier.

'Mrs Campbell, don't make mat-ters worse, open this door—NOW.'

But Meg Campbell had other ideas...

*

Inspector Nisbet looked up in annoyance at the interruption, his expression turning to one of surprise.

'What the...Mrs Campbell! I'm sor-ry, but I must ask you to...'

She turned the key in the lock just before McGinn began banging noisily on the other side of the door. She ignored it, crossing to the desk and sitting down across from Nisbet, whose expression was now thunderous.

'Mrs Campbell, I won't stand for this,

get out of my office immediately.'

'Naw. Fur a start, it's Tait's office, no' yours...'

Nisbet rose from his chair.

'I've had enough of this nonsense; I've a good mind to charge you with breach of the peace.'

'Let him go.'

'What?'

'Colin, ma son. Let him bloody go. Ah'm here tae tell ye whit *really* happened.'

Nisbet sat back down as the thumping on the door continued. He stared at the woman; she appeared harmless enough. He called out.

'It's all right, Sergeant, Mrs Campbell is just wanting to talk.'

'Ye're damned right Ah dae—let ma son go, he's done nothin'.'

Nisbet shook his head.

'I can't do that, Mrs Campbell. At the moment, it's likely that your son will be charged with the murder of—'

Meg Campbell leaned across the desk.

'I said let him go, ya sanct...san...ya arrogant bastart!'

Nisbet half rose once more from his chair.

'Mrs Campbell, I'm not going to sit here and listen to this, I've...'

'It wis me!'

Nisbet dropped heavily back down on the protesting chair.

'What?'

'It wis me—Ah killed that bastart husband o' mine.'

Nisbet stared at her in disbelief.

'You? But...but..?'

She sniffed as her voice started to break.

'The bastart said he wis goin' oot after Mary. He knew that she wis seein' thon Benson boy an' he wisn'ae hae'in' it. Said she could do better; mind he was probably richt, although God knows he never showed the lassie much affection. But then, jist that day she'd telt us that she wis expectin' Benson's child an' that must hae been the last straw. Ah thought he wis goin' tae the nicht shift at the steelworks but he didn'ae, he must've gone doon tae the pub. When Mary never came hame, Ah went oot lookin' for her. Ah caught up wi' him doon at the side o' the loch, washin' his face an' his hands, mumblin awa' aboot "how the hoor had deserved it." Ah reckoned on whit he'd done so Ah picked up a rock an'...weel, ye ken the rest.'

'You knew that he'd killed Mary?'

She shook her head.

'No' at first, but once he had a guid drink in him, there wis nae controllin' him, nae tellin' whit he micht dae. Like Ah said, Ah went oot lookin' for Mary but Ah couldn'ae find her. Ah saw him come oot o' the coal yard entrance an' Ah followed him doon tae the loch side. The bastart wis aw covered in coal-stoor, he must've killed ma lassie an' dumped her in that coal wagon where ye found her. But it wis only when he wis washin' his face that Ah saw the scratches on his cheek, then Ah knew for definite whit he'd done. Ma lassie must hae put up a fecht, at least she hurt the bastart.'

The tears were streaming down her haggard face. She wiped her nose on a grubby sleeve.

'Ah loved that lassie—she wis the licht o' ma life an' that bastart Hugh Campbell took her frae me. He deserved it, he deserved worse. Ah should have let him bloody hang...'

Nisbet continued to stare at the woman, who had

now pulled a rather dirty handkerchief from the pocket of her apron. She blew her nose noisily.

'So, like Ah says, ye can jist let Colin go. Ah'm prepared tae make a statement swearin' that Ah killed ma husband an' that Ah'm sure he killed ma poor lassie.'

'And how do I know that you're not just covering for your son? There's plenty of evidence against him.'

Meg Campbell gave a humourless smile; Nisbet stood up suddenly and walked around the desk. He spoke with a sarcastic sneer of disbelief.

'No—I've heard enough of this nonsense, Mrs Campbell; as far as I can see, you're just making an excuse to get your son out of trouble, that's all, and you're wasting my time.'

'Is that a fact? Weel, Ah've told ye how Ah done it, wi' a rock frae oot o' the loch. Why don't ye ask Colin whit *he* used tae kill Hugh? Because, as far as Ah ken, whit he wis killed wi' isn'ae common knowledge, is it? An' neither are the bloody scratches on his face—ask Colin if he noticed *those*, why don't ye?'

Nisbet's sneer faded; he didn't reply.

'Aye, Ah thocht not.'

He stared down at her for a moment, then leaned closer, speaking in an angry near-whisper, his lips drawn back over his teeth in a snarl of rage.

'You'd better be telling me the bloody truth, Mrs Campbell. Perjury is a serious crime...'

She glared back up at him, then gave a derisory snort.

'Aye, ye're jist like yer bloody faither, a stubborn, narrow-minded bully. Ye've even got the same straw-like hair— goin' baldy too, jist like thon weasel, Willie Montgomery.'

Nisbet straightened up, his mouth hanging

open, but he regained his composure quickly.

'How dare you...what on earth are you talking about?'

'Huh! How dare Ah? Aye, ye dinn'ae recognise me, dae ye. Gabriel Nisbet. Huvn'ae a bloody clue who Ah am. Mind, Ah suppose there's little reason why ye should—nae doubt Flora Nisbet telt ye Ah wis deid.'

She gave a grim smile and sat back with her arms folded across her scrawny chest, glowering up at the inspector as he gaped down at her.

'But Ah recognised *you*, that first day ye came tae the hoose. Aye, it wis jist the look o' ye at first, but when ye telt me yer name, then it aw came back tae me. Fifteen, Ah wis, jist a wee lassie, when Ah got caught tryin' tae nick a pack o' fags oot the wee shop on Maryhill Road. Oh, Sergeant bloody high-and-mighty Montgomery wis *so* understandin', said he'd let me aff if Ah went up the close wi' him. Jist for a few minutes—an' that wis aw it took, a few bloody minutes, big fat sweaty bastart that he wis. Puffin' an' pantin, his troosers roon' his knees. Ah jist stood an' took it, reckoned it wis better than the leatherin' ma faither wid ha'e given me for thievin.'

Nisbet looked as if he'd seen a ghost.

'Aye, but it wisn'ae sae bloody guid nine months later, when *you* arrived. As soon as ye cam' oot, Ah could see the bloody resemblance.'

Apart from the twitching of a jaw muscle, the inspector's features appeared to have been set in stone, although the colour had drained from his face as Meg Campbell continued.

'Ma mither and faither practically disowned me. Ah wis feart tae tell them who the faither wis, of course, not that they'd hae done anythin' aboot it. Ma mither packed me off tae thon big hoose doon past Barloch, Myrtlebank; God knows how, but she got me a job as a kitchen maid. Never saw you again, until last week. Ma mither forbade me tae get in touch, she'd told the neighbours that Ah'd died frae complications o' childbirth. Aye, bloody complications richt enough—micht as weel hae been bloody deid.'

Mother and son regarded one another for a few moments in a tense, emotionally-charged silence, then Meg Campbell spoke again, her voice softer.

'So there ye are, Gabriel Nisbet. Ah hope ye're satisfied—ye've a half-sister deid an' ye're mither's a murderer.'

*

Sergeants Tait and McGinn, along with Constable McInnes had been aware of the raised voices but had been unable to make out any of the conversation. They stood silently, Tait puffing ruminatively on his pipe, McGinn drawing furiously on his cigarette. Finally, the office door was thrown open and Inspector Nisbet stormed through. The man's face was white as a sheet and, as he spoke, his voice seemed half-choked.

'I want a statement taken from the Campbell woman. She's just confessed to the murder of her husband, Hugh.'

There was a stunned silence as the other three officers exchanged astonished glances. McGinn finally spoke.

'An' what about the daughter, Mary?'

'She claims that her husband strangled the girl when he found our that she was expecting. She maintains that she followed him from the coal-yard entrance down to the loch, where he appears to have been attempting to wash himself. She says that she noticed the scratches on his face and assumed that he'd killed the girl. She claims that she came up behind him and struck him with a rock, just as Doctor Miller has suggested.'

McGinn frowned.

'That's no' common knowledge, is it, sir?'

Nisbet shook his head.

'Nor are the scratches on Campbell's face, for that matter.'

'So does that let Colin Campbell off the hook, sir?' asked Alan.

Nisbet turned and stared at Alan,
his eyes seeming unfocused.

'Of murder, possibly. I want him interviewed again,
lean on him a bit. Ask again what he used as a murder weapon, although I have the suspicion he won't
know—unless he's in collusion with his mother...'

He paused staring down at the floor, a
haunted expression on his face.

'I think the woman's telling the truth. Colin Campbell may still be an accessory, if he knew
what had happened, but his mother has said that
he had no knowledge and it'll be hard to prove anything against him if she's admitting her guilt.'

'So can he be released?'

Nisbet turned his gaze towards McGinn, as
if he hadn't understood the question.

'What?'

'Can we release Campbell if his mother's confessed?'

'Em...no, see what he has to say once you tell him about
his mother, then you can release him, but it'll be with the
proviso that he stays here. I don't want him going back to
sea until we're certain that he's not implicated in some way.'

He shook his head, as if trying to clear his thoughts.

'In fact, it's entirely possible that *he* may
well end up confessing in an attempt to save

274

his mother, so be prepared for that...'

He looked around at the thee officers, a look of abject defeat on his austere features. His shoulders slumped.

'God almighty, this whole thing's a total bloody mess.'

McGinn threw his cigarette into the fire.

'What about Benson, sir?'

Nisbet frowned.

'Benson? Oh, yes, I suppose he *can* be re-leased, seems he played no part in any of it.'

*

Without another word, Nisbet strode to the door, then turned and looked across at McGinn.

'I'm going back up to Paisley to start my re-port—it'll take bloody ages...'

McGinn looked surprised and made to follow his superior.

'Em...but I though you wanted me to in-terview Colin Campbell?'

Nisbet looked away once more.

'Yes...yes, I do. You stay here, I'll catch the train, could do with a bit of fresh air...clear my head...'

With that, he opened the door and walked outside, leaving Alan and McGinn staring at each other.

'Should we go after him, d'you think?' asked Alan.

'No, best leave him to it; not like him to turn down a lift, mind. He's probably just furious that he got it so badly wrong. God, he's an odd bug-ger... Right, McInnes, we'd best do what the man says an' have another word with Campbell junior.'

He was interrupted by a chilling wail that turned into near-hysterical sobbing. He lifted a pen and a piece of paper from the desk.

'On second thoughts, maybe we should
get Meg Campbell's statement first...'

He gave Alan a knowing wink.

'...before she changes her bloody mind!'

*

'Ah telt ye, Ah'm sayin' nothin until Ah've got a lawyer.'

'Aye, you told us, but things have changed, Campbell.'

They were interviewing Colin Campbell in his cell—
the small local police station had run out of space! The
surly figure, seated on the narrow, untidy bed, sneered.

'Aye? How've they changed?'

McGinn folded his arms.

'Your dear old mother has just confessed to the
murder of Hugh Campbell, her husband.'

There was a long pause as the information pen-
etrated Campbell's brain. Alan, standing with
his back to the cell door, saw the man tense and
he reached for his truncheon—just in case.

'Whit? Naw, ye're lyin', ye're bloody lyin'
tae try an' get me tae say somethin'...'

McGinn was holding the statement that Meg
Campbell had signed. He raised it up.

'It's all here, Campbell, chapter an'
verse. D'you want a wee look?'

'Naw, she's talkin' rubbish, it's aw a pack o' lies—it wis
me that killed him. An' he bloody deserved it tae.'

McGinn smiled; this was exactly what Nisbet had anticipated.

'Right, I see, it was *you*, was it—
you killed your step-father?'

'Aye, see, Ah'd had enough o' him beatin' up ma mother, so Ah followed him an' killed him.'

McGinn leaned towards the man.

'An' what about Mary—what about your sister?'

Campbell looked confused.

'Eh? Whit d'you mean—Ah never touched her...'

'Then who did?'

Campbell shrugged.

'How the hell should Ah know—you're the bloody polis, you tell me.'

McGinn paused, glancing round at Alan and giving him a knowing look. Campbell clearly knew nothing of the scratches on his step-father's face.

'So, just *how* did you kill him, Campbell?'

Campbell hesitated very slightly.

'Em...like Ah telt ye before, Ah strangled him wi' ma bare hands.'

'Funny that—the police doctor says he died of a head injury.'

'Aye...weel...em...efter Ah'd strangled him Ah hit the bastard on the heid, just tae make sure.'

'You hit him on the head, did you?'

'Aye.'

McGinn paused and leaned back against the stark, green-painted wall.

'I see—what did you hit him on the head with, Campbell?'

Alan noticed Campbell's eyes dart from side to side, as if searching for an answer.

'Em...a bit o wood. Aye that's it, Ah battered him on the heid wi' a bit o' wood.'

'What kind o' wood?'

'Whit d'ye mean?'

'I mean just what I said—what kind o' wood? A branch, maybe, a bit of log that just happened to be handy?'

Campbell gave a leering smile.

'Aye, very good, Mister Polisman. Tryin' tae catch me oot again. Naw, it wisn'ae a branch, it wis a bit o' an old fencepost. That's it—it must've washed up on the shore o' the loch.'

'So you're tellin' me that, after stranglin' your step-father, you hit him over the head with a bit o' fence-post?'

'Aye.'

Again McGinn looked round at Alan, this time giving him a knowing wink.

'Right, that's all. I think we've heard enough, McInnes, don't you?'

Campbell stared at his inquisitor as Alan opened the cell door.

'Whit—are you no' chargin' me?'

Sergeant McGinn smiled beatifically.

'No, Mr Campbell, we're not. What you've told us is a pack of lies and you know damned well that it is. We might charge you with pervertin' the course of justice but you're sure as hell no' guilty of the murder o' Hugh Campbell.'

*

Colin Campbell was released, under strict caution to remain in Barloch for the time being. McGinn, accompanied once more by McInnes and, on the strength of her statement, duly charged Meg Campbell with the murder of her husband. The woman was now almost catatonic, seemingly incapable of speech. She had eventually been led to the cell recently occupied by her son to await transfer to Greenock's Gateside

Womens' prison; her final comment was simply a mumbled, "The bastart deserved aw' he got."

Sergeant Tait had also released Billy Benson, personally escorting him down to McGeoch's coal-yard to assure Mrs McGeoch that the young man was entirely innocent. Fortunately, Mrs McGeoch, being the kind-hearted soul that she was, told Benson that his job on the lorry was re-instated. However, when Tait returned to the station, his expression was grim.

'It's a bloody shame—it's like the licht's gone oot in the poor lad's eyes. There's nae doubt that he loved that lassie, wayward an' all as she may hae' been.'

'D'you think he'll stick the job?' asked Alan.

Tait shrugged.

'Time'll tell, Ah suppose. Let's just hope so— she wis definitely a good influence on him.'

McGinn looked at his watch.

'It's gone five—I'd best get up to Paisley an' start on my own report.'

He extended a hand to Alan.

'It's been good workin' with you, McInnes. I hope you've learned a thing or two.'

Alan shook the sergeant's hand in the customary manner.

'Aye, I have, Sergeant. Thanks very much.'

McGinn then extended his hand to Sergeant Tait.

'You too, Tait.'

He nodded in Alan's direction.

'He's a good' un—might make a detective o' him yet.'

Tait smiled as McGinn turned back to face Alan.

'McInnes, if a position in the CID comes up, d'you want me to let you know?'

Alan glanced at Donny Tait, who nodded.

'Aye, Sergeant, if you wouldn't mind, that'd be great.'

McGinn smiled.

'Right then, I'll be off. Might be back to tidy up any loose ends. If not, look after yourselves.'

He gave them a wink and was gone.

*

Alan had finished his dinner and was listening to the wireless while his mother put away the dishes. He had left the station not long after McGinn, and Sergeant Tait had told him to take the following day off as leave. Kerr Brodie had, apparently, recovered sufficiently to cover his shift and Tait reckoned that Alan deserved a day off; he had agreed wholeheartedly!

Their "situation" hadn't been discussed, but an unspoken understanding seemed to have been reached, much to Alan's relief. Perhaps, one day...time would tell.

Gilbert McInnes was dozing by the fire, the stump of his leg resting on a stool. Isa dried her hands, crossed to the back door and reached for her coat. Alan turned down the volume on the wireless..

'You're goin' out, Mother? It's gettin' dark.'

She looked slightly abashed.

'Och, I'm just taking a wee bit dinner down for Donny—he's got enough on his plate with all this carry on.'

'But it's pretty much over and done with, Mother. Meg Campbell's away to the jail in Greenock and both Benson and Colin Campbell have been released.'

Isa appeared very slightly flustered.

'Aye, but Donny's no' getting any younger, Alan, and it's been a difficult time for him. We're not

used to a carry-on like this in Barloch. Anyway, it's just a wee bit brisket that's left over...'

Gilbert McInnes grunted and sat forward.

'Whit's that, Isa? Where're ye off tae at this time o' nicht?'

She crossed to the door, the dish of
food grasped in her hand.

'I'm just taking a wee bit dinner down to
Donny Tait, Gilbert, I'll not be long.'

Gilbert McInnes glowered up at his wife.

'Donny Tait again, is it? Seems like ye
cann'ae keep awa' frae the bloody man.'

Isa's face reddened.

'There's no need for language like that, Gilbert.
Donny's had a hard time recently, with these kill-
ings. He'll be fretting, no doubt, and as likely as
not he'll not have made himself any dinner...'

'Ach, awa' ye go then, woman, awa' an see yer fancy man.'

Alan stood up angrily.

'Don't you speak to Mother like that!'

Gilbert had picked up his pipe and
was filling it from his pouch.

'An' dinn'ae you lecture me on things
aboot which ye know damn all.'

Alan stood, dumbfounded; Isa had started to weep, softly and silently, and Alan crossed
to her, placing a hand on her shoulder.

'He didn't mean it, Mother, he's just half-asleep.'

'Ah'm no' bloody half-asleep, Alan McInnes.
Jist let yer mither go, Ah'm past carin'.'

Isa McInnes pulled away and stormed out, slamming the door behind her. Alan turned to his father.

'What the hell are you playin' at, Father? You've really upset Mother!'

Gilbert McInnes lit his pipe, staring into
the fire with a melancholy look.

'Ay, weel, twa people can be upset—an' ye ken
damned fine why that is. Ah'm sayin' no more.'

Chapter 24

Despite his exhausted state, Alan didn't slept at all well; he lay for what seemed like ages, staring at the ceiling, replaying the conversation with his mother, replaying the week's events...

Finally, he fell into a deep but troubled sleep, filled with dreams that verged on nightmares. He was awakened by someone gently shaking him and calling his name.

'Alan—Alan, c'mon, son, you need to waken up.'

He opened his eyes to find his mother sitting on the edge of the bed, the appetising smell of bacon filling his nostrils.

'Wh...what is it, Mother? I'm off duty today.'

She gave a sad smile.

'I know, but Don...Sergeant Tait's just been on the telephone, asking if you can go down right away.'

Alan sat up, reaching for his watch.

'It's half-past nine—Sergeant Tait said I could have the day off! Did he say what the trouble was?'

His mother pulled a face as if she'd eaten something unpleasant.

'Something to do with that man McGinn.'

Sergeant McGinn was obviously still out of favour.

'Anyway, Sergeant Tait said it was urgent so I've brought you up a bacon sandwich and a cup of tea, I'll leave you to get ready.'

*

Forty minutes later, Alan was walking down School Street

towards the police station, having gulped down his breakfast and hastily donned his uniform. After the week's events, he had been looking forward to a day of rest but, as he reached the police station, the presence of the Wolseley indicated otherwise. He wondered briefly if he was about to get a dressing-down from Inspector Nisbet—after all, the man *had* said he "would deal with him later." He turned up the path, straightened his tie and opened the door.

Judging by their expressions, Sergeant McGinn was in what appeared to be in rather serious conversation with Donny Tait, although Nisbet was absent, presumably already ensconced in Tait's office. Kerr Brodie, his face bruised and his nose still swollen, was nursing a large china mug of tea and listening in on the discussion. McGinn nodded at Alan.

'Mornin', McInnes, sorry to disturb your day off.'

'That's all right, Sergeant, at least I had a long lie. Has something happened?'

McGinn frowned.

'That's the thing, McInnes, I don't know. See, Inspector Nisbet appears to be missin'.'

Alan gave an inward sigh of relief; at least he wasn't "in for it!"

'Missing?'

'Aye, that's what I said. Seems he never went back to the office yesterday, despite what he told us, and he hasn't turned up for duty this mornin'. I though I'd best come down and see if he'd turned up here but, obviously, he hasn't.'

'He seemed tae be in a bit o' a state when he left yesterday,' added Tait. 'Jist walked oot wi' hardly a word.'

McGinn nodded.

'Aye, that wasn't like him, usually he has a lot more to say, especially when he's tied up a case.'

'I take it ye've tried his home?'

'I have, but it seems he lived alone and there was no reply when I called. I phoned the City police, apparently his wife walked out on him about a year ago—mind you I don't think he'd be the easiest bugger to live with.'

He looked at Sergeant Tait.

'Is it all right if I borrow McInnes for a while? We'll head down to the railway station, see if he actually boarded a train and at what time.'

'Aye, that'll be fine. Brodie's back, although he looks like he's been through the wars.'

McGinn grinned.

'Right, McInnes, let's head down and see what we can find out.'

*

It only took a couple of minutes in the Wolseley before they pulled up at the southern ramp that led up to the station. They reached the platform, where a few passengers were waiting in the sunshine for the next train to Glasgow. The stationmaster noticed their approach and walked towards them.

'Mornin', Alan. Everythin' all right? Thought aw' the fun an' games was over an' done wi'?'

'Just another wee enquiry, Mr Oliphant.'

Alan introduced McGinn and the two men shook hands, the same immediate bond being formed.

'My inspector left the office yesterday afternoon, said he was catchin' a train to Paisley. Thing is, Mr Oliphant, he never arrived at Paisley headquarters an' he's no' turned up for duty today. We're just checkin' to see if he actually got on the train.'

McGinn gave a description of the inspector and Bert Oliphant rubbed his beard thoughtfully. After a few moments, he shook his head.

'No, Ah was on duty yesterday an' Ah cann'ae say Ah sold a ticket tae anyone answerin' that description. As you'd imagine, Ah ken pretty much everybody who get's a train frae here an' Ah could pretty much pit a name tae' every passenger yesterday. Ah'd ken a stranger if he cam' alang, so yer man wasn'ae amongst them, Ah'm sorry.'

'I see...'

They were interrupted by the brief ringing of a telephone bell; it stopped suddenly.

'D'you need to get that?' asked McGinn.

'Naw, Combe'll have answered it—'

He was interrupted by the voice of Alex Combe, the porter.

'Mr Oliphant, ye're wanted on the telephone.'

Oliphant turned around.

'Can it no' wait—Ah'm talkin' tae these gentlemen.'

'It's a Mr Kilgour at the Marchburn Farm, doon off the Glensherrie road—says there's a railway worker at his door, needs tae speak tae ye urgently.'

Oliphant swore under his breath.

'Excuse me a minute, Ah best see whit he wants.'

McGinn lit a Capstan and the two officers stood in the warmth of the sunshine for a few minutes. When Bert Oliphant returned, his expression was serious; he repeated the conversation and, as McGinn and Alan walked rapidly back towards the car, the look on their faces was equally grim.

It took less than ten minutes to reach the entrance to Marchburn Farm, a couple of miles down the main Glensherrie Road. Standing at the farm road-end was a grizzled man, clad in a pair of oil-stained overalls, a well-worn tweed jacket and a flat cap. He gave them a desultory wave and McGinn drew the car onto the verge. The two officers got out, the man nodding a salutation they approached.

'Richt, jist up alang here, gentlemen.'

They followed the plate-layer, who had identified himself simply as "Boaby" and walked up the steep road leading to the farm. About half-way up the road, they came to a rough, overgrown track leading off to the left, down a steep slope towards the March Burn. They could hear the gurgling and splashing of the dark, swift-flowing water, still in spate from the recent downpour. Once they had picked their way carefully down to the riverbank, ahead of them they could see a high, steel railway viaduct towering above the valley floor, supported on heavy stone buttresses and two tall, ashlar pillars. The valley itself was heavily-wooded, the undergrowth thick and lush. As they approached the foot of the lofty structure, the peace was disturbed by a sharp whistle from above, followed by an ominous rumbling and clattering as a steam-hauled train crossed the lofty girders of the March Burn viaduct. A second overall-clad figure stood ahead of them, the fragrant smell of pipe tobacco wafting towards them in the gentle breeze. It appeared a near-idyllic sylvan scene, but for one thing.

On a large, flat rock in the centre of the fast-flowing

water lay a twisted figure, the angle of the neck and the dark red stain on the grey stone beneath precluding any possibility of life. The four men regarded it for a moment, then McGinn turned to Alan, shaking his head sadly.

'No doubt, eh?'

"Fraid not, Sergeant. It's the inspector all right.'

*

Before setting out, McGinn had instructed Bert Oliphant to telephone Sergeant Tait and ask for the police doctor to be called, as well as an ambulance. Dr Miller duly arrived and, suitably attired in his green Hunter boots, knelt on the rock to examine Nisbet's remains. McGinn was taking a statement from the worker named Boaby, while Alan looked on, realising that, already, the effect of violent death seemed to have had less effect on him than it had just a few short days ago. McGinn, notebook in hand, was speaking.

'What made you look over the viaduct, Boaby?'

'Weel, we wis inspectin' the track, jist as usu-al, ye ken. We got half way ower the viaduct when Ah saw an empty bottle sittin' richt at the edge. Ah looked closer, it wis a half-bottle o' whisky.'

'And why did *that* make you look over the edge?'

'Weel, if it'd been flung oot o' the windae o' a train, ye ken, it wid either have gone ower the edge or smashed when it hit the stane. But it wisn'ae broke, ye ken, which seemed funny tae me. Looked mair like it had been dropped, if ye ken whit Ah mean. So, Ah looked ower...an' there he wis. Poor bug-ger—we cam' doon as quick as we could but it's a hell o' a long way doon, there wis nae hope, ye ken.'

'No, I don't suppose there would have been.

Right, thanks Boaby, we'll get a full statement from you back at the station.'

Dr Miller approached, the knees and lower
part of his trousers soaking wet, despite his rubber boots; he looked particularly disgruntled.

'Damned awkward place to carry out an examination—I thought a filthy coal wagon was bad enough but
the middle of a bloody river is worse. I'm soaking.'

'Sorry, Doctor, can't be helped.'

'No, I suppose not. Anyway, cause of death could
be either a broken neck or a fractured skull—the victim has suffered both, as you can probably see.'

He paused, a mournful expression on his face. The
man had, undoubtedly, seen death many times but
probably seldom where he had known the victim.

'It's Nisbet, of course—you knew that, I'd imagine?'

'Aye, we recognised him right away.'

'Hm. Suicide, by the looks of it—you say
there was a bottle found on the bridge?'

'Aye, an empty half-bottle o' whisky.'

The doctor nodded.

'Yes, that makes sense, there was a strong
smell of alcohol from his mouth. God, what
the hell got in to the man, I wonder?'

'As do I, Doctor. The murder case was concluded, maybe he felt he'd not handled it correctly.'

Dr Miller raised an eyebrow.

'Turned out it was the Campbell woman that murdered her husband; in turn, she implicated her husband in the murder of the daughter. Seems that neither Billy Benson nor the son, Colin, had anythin'
to do with it. The inspector had been certain that

it was Campbell junior that had killed Hugh.'

'Hm; but we can all get it wrong, it's hardly enough to make one want to jump off a bloody bridge. I suppose we'll never know now, unless we find a note. Once we get him on to the bank, you can have a look through his pockets, just in case. I certainly didn't see anything out there but it may have washed away, I suppose.'

'Any idea how long he's been there, Doctor?'

'I can't give an exact time of death yet, of course, need to get him on the table, But, given the conditions, I would think he's been here overnight at least.'

McGinn and Alan exchanged a glance.

'I see—he left the office yesterday afternoon, sayin' that he was goin' to catch a train back to HQ. Seems he never got on the train an' he never arrived back at the Paisley station. We'll check his house later in case there's anythin' there, but your estimate suggests that he never went home either.'

The rustling of the undergrowth caused them to turn; two uniformed ambulance men were approaching, one carrying a rolled-up stretcher. The expressions on their usually impassive faces suggested that they, too, didn't relish the idea of wading through a fast-flowing river. Ambling along behind them, cigarette in mouth, was the jaded police photographer, his large camera dangling from his scrawny neck. As he reached the bank he began his task, photographing the body from every angle, seemingly impervious to the conditions or the tragedy of the situation. It took him ten minutes, then he ambled off, hardly a word having been exchanged.

A few minutes after his departure, the ambulance men carefully laid their stretcher, bearing the body of Gabriel Nisbet, on the riverbank. McGinn went through the corpse's pockets; he found the obligatory notebook and pencil, as well as a wallet, still containing a photograph that McGinn concluded to be that of the inspector's estranged wife. Some pocket change and a handkerchief made up the rest of the contents; there was no suicide note. As McGinn leafed through the notebook, his brow furrowed.

'Looks like there's been a page torn out— McInnes, have a look about, he's maybe written somethin' an' left it somewhere.'

He turned to the platelayers.

'Boaby, you didn't see anythin' up on the viaduct—a wee piece of paper like this?'

He showed the two men the notebook, but they shook their heads as Boaby answered.

'Naw, jist thon half-bottle. If it wis there, the wind wid likely hae carried it off onywey, ye ken.'

McGinn continued to stare at the notebook, as if willing it to divulge the contents of the missing page. Dr Miller cleared his throat impatiently.

'Well, that would appear to be that, nothing more to be done here, I suppose.'

Nodding at the ambulance men, he made to leave.

'Right, let's get him off to the mortuary.'

The two men lifted their tragic burden and made off, rather awkwardly, through the thick undergrowth. The two plate-layers were dismissed, being told to report to the police station the following morning to give a formal statement; they, too, ambled off towards the track. McGinn stood in thought for a few minutes until Alan returned, shaking his head. '

'Nothin', Sergeant, no sign of a note anywhere.'

McGinn shrugged and the two men stood in silence, their eyes irrevocably drawn to the large, flat stone in the middle of the river. The dark red stain was still in evidence, no doubt to be washed away by future rains and floods. Finally, McGinn broke the silence.

'Y'know, he was an odd bugger, but he was still a bloody good policeman. You wonder what the hell gets in to people's minds, to make them do such a thing.'

He shrugged, straightened himself then pulled out his cigarettes, the wind blew out three matches before he finally managed to get one lit. Blowing out a cloud of smoke, he, too, turned towards the track.

'Right, best get back, there'll be even more bloody paperwork to deal with now.'

Alan stood for a few moments more, watching the retreating back of the sergeant as he followed the stretcher, bearing away the remains of his former superior officer. A gust of wind soughed through the trees above, sending a shiver down Alan's spine; somehow, the valley now seemed melancholy, sinister almost. Finally, he set off through the ferns and the grass, along the bank of the fast-flowing March burn. Had he glanced towards those waters, he might have noticed the small, sodden scrap of paper being carried through the mossy rocks, dislodged from under the body when it was lifted by the ambulance men; but he walked on, head cast down, oblivious. Gabriel Nisbet's secrets remained behind, forever safe in the March Burn valley...with only the sigh of the wind as witness.

Hogmanay

The crowd applauded enthusiastically as the accomplished little ceilidh band played the final chord of the eightsome reel. Young and old, the dancers retreated to their tables for well-earned refreshment, the ladies dizzy and with aching arms, the men perspiring and red-faced. Alan looked at his watch—ten minutes to go. His heart was pounding, although not from the exertion of the dance; he squeezed Nancy's hand and excused himself.

'Make sure you're back in time for the New Year, sweetheart,' she trilled. 'Someone's brought a wireless this year so we'll be able to hear the pips!'

*

He splashed some cold water on his face and regarded himself in the slightly rust-marked mirror of the gents toilet as the strains of the St Bernard's waltz filtered through from the hall. He considered himself reasonably handsome; his hair had been neatly cut, he had shaved more carefully than usual, his shirt was pristine and his suit was well pressed—all thanks to Isa McInnes, of course. He smiled; what would his mother have to say when he told her his news? He felt in his jacket pocket, his fingers closing around the little blue velvet box that contained the small, yet exquisite, diamond solitaire ring. The smile faded for a moment; what if Nancy said no...? As his shoulders drooped almost imperceptibly, the other thoughts that had been troubling the young policeman crowded into his mind.

It had been a month since Sergeant Tait had announced that he was considering retiral sometime in the New Year. Following a gruelling interview with the divisional Chief Superintendent, Alan had been advised that they would consider promoting him to sergeant and would take over Tait's duties once the older man finally retired. It had seemed a particularly good omen...until that morning.

His mother had answered the telephone, then had come upstairs to his room.

'Alan, son, that's that man McGinn on the phone for you.'

It seemed that Isa still hadn't forgiven Gordon McGinn for his rather heavy-handed treatment of Colin Campbell. Alan smiled; it didn't do to cross Isa McInnes. He had made his way downstairs and lifted the receiver.

'Sergeant McGinn? McInnes here.'

'Mornin' McInnes, how are you—recovered from all the excitement?'

'Aye, pretty much. Back to stolen bicycles and broken windows.'

McGinn chuckled.

'Aye, well, that's the life o' a local bobby—speakin' o' which, I hear congratulations are in order—Sergeant! Well, sergeant-to-be, that is!'

'News travels quickly, then! But, yes, I've had an interview with the Chief Super; once Sergeant Tait retires, I'm hopin' to take over at Barloch. Mind you, the Super *did* say he thought I was a wee bit young!'

McGinn chuckled.

'Aye, well, if you're the right man for the job, McInnes, age shouldn't make too much o' a difference. You've had a fair bit o' experience now, after that last carry on; that'll certainly carry a bit o' weight with the Chief Super.'

There was a rather ominous pause.

'Look, McInnes, I hate to throw a spanner in the works, but the thing is, I've had a promotion too—it's Inspector McGinn now!'

'Congratulations, sir. Well deserved, if you ask me.'

'Thanks, McInnes, but I don't think we need to dwell on the reason...'

'No, I suppose not.'

'Anyway, see, the thing is, I now have a vacancy for a detective constable. I remembered that you had expressed an interest in joinin' the CID and... well, I wondered if you might like the job?'

Alan stood with his mouth agape; this was unexpected, to say the least.

'Still there, McInnes?'

'Em...aye, I'm still here...that's a bit o' a surprise, sir.'

'Not really—you seemed interested and you certainly had a few good theories in that last case, even if you didn't exactly go about them in the correct manner. Listen, McInnes, I don't expect an immediate answer an' you might want to talk it over with Tait—an' maybe with that lassie o' yours. Look, I know you've got a promotion' comin' and this would maybe seem to be a step backwards, but if you play your cards right, you could be lookin' at a promotion within six months, a year at the most. You're a bright young lad and, personally, I think you've got what it takes to make a bloody good detective.'

Alan could feel the blood rush to his cheeks at this praise and he managed to blurt out a mumbled "I see" before McGinn continued..

'But let me tell you a few things about the job. For a start, you can forget the regular shift pattern—if we have a big investigation, it'll be all hands on deck for as long as we need you. The hours are long, the work's hard an' I'll no' deny that it can be dangerous at times. But, in my opinion, bein' a detective is *real* police work, not chasin' about after stolen bikes an' broken windows, as you put it yourself.'

Alan's thoughts were in turmoil; his life had appeared to be pretty much charted out for him but here was an opportunity to do what he *really* wanted, to make a difference. McGinn continued.

'But I'll be honest wi' you, McInnes, it doesn't always work out the way we'd like. Have you heard about Penman?'

'What—the bookmaker?'

'Aye, the very same. He's due to go for trial at the start o' January; he'd given us names, details, possibly enough to go for a prosecution, in the hope o' gettin' a lighter sentence...'

There was a pause; Alan heard the strike of the match, the exhaling of the smoke; for a moment, he could almost smell the tang of Capstan full-strength.

'That was until last week.'

'Why, what happened?'

'Well, remember that fancy motor o' his, the Jaguar?'

'Aye—a nice car, as I recall.'

'It was, but now it's just a burnt-out wreck.'

'What? Why—what happened?'

'Arson, if I'm no' mistaken, a wee warnin'. But it seems that wasn't deemed to be enough. Just yesterday, his wife was attacked on her way home from visitin' her old mother. Got a broken arm and a few nasty bruises. Nothin' was taken, but my guess is that she was told, in no uncertain terms, what would happen if Benny Penman gave evidence.'

Alan was shocked; he hadn't realised that such things really happened.

'Needless to say, Penman's now denyin' everythin' that he told us, says he can't remember a thing. The man's scared out o' his wits; he knows that, if he were to give evidence, either somethin' would happen to his wife or to him, once he's inside. Probably both, if I'm bein' honest. So we're back to square one regardin' the stolen booze an' fags. We know who's involved but, without Penman's testimony, there's bugger all chance o' gettin' a case to court.'

'There's *nothin'* you can do?'

'No' a thing. He'll stand up in court an' say he hasn't a bloody clue who stole the stuff. He'll go down for a long stretch but he'll be safe enough, as long as he keeps his mouth shut. That's how it goes, once the big boys are threatened. Y'see, McInnes, it's no' a very nice world that us CID types inhabit. We're dealin' with the *real* bad bastards that are out there, so have good think. Y'know, the life o' a local sergeant isn't a bad one, play your cards right—especially at your age—an' you could make inspector by the time you're forty. Nice wee house, decent pension, a couple o' kids, your own motor; I'm just sayin'. Look, I'll phone in a week or so an' you can give me your answer. Oh, an' a happy New Year when it comes!'

The waltz had come to an end and the band leader was inviting everyone on to the dance-floor. Alan straightened his tie and exited; the door to the hall opened and Nancy popped her head round.

'There you are, Alan—what kept you? It's nearly midnight—come on'

'Nancy, I...'

She smiled; her cheeks were flushed, her eyes were sparkling, she looked stunningly beautiful in the scarlet, sleeveless dress.

'Come on, Alan, we don't want to miss...'

'...there's somethin' I wanted to ask...'

His hand closed around the little velvet box.

'Och, can it not wait, Alan.?'

A loud shout went up in the hall.

'TEN...'

'Nancy...'

'NINE...'

She gave him a smile and held out her hand in invitation.

'EIGHT...'

'Come on, silly, we can talk later.'

'SEVEN.'

'But it *can't* wait, Nancy.'

'SIX...'

'Of course it can.'

'FIVE...'

With some reluctance, Alan let the ring-box fall back in to his pocket and he followed Nancy back in to the hall.

'FOUR...'

She dragged him into the melee.

'THREE...'

The excitement was now palpable—a new near; a new decade. The band leader tried to quieten the crowd as he fiddled with the dial on a transistor radio. As he held it up to the microphone, the brief crackle of static sounded through the small public address system. The crowd ignored him, however, content with their own, more traditional, count-down, one with which the radio couldn't hope to compete.

'TWO...'

The band-leader gave up; he hastily placed the radio on the floor and turned to his fellow musicians.

'ONE...'

1960 had begun!

Amidst a cacophony of "Happy New Years", of hugging, hand-shaking and kissing, the band struck up the obligatory Auld Lang Syne. The excited, happy crowd immediately began to sing enthusiastically as the circle formed. Alan took Nancy's hand as they dashed in and out, the trials and troubles of 1959 forgotten in that joyous moment that only the Scots know how to truly celebrate. Then it was over; the crowd retreated for another quick refreshment before the bandleader asked them to take the floor for a Dashing White Sergeant; there was to be no respite, apparently...

Nancy ran across the dance-floor to where her friends, all fellow-teachers, were seated, urging them up to form the necessary sets of six. Alan looked on, his heart heavy; the moment had passed. There would, undoubtedly, be another opportunity but he had really hoped for tonight. Nancy turned around, noticing his rather dejected expression. She flitted back across the dance-floor, grabbed the lapels of his jacket and, pulling him towards her, kissed him full on the lips; there were a few cat-calls, a few jealous glances from the younger males. She gazed up at him and grinned.

'Alan McInnes.'

He held her tight as he gazed into her pretty hazel eyes.

'What?'

'Happy New Year! I love you, you dope!

Now, what was it you wanted to ask?'

He couldn't help but smile at the beautiful, vivacious vision before him, realising that now was not the time.

'Och, nothin', Nancy, it can wait.'

She kissed him again; as the band struck up, she grabbed his hand and shouted

'C'mon, sweetheart, the Dashing White Sergeant's about to start...'

*

Along the length and breadth of the mighty River Clyde, boats large and small sounded their horns, their hooters, their sirens, to herald in the New Year, the new decade. The sharp "toot" of the tugboat, the deep, melancholy "moo" of the liner, the characteristic "whoop" of the naval frigate. Hands were shaken, bottles were opened, dubious renditions of Auld Lang Syne sounded across the dark, rippling waters.

But, even in that moment of celebration, the illicit trade continued. Shadowy figures prised open crates in the dark, deserted docks of Glasgow. A shipment mislaid, a consignment lost...all for a few pounds, to be spent the following week in the public-house, the bookmaker's, the brothel...

"Aye, we're the boys awright!"

Acknowledgements

As "Barloch" (my fourth novel published by Sparsile Books) finds itself in print, once again I feel a slight sense of astonishment at seeing my name on the cover! This book offers a somewhat different approach, set in a past that, perhaps, we view with "rose-tinted" spectacles. However, once you have read it, you will realise that the tint quickly wears off and that life was not quite as rosy as we may choose to believe!

As always, my profound gratitude goes to Lesley Affrossman, my publisher, Jim Campbell, my editor and also to Stephen Cash for proof-reading and pointing out a few glaring errors! You're ongoing faith in my writing still amazes me and I can't thank you all enough. Thanks and love to my family for, once again, tolerating my absences as I either rattle the laptop or sit in a daze, contemplating the latest twist in a plot (well, that's what I tell them!). And to all my friends who support me, who buy my books and sometimes even tell me that they like them, cheers guys.

I am very grateful to my dear friend and fellow author, Alex Gray, for all her encouragement and support throughout my (considerably shorter) writing career; also for her final, and valued, edit of Barloch. It's always astonishing what you can miss, no matter how many times you read it!

Finally, a rather belated thanks to someone no longer with us; however, it is my hope that, somewhere in "the ether" my 6 th year studies English teacher, Miss Watson, is looking down with a smile and a sense of pride. It`s a long way from my "Comparison of Ian Crichton Smith and George Mackay Brown" but there is no doubt that she inspired me and nurtured my writing and love of language. Thank you, Jean!